PAST CRIMES

PERFECTLY CRIMINAL III

With contributions from

CATHERINE AIRD

MAT COWARD

EILEEN DEWHURST

MARJORIE ECCLES

MARTIN EDWARDS

SUSANNA GREGORY

EDWARD D HOCH

H R F KEATING

GILLIAN LINSCOTT

EDWARD MARSTON

AMY MYERS

ANNE PERRY

RUTH RENDELL

ANDREW TAYLOR

ALISON WHITE

TONY WILMOT

PAST CRIMES

Perfectly Criminal III

The Crime Writers' Association's
Annual Anthology edited by Martin Edwards

with contributions from

CATHERINE AIRD
MAT COWARD
EILEEN DEWHURST
MARJORIE ECCLES
MARTIN EDWARDS
SUSANNA GREGORY
EDWARD D HOCH
H R F KEATING
GILLIAN LINSCOTT
EDWARD MARSTON
AMY MYERS
ANNE PERRY
RUTH RENDELL
ANDREW TAYLOR
ALISON WHITE
TONY WILMOT

SEVERN
SH
HOUSE

This first world edition published in Great Britain 1998 by
SEVERN HOUSE PUBLISHERS LTD of
9–15 High Street, Sutton, Surrey SM1 1DF.
This first world edition published in the U.S.A. 1998 by
SEVERN HOUSE PUBLISHERS INC of
595 Madison Avenue, New York, N.Y. 10022.

British Library Cataloguing in Publication Data

Past crimes : perfectly criminal III
1. Detective and mystery stories, English
I. Edwards, Martin, 1955-
823'.0872'08'0914 [FS]

ISBN 0-7278-2232-2

Typeset by Hewer Text Ltd,
Edinburgh, Scotland.
Printed and bound in Great Britain by
MPG Books Ltd, Bodmin, Cornwall.

LIST OF CONTENTS

FOREWORD

The annual anthology of short stories by members of the Crime Writers' Association has become an eagerly awaited event. Martin Edwards as editor sets a theme for each volume so that it isn't a ragbag of oddments but a rare opportunity for readers to experience a concept turned this way and that by a marvellous range of talents. This year's theme is Past Crimes and Martin has cleverly insisted that each story should be set in a time before the birth of the CWA in 1953.

The art of the short story is very different from that of the novel. Even as some brilliant writers of short stories shun a full-length work, so not every successful novelist can succeed as a short story writer. But the rewards offered by the medium are many and varied. A short story can offer an opportunity to display technical virtuosity as the writer produces one of those 'twist' endings that surprises the reader into stunned admiration; or the chance to create an atmosphere, an evocation of a moment in time that would be impossible to sustain in a longer work. And some ideas just insist they are short stories, not novels.

For the reader, an anthology offers stories that can be swallowed in one gulp rather than having to be spun out over several sessions. The short story is a *bonne bouche* rather than a banquet, something to relish and remain hungry for more.

It would, indeed, be a shame to devour all the offerings in this great collection at a sitting, for the other advantage of

Foreword

Past Crimes is that it gives you the opportunity to sample the work of a very varied range of writers. Ration yourself, read one at a time; savour each flavour before passing on to try another of the treats.

You can carry *Past Crimes* around, read it on the train or while waiting in a queue. It can be kept by your favourite chair for a treat after lunchtime or in the evening, or by your bed for a stimulating end to the day. Or are you one of those who love to read in the bath?

Wherever these stories are read, I can guarantee that each of them will give you enormous delight. After the anthology has been finished, I hope you will look for the full-length novels of any of the writers you haven't read before, and catch up with the latest offerings of those you have. Happy reading!

Janet Laurence
Chairman, Crime Writers' Association

INTRODUCTION

In this book, members of the Crime Writers' Association, ranging from international bestselling authors to relative newcomers, explore the endless possibilities of stories about crimes of the past. In recent years, readers' enthusiasm for mysteries with a period setting has soared. Authors have supplied the demand with relish and there has been much notable work: *The Name Of The Rose* and the Brother Cadfael series by the late Ellis Peters are but two examples. Yet a puzzle to tax even the most ardent crime fan is: why has the boom occurred?

Peter Lovesey, himself a former editor of the CWA's annual anthology and an accomplished exponent of the history–mystery, has pointed out in an essay that 'there were surprisingly few historical mysteries written prior to 1970', particularly if one excepts the books of John Dickson Carr and one-offs such as Agatha Christie's *Death Comes As The End*. He suggested that 'one day some assiduous research student may earner a higher degree by explaining why it was that in 1970 the floodgates opened'. My own guess is that, during and after the heady days of the 1960s, crime novelists setting their books in the contemporary world became increasingly concerned with the delineation of character and exploration of matters of current social concern. The traditional elements of the classic detective story, and in particular its emphasis upon elaborate plotting, were not easily integrated within books set

INTRODUCTION

in the nuclear age. As a very broad generalisation, it seems to me that those readers and writers who have hungered most for classic detective stories have found the right ingredients in books set in the past. The distance of time may, for instance, make the conventions of detective fiction seem more plausible. The chance to learn about life in societies very different from our own is an added bonus.

What is so impressive, though, about the period mystery today is the sheer diversity of high calibre work that is being produced. The medieval and Victorian ages have provided a backcloth for many books, but increasingly writers have rung the changes by setting their stories in a wide range of times and places. The stories here span from Greek myth and legend to small-town England in the early 1950s: I chose as a cut-off date for the past crimes in this book the date of formation of the CWA, 5 November 1953.

To my delight, the two last CWA anthologies have each yielded the story awarded the Dagger by an independent panel of judges for the best short mystery of the year; Ian Rankin's success in 1996 was followed by Reginald Hill's in 1997. But again I have been keen above all to provide readers with freshness and variety of content and mood. Only one of the stories in the book – *Expectations* – has ever appeared in print before; the rest were written especially for *Past Crimes*. I have also been keen to mix in with the famous names, such as Anne Perry and Diamond Dagger winner H R F Keating, a number of younger authors and those who are not generally associated with the historical sub-genre.

I would like to thank all the contributors for their enthusiastic support and Janet Laurence for her foreword, as well as Eileen Dewhurst and Helena Edwards for help with the proofs and those at Severn House who have worked on this book.

Martin Edwards

EXPECTATIONS

Ruth Rendell

One does not readily associate Ruth Rendell with the historical mystery, even though several of her novels – notably those written as Barbara Vine – deal in compelling fashion with crimes of the past. But Expectations *is a splendid, albeit brief, tale with a pleasing twist in the last line which reveals the significance of the title.*

No varnish can hide the grain of the wood, as my cousin Matthew once said of my late husband, adding that no man who was not a true gentleman at heart ever was a true gentleman in manner. George, however, succeeded in passing himself off as well-born and well-educated and in his last years only his wife and daughter knew the real man behind the smile and the black clothes and those snow-white pocket handkerchiefs. I and Estella alone knew the criminality hidden under the mellifluous speech-making and verse-quoting and his handsome looks.

But a gentleman who is upright and admirable is not found stabbed to death on Epsom Racecourse as George was three weeks ago. A man as virtuous as some of his acquaintance believed him to be does not leave on his death a contented widow and a joyful daughter. The truth is that, shocked as I was when the news of his murder was brought to me, I was also relieved. These twenty years gone by have sometimes been almost intolerable – though what course is there for a woman but to tolerate? – and George's death, horrible though the circumstances of it were, lifted the load from my shoulders in the twinkling of an eye.

His grave is in our village churchyard. Living in London, I missed the countryside and longed to go back. The brewery and all the property of course became George's on our marriage. I only deceive myself if I deny that it was to possess them that George married me but I am glad he kept Satis House, in spite of disliking it so thoroughly. I have returned to it and am about to take my place in country society with my daughter who comes out in a year's time. By then my mourning will be over and I shall give a ball for her. There will be some hearts broken when the young blades thereabouts set eyes on Estella. Her very name means a star. I always vowed that if I had a girl she should be called Estella, and George for once put up no opposition. He, of course, wanted a son.

She is far more beautiful than I ever was. She is tall like her father and has his dark curly hair. It is extraordinary to me now the effect he had upon me when Arthur brought him home to meet me all those years ago. I fell in love with him that first evening. But even then, blind as I was to everything but George's beauty and George's grace, I retained sense enough to wonder why my half-sibling – I will not dignify Arthur with the name of brother – was so desirous that his friend should like me and I return that particular regard.

Arthur was envious because our father left the greater part of his property to me, his elder child. Perhaps I should have reminded him more often that his riotous and undutiful behaviour almost secured his disinheritance. It was only on his deathbed that Papa relented and left him a share in the brewery. But that and the income which came with it was insufficient for Arthur, as I soon understood, though it was not until just before my marriage that I knew of the conspiracy got up between him and George.

Should I have refused George money? Would a prudent young woman have refused? I was so afraid to lose him. Of course I had suitors enough, but I wanted none of them. I wanted George. And the truth of what he said to me was undeniable.

"Why not a thousand pounds now, my dearest, bearing in mind that it will all be mine once we are married? Mine to husband for you and watch over diligently when you are my wife?"

So I agreed. Then, and again and again.

Three weeks before our wedding George was staying in the house and one night, unable to sleep, I came downstairs to find myself a book from the library. They were inside, Arthur and George, sitting over the dying fire with, no doubt, the brandy bottle. The door was a little ajar and I heard their voices.

I had been so certain they would have retired by now that I had come down in my nightgown with only a shawl thrown about me. So I paused at the door, uncertain of what to do next.

Then I heard Arthur say, "She shall have my share of the brewery, my boy, but I'll want a great sum for it, so mind you tell her not to jib at the price."

George laughed. "I'm likely to do that, am I? What, when you and I are dividing the sum between us?"

The man I had been used to call my brother said, "You'll be off then, Compeyson, will you?"

"Don't speak too loud." George's voice was almost too low for me to hear. "The long and the short of it is that I'll only marry her if she won't buy you out. But she will, she will.

Why, she's so much in love she'd follow me to the ends of the earth in her petticoat."

It was true. But I trembled as I stood there, drawing the ends of the shawl about me, returning to bed slowly, moving like a sleepwalker. There was no sleep for me that night. I had no one to advise me, though I knew, ignorant as I was, what advice the wise would give. But I loved him. In spite of his treachery, I loved him. I saw the grain through the varnish but still I loved him.

Next day and the next and the next George pleaded with me. When he was my husband, he said, it was only fitting that he should hold the brewery and manage it all. For a while I played the same game as he played. I asked Arthur's price and pretended to be appalled at the sum. I counted the days to our wedding day, nineteen days, then eighteen days. My clothes were bought, I had had three fittings for my wedding gown. George said all that would be needful was for me to sign a paper he would bring me.

Over the first paper I succeeded in spilling ink. Fifteen days, fourteen. I sent to the town for an attorney. He came and looked at the paper, he took it away with him and the days passed, thirteen, twelve, eleven, but he returned with the paper and pronounced it a legal document. There was no obstacle to my signing it. Except myself. I took my courage in my hands and told George I would be happiest to have *him* buy Arthur out, that I was a mere woman and unfit for business. Once we were married he would have an ample sum with which to purchase Arthur's share.

That was six days before the wedding. George was gone and I saw and heard nothing of him. I had no sleep, I could scarcely rest. But the wedding dress was finished and the bride-cake made and at last the day of my marriage came. Arthur was to give me away but I heard nothing of Arthur.

4

Expectations

George was to be my husband and I had received no sign from him for a week.

It was twenty minutes to nine in the morning and I was seated at my dressing table in front of a gilded looking glass. My maid had dressed me in satin and lace, all white, and put bridal flowers in my hair and Mama's diamonds about my neck. Half-packed trunks stood about the room. I remember the moment when the note came. My veil was but half arranged, and I had but one shoe on, the other being on the table near my hand with trinkets and gloves and a Prayer Book and some flowers, all confusedly heaped about the looking glass.

My maid came in and put the note into my hand. Time and the whole world seemed to stop and I thought, if this letter tells me he is gone time shall indeed stop and I will remain for ever in this moment. I will wear this dress for the rest of my life, with one shoe off and one on, until my hair is white and my skin is yellow. The feast shall remain spread until dust covers it and the bride-cake be a nest for spiders to veil with their webs.

I opened George's letter. "My dearest," he wrote, and he went on to say he loved me, he had been unavoidably absent these past days but he would be awaiting me in the church. I let my maid arrange my veil, I put on my shoe, the rings on my fingers and then the gloves. I took up the flowers and the Prayer Book and descended the stairs to meet Arthur at the foot and have him take me to be married.

Love was faded within the year. The varnish was stripped away and I saw only the grain, but yet I was married, I was Mrs George Compeyson with the dignity of a wife. I had my child to watch grow in health and beauty. Satis House, the name that means a sufficiency, awaited me for my widowhood, and they used to say, when the name was given, that whoever had that house could want nothing else.

5

Enough of my fortune remains after George's depredations for me to live in comfort and give Estella twenty thousand pounds on her marriage.

If I sometimes feel a little low and see myself growing old, my life wasted, I go into that room that was once my bedchamber and sit at the dressing table. There, staring into the looking glass, I tell myself to be thankful for what I did and what I did not do, for a year of love and a lovely child, and that I am not still in that white dress and veil, one shoe off and one shoe on, doomed to be for ever Miss Havisham.

DIALOGUE

Gillian Linscott

Although she has written novels where the action takes place in the present day, Gillian Linscott is probably best known for her historical crime fiction. Murder, I Presume, *set in London and Africa at the height of Queen Victoria's empire, was a notable venture into the sub-genre and in recent years she has written several books and a novella featuring the suffragette and amateur sleuth Nell Bray. With* Dialogue, *she stretches back much further in time to present a classic murder mystery set in ancient Greece. Appropriately, the tale is told almost entirely in conversation.*

*A*thens 417. *Summer sunrise*

"Wake up. It's Nicomachus. We're in terrible trouble."
"A death."
"Don't bellow it out to the street like that."
"Give the door another bash."
"Hold it, he's come to the window. Socrates, let us in."
"Nicomachus, Simonides, Melesias. I realise you three are

hungry for my company, but this early it's a touch too flattering."

"Someone's just died."

"That's the case almost any morning."

"Philocleon."

"How?"

"Poisoned."

"Come in."

"Thank the gods. What happened was, yesterday evening we went—"

"You see, we'd decided Nico here needed cheering up, because of his brother—"

"Philocleon decided."

"We all four of us decided really, but it was Philocleon who—"

"Will you please all stop yapping away like the three-headed hound and sit down. Simonides, you're the oldest so should be the wisest. Would you care to tell me as plainly as you can what's happened?"

"We all four of us met in the Agora, just before sunset. Philocleon suggested we should go off to his favourite brothel, the Little Honeypot, and we were there for most of the evening. It was dark when we came out and I was in favour of going home. But Philocleon wouldn't have that. Don't break the party up. Let's go back to someone's place for a few more drinks. So we ended up going back to Nico's."

"Tactless, wasn't it? A son in exile and a household in mourning?"

"Nico's mother was away at her sister's, but yes, I agree. As you know, Philocleon could be very insistent."

Nicomachus said, shame-faced, "The fact is, Socrates, even before we went back to my house we'd drunk a fair amount."

"Go on, Simonides."

Dialogue

"The place was in darkness, but Nico woke up a couple of slaves and the little flute girl, Antheia, and we had another drink or two."

"Just the four of you?"

"That's right. It has to be said that Philocleon was behaving boorishly by then . . ."

"He kept grabbing the flute girl's boobs to try and put her off her note. Peep peep peep – PARP."

"Be quiet, Melesias. It's out of place now. Anyway, after a while Nico and I had had enough. Nico dropped a gentle hint by letting the wine in the mixing bowl run out, but Philocleon was waving his empty cup around wanting more. Nico said all right, just one more then, but it turned out that the big jar of wine by the wall was nearly empty. Neat wine, that is, no water in it. Frankly, anybody less thick-skinned than Philo would have left it at that and said goodnight. Instead he grabs the big jar and starts glugging the dregs of the unmixed wine straight into his mouth."

"Not a pretty sight."

"I said, be quiet, Melesias. Almost at once, he started choking. Then he writhed around on the floor, yelling his mouth was burning, he'd been poisoned."

"We laughed."

"We weren't to know—"

"Of course we weren't, that's the point. We thought it was just Philocleon fooling around as usual. Even when he started vomiting all over the place, we thought it wasn't surprising given the skinful he'd drunk. And by the time we'd realised it wasn't a joke he . . ."

". . . was dead. I don't like Melesias' tone but that was just how it happened."

"Why have you come to me?"

"Who poisoned him, Socrates? It's what the authorities will be asking us."

9

"How would I know? I wasn't there."

Simonides said: "We thought you'd know what questions to ask."

"None that you can't ask yourselves."

Silence, then Nicomachus, "You mean how? How the poison got in the wine jar?"

"How, if you like. What's the answer?"

"I don't know. I have simply no idea."

"Very well then, you'll allow me to ask a question or two. You were the host. I take it that the jar of unmixed wine came from your storeroom."

"Yes. The slave Hermon brought it in. I unsealed it."

"And was that the jar you were all drinking from last night?"

"Yes."

"How did you drink it?"

"Well, the usual way."

"Describe the usual way."

"Just what everybody does. I'd tell Hermon to pour the wine in the mixing bowl and watch while he did it. Then the little slave lad would pour in water from a pitcher, also while I watched. Then I'd taste it to see that the mix was right and tell Hermon to pour it into the guests' cups."

"If Philocleon hadn't picked up the storage jar and drunk the last of the wine neat, is that what would have happened to it?"

"Yes, I suppose so."

"Did Philocleon give any warning that he intended to drink it straight from the jar?"

"None."

Simonides said: "It was a very bad mannered thing to do, after all."

"Nicomachus, what you say gives us some idea of when the poison was put into the jar, doesn't it?"

Dialogue

"I'm sorry, Socrates. I don't see. My mind—"

Melesias cut in. "He means, if we were drinking from that jar all night, the poison must have been put in after we had our last round together or we'd have all got it. Obvious."

"And if you choose to go down that road, you ask yourselves who had a chance to put the poison in unobserved."

Melesias said: "Well, any of us."

Simonides and Nicomachus started protesting, but Melesias cut across them. "No, think about it. The amount we were drinking, every so often one of us would have to get up and go out in the yard. Any of us could have dropped the stuff in on our way in or out."

"Without the rest of us seeing?"

Melesias said, "Do you sit there watching when your friend goes out for a piss, Simonides? Not unless you're completely besotted with him, you don't, and even you and Nico are past that stage."

"Do the two of you accept what Melesias says, that any of you could have done it?"

"It's monstrous to—"

"He was our friend after all—"

"If you're not going to think about it logically, I'm going back to bed. Is Melesias right, yes or no?"

"Yes, but—"

"Yes, only—"

"Could anybody else besides you three have put poison in the jar?"

Simonides said, "The two slaves or the flute girl. I'm sorry, Nico, but they could."

"Hermon's been in the family since my father was a boy. I'd trust him above anybody. As for the lad, he's simple. He can do little tasks like carrying water, but he's got the mind of a five-year-old child."

"Antheia then, the flute girl. Philocleon was annoying her."

11

Melesias said, "Talk sense, Simonides. If flute girls took to poisoning every man who squeezed their titties, Athens would be depopulated."

"I am trying to talk sense, and if you think it's a matter for joking—"

"Be quiet." Socrates' roar stunned them into silence. When he'd got their attention he said, more quietly, "You realise Melesias has just changed the question? We were asking how. Now we're asking why."

"You mean why would the flute girl want to kill Philocleon?"

"Why should anybody want to kill Philocleon?"

They considered it, sitting in silence. The rising sun coming in through the window showed their grey and shocked faces, the stains of wine and vomit on their clothes. Simonides spoke first.

"I can see no reason."

"Nicomachus?"

"Nor can I, Socrates. He was one of the most easy going men alive. Rather addicted to practical jokes perhaps—"

"And to drinking and whoring." That was Melesias. The other two turned on him, but he appealed direct to Socrates. "I can't see the point of this if we're not going to tell the truth. He was a good friend of us all, but Nico and Simonides know as well as I do that he had his little weaknesses. Like borrowing money off his friends and forgetting to pay it back."

Simonides said, "People don't get poisoned for borrowing a few hundred drachmae or playing practical jokes."

"What do they get poisoned for then, that's what Socrates is asking. What had he done to any of us in that room that we'd want to poison him?"

No answer from anyone. They sat there, looking at Socrates.

"It's no good staring at me like that. If there's an answer, it's in your heads, not mine, and you're none of you fit for anything at the moment. Go and take a bath, put on clean clothes. I'll meet you in the usual place by the wrestling ground at noon, then we'll see if any more promising questions occur to us."

Nicomachus and Simonides filed out unwillingly. Melesias, pretending to tie a sandal strap, stayed behind.

"Socrates, the why question. There's something I didn't like to mention with Nicomachus there. You know his elder brother had to go into exile because he was accused of plotting with the Spartans."

"The whole city knows it."

"And half the city knows why. An anonymous message accusing him, left on the doorstep of the Council."

"Yes."

"Supposing Nicomachus or one of his friends found out who'd left that message. They'd be angry, wouldn't they?"

"Are you saying that has something to do with why Philocleon died?"

"I don't know, but you can't help ideas coming into your mind, can you?"

The way Socrates was looking at him disconcerted Melesias and he left in a hurry, going the opposite way from Simonides and Nicomachus.

As they walked along, Simonides said to Nicomachus, "Melesias is telling Socrates about what happened at the Honey Pot. I'm sure he is."

"Why should he do that?"

"To give me a reason for poisoning Philocleon."

"As you said, people don't get poisoned for practical jokes."

"Except most of the clients of the Honey Pot last night must have heard me telling Philocleon I was going to kill him."

"You didn't mean it. You were just annoyed, that's all. And it was a nasty trick he'd played on you."

"Substituting a pox-rotted old bag who'd been had all ways by every sailor in Piraeus for the girl I'd paid for, then saying it was a philosophic proof that all women are alike in the dark—"

"Calm down, people are watching. But you didn't kill him, did you?"

"No, of course I didn't. But it will look bad for me when Melesias starts putting the story round. You know he'd like to make trouble between us. He's jealous."

"Will Socrates believe him?"

"Does he believe any of us?"

They walked on through the increasingly crowded streets, two battered party-goers with hangovers.

By noon, the whole city knew. When Nicomachus, Simonides and Melesias met Socrates in a quiet corner by the wrestling ground, the men exercising kept twisting themselves into contortions to look at them over their shoulders. In spite of clean clothes and baths, they looked no better than in the early morning. Nicomachus in particular was as tense as a sail in the wind.

"You know what will happen if we can't do something about this? They'll take Hermon and the slave lad and torture them on suspicion."

Simonides just nodded, but Melesias looked terror-stricken. "If that happens, they're bound to accuse us all to save their own skins."

Simonides said, "Nobody would take a slave's word against a citizen's."

Dialogue

"Even a citizen whose brother's supposed to be in league with the enemy?"

"Don't you dare mention that, Melesias. We know it's not true."

Nicomachus ignored them both and spoke to Socrates. "I'm head of the household now my father's dead and my brother's in exile. It's my duty to save our slaves from being tortured."

"In that case, I hope your heads are clearer than this morning. We've asked ourselves how Philocleon died and we've asked ourselves why anyone should have wanted to kill him. So far, we've got nowhere. Do any other questions occur to you?"

Melesias, still looking shaken, glared at Simonides. Simonides looked anxiously at Nicomachus, who answered for all of them.

"No, Socrates."

"I shall have to try to find one for you, then. We agreed, I think, that we could think of no reason why anybody should want to kill Philocleon?"

Melesias scuffed the edge of his sandal backwards and forwards in the sand, but no one said anything.

"Very well. Let us assume that there really is no reason why anybody should want to kill him. Does a man kill another man for no reason at all?"

"Unless he's mad, no."

"And to speculate about the reasoning processes of a madman would be ridiculous, wouldn't it, Simonides?"

"Of course, Socrates."

"So if we are to reason without making ourselves ridiculous, we must assume that Philocleon was not killed by a madman. But we've already agreed that a man who is not a madman does not kill without a reason. Is that right?"

"Yes."

15

"And we have found no reason why Philocleon should be killed, isn't that right too, Melesias?"

"I suppose so."

"Then our conclusion must be that our friend Philocleon wasn't killed at all. Any moment now he'll walk in laughing and ask us to lend him twenty drachmae or come and have a drink with him."

The three of them stared at Socrates as if he'd gone mad. Simonides said, stiffly, "I know you like to make a joke of things, but it's inappropriate here. Philocleon is dead."

"And yet we've just proved that it's logically impossible that he should be. Can't any of you cut this knot for us? Simonides, you used to have a brain."

"Perhaps it was an accident."

"What do you mean? That somebody put poison into a wine jar without intending to?"

"At any rate, without intending to kill him. As a joke perhaps."

"In which case, how would he know that Philocleon was going to drink straight from the jar? Is that the way he usually drank?"

"Of course not. It was childish bad manners, even by his standards."

"So a person who put poison in the jar couldn't have known that Philocleon would pick it up and drink from it. What would he expect to happen?"

"That it would be poured into the bowl, mixed with water and served to the guests."

"As Nicomachus described to us, very lucidly. Let's go back to that. Something happens before it's served."

Simonides gasped as if somebody had punched him in the stomach. "Nico. He'd taste the wine first. The poison wasn't meant for Philocleon at all. It was meant for Nico."

"Very well, let's assume that's the case. We'll ask the

question we asked about Philocleon. Why should anybody want to kill Nicomachus?"

"We can be more precise than that," Simonides said. "Let's ask why should anybody in that room have wanted to kill Nico?"

He was quivering like a hound on the scent. Socrates gave him a curious look, but his voice didn't change. "What do you two think? Shall we proceed as Simonides suggests?"

Nicomachus nodded. Melesias said, "We've no choice now, have we?"

"Right. Will you do it, Simonides, or shall I?"

"Go on."

"To the three of you, then. Would either of the slaves want to kill him?"

Simonides said: "He's good to them. They certainly wouldn't get a better master."

"The flute girl?"

"Same applies."

"Philocleon?"

"I can't think why he'd have wanted to. Anyway, he wouldn't have put poison in that jar then gulped it down himself, would he?"

"Quite so." Socrates shifted his position, apparently intent on a pair of wrestlers struggling shoulder to oiled shoulder. "So if we are looking for a potential killer of Nicomachus we rule out the slaves, the flute girl and Philocleon. Leaving—"

Melesias grabbed Socrates by the shoulder, pulling him forward so that their faces were only a little way apart, spluttering saliva all over him in his anger.

"You've fallen for it, Socrates. You've let Simonides lead you along like an old goat to the sacrifice. Two people left, him and me – and of course Simonides wouldn't poison his darling Nico, would he? So who does that leave?"

Socrates pulled himself away quite gently and wiped the spittle off his face, good humour unruffled.

"Are you going to answer your own question, Melesias?"

Without saying anything, Melesias left them at a heel-hammering walk, fists clenched. Nicomachus had gone very pale.

"You don't think he was really trying to kill me, Socrates? Why?"

Simonides, not Socrates, answered him. "He's eaten up with envy because you preferred me to him. He's just been waiting for his chance, that's all."

Nicomachus looked from one to the other, still waiting for Socrates's verdict, but for once he wouldn't speak.

Simonides said, "Come on, Nico. I'm taking you home."

They went together, leaving Socrates standing there, staring into space.

After dark, at Nicomachus's house

"Socrates, what are you doing here? Has something happened?"

"What sort of something? Hermon didn't want to let me in. He says you're ill."

"Shocked, more like. Beaten down. So much at once. Has Melesias been arrested?"

"You expected it? No."

"What then?"

"I simply wanted to continue our discussion, just the two of us. It was broken off, if you remember." The room was dim, with only two small lamps burning. Socrates's eyes went to the dark shape of a jar against the wall. "A new one?"

"Yes."

"Aren't you going to offer me a cup of wine?"

"Of course, I'm sorry."

Dialogue

Nicomachus mixed it himself, without calling a slave. When they were sitting down, Socrates said: "I should have called to commiserate with you about your brother going into exile. I suppose you never found out who made the accusation."

"No."

"A shabby thing to do, a false accusation in an anonymous letter."

"Yes."

"I don't suppose the man responsible would have delivered it himself, do you? By messenger in the dark, more likely."

"I suppose so."

They drank in silence for a while, then Nicomachus got up courteously to refill their cups.

"You're a good host, Nicomachus. Everything done properly."

"I hope so."

"Which raises a question which has been puzzling me. I came to see if you could help me with it." Nicomachus said nothing. "A good host doesn't give his guests wine from a jar that's nearly empty. It would be cloudy with the dregs. If a jar's nearly empty – so nearly empty that a bad-mannered guest could pick it up and drink from it – doesn't the host tell his slaves to take it away and bring a fresh one?"

"It was late. We were all drunk."

"In fact, in a well-run household, which yours is, a good slave like Hermon would do it without being told, wouldn't he?"

Nicomachus took a great gulp of wine and said nothing.

"Or rather, he wouldn't do it himself. He'd leave such a job to the lad – a simple lad just about capable of carrying things around. Things like jugs or jars." He waited a few heartbeats for Nicomachus to say something then added, in a low voice. "Or anonymous letters."

19

Very slowly, like a man underwater, Nicomachus put down his cup. Socrates went on, in the same low voice.

"If a man wanted to denounce his brother, a simple lad who wouldn't ask questions would be just the messenger he needed. But then the man might have doubts. Suppose the lad, in his innocence, prattled about it? Suppose somebody who mattered heard him? What do you think that man would do then, Nicomachus?"

Silence.

"I seem to be answering all my own questions tonight. I think he might poison the lad, Nicomachus. Poison him in front of friends, who'd see nothing but a slave lad dying of a seizure. A pity, but these things happen. The master is a conscientious master, you see. He knows his slaves. He might know that particular lad has been in trouble before for drinking up the dregs in the wine jars. Only this time, a drunken guest spoils the plan by getting there first." Nicomachus was hunched forward, arms hanging down, shoulders rising and falling in great sobs.

Socrates said, "In the eyes of the gods, would this man be innocent of killing his friend Philocleon, who is dead, but guilty of killing the slave lad, who is alive? A question I thought we might pass some of the night in discussing." He waited, drinking his wine. After some time Nicomachus's convulsive sobs changed to a few pumped-out words, repeated time after time.

"What shall I do, Socrates? Oh, what shall I do?"

"That's another question."

MASKS AND FACES

Eileen Dewhurst

The authentic atmosphere of Masks and Faces *owes much to Eileen Dewhurst's own memories of life just before and during the Second World War. The skill with which she gives readers an insight into the mind of the boy Richard is typical of the best of her varied output. Dewhurst's career as a novelist stretches back over twenty years, but it is only in recent times that she has turned her attention to the short form, with very successful results. This is, I believe, the first time that she has experimented with a 'past crime'. I hope it will not be the last.*

T he child, already unnerved by the barely suppressed anxiety of the adults surrounding him, hung back from the dim interior of the shed until his mother took him by the hand.

"Come along, Richard!" She had assumed the uncharacteristically hearty voice she used when urging him into the dentist's surgery. "There's nothing for you to be afraid of. It's going to be rather fun, in fact. And do you know? You're stealing a march on Mummy and Daddy, we have to wait I don't know how long for *our* gasmasks to be fitted! *And* they won't have Mickey Mouse on them!"

"Don't want a Mickey Mouse," the child muttered as, blinking, he exchanged the sunny daylight for the spaced bare bulbs above the long trestle table on which the things he was trying to keep his eyes away from were tumbled in heaps. "Don't want—"

"Hallo, there!" A woman his mother knew, a woman whose voice was always hearty, was standing the other side of the table and picking an object from the hateful pile in front of her. Holding it out to him.

The child shrank back. "No!" he shouted. It looked even worse than he had been afraid of: black rubber to trap his head, a terrible snout to stop him breathing. The silly goggle Mickey eyes and protruding Mickey nose didn't help at all. "Won't!"

"Darling, all the other children . . . D'you want to be the only one at school tomorrow not to be able to say he's been fitted with a gasmask? To have to tell all your friends it's because you were too frightened? I'm sure you don't want that, Richard, sweetheart."

He didn't, of course, and he suddenly felt braver. But for a few minutes he played hard to get, and when he let it happen it *was* frightening – the rubber smelled nasty, like dentist's gas, and was tight to each side of his head, and when he spoke his voice came out all deep and bubbly.

But the tightness was what the woman behind the trestle table was looking for, as was his struggling awareness of his every breath, and when she took the mask off (he had to hold his hands together very tightly so that they didn't flutter up and try to free him before the woman was ready) she told him and his mother how satisfactory it was when the first mask was the right fit and she didn't have to put the child through a second *ordeal*. The woman pronounced the last word on an emphatic whisper but the child wasn't listening, he was straining towards the daylight behind him and anyway he hadn't yet learned what the word *ordeal* meant.

Their walk home took them past the town hall. Soldiers were piling sandbags against its red brick walls.

"Why are they doing *that*?" the child asked.

"Because there might be a war," his mother said, trying to speak lightly. "Against Germany."

"But why should that—?"

"If there is, German aeroplanes might drop fire bombs as well as gas bombs. Sandbags would stop the fires spreading. But I don't think they'll drop either because I don't think there'll be a war."

She was right, of course. The Prime Minister came back from Germany waving a piece of paper on all the newsreels and telling everyone that he'd won 'peace in our time'. The sandbags disappeared, and Richard's mother put his gasmask at the back of a shelf under the stairs.

But less than a year later the sandbags were back in place, and there were gasmasks for all. Richard had to go back into the shed with his and have it exchanged for a larger and more grown-up one without a Mickey Mouse. He didn't like trying on the second one any more than he'd liked trying on the first, but he was almost a year older and anyway, he knew this time what to expect. But the fear came back for a moment when he saw his mother in hers, it made her look so strange and inhuman.

"Take it off, Mummy! Oh, take it off!"

He was ashamed the moment he'd cried out, especially as a girl alongside him, a bit older than himself, was sniggering at his sudden terror.

His mother, though, seemed to understand, and quickly pulled the mask off. "That better, darling?"

He nodded dumbly, looking away from the girl.

"You can, of course, Mary," the woman behind the table was telling his mother, "carry the mask in its cardboard box, it's got a string long enough to go over the shoulder, but down there" – indicating the shadowy end of the trestle – "we have some cases for sale. A proper strap rather than a string, and really *very smart*."

"You'd like that, wouldn't you, darling?" his mother asked.

He would like it, but he said yes without enthusiasm because the restoration of his self-respect demanded it, hoping his mother wouldn't be put off. So it was a relief, after she had thanked the woman and they had agreed to have coffee together at the next WI bring and buy sale, when she led him along the shed until they reached another heap, one he didn't mind looking at, and let him choose a shiny black case with a buckle on the strap for making it as long or as short as you wanted. Richard liked it so much he came out of the shed feeling very different from the way he'd felt when he'd gone in, quite jaunty in fact, swaggering along with the black box swinging in rhythm with his feet.

"I've got a gasmask case, I've got a gasmask case!"

The words had a tune, but he didn't sing them aloud because he wanted to keep to himself how pleased with life he had started to feel.

As they walked away from the shed she told him that he mustn't be upset when he saw Daddy's gasmask. "You see, Richard, Daddy's joined the ARP, he's an air raid warden, and people with important jobs in civil defence wear what are called service gasmasks."

"Uh-huh. Are there going to be air raids?"

"There may be, darling, we have to be prepared. But we've got the cellar, we'll be safe. Now, Daddy's gasmask . . . Being a service gasmask it's different from ours."

24

Masks and Faces

"How different?" *I've got a gasmask case, it's very black and shiny/I like my gasmask case, it's* . . . He couldn't think of a rhyme for *shiny*.

"Well, you know how ours has a sort of – a sort of *snout*? A bit like a pig, if you're going to think of an animal. The service gasmask has a long tube for breathing that looks like a – well, a bit like an elephant's trunk; it's sort of ridged like one and just about as thick. I'm telling you before you see Daddy wearing it, Richard, so that you won't get a shock."

"Oh," he assured her, "I won't get a shock." She hadn't realised, he decided, that he had grown up. "Will Uncle Freddy have an elephant's trunk, too?" Uncle Freddy was his father's brother, who a few weeks ago had come to stay with them because his wife had gone away. Richard had asked where and why she had gone and been told she was in hospital. His mother and father had looked at one another before answering him, and he had had a feeling they weren't telling him the truth. He wasn't interested enough, though, to ask them why. And he liked having Uncle Freddy around, he was fun and didn't talk to him as though he was still a child.

"Yes, darling, Uncle Freddy will have a service gasmask because he's an air raid warden as well." Richard's mother seemed to like having Uncle Freddy around, too.

"Dad's and Uncle Freddy's gasmasks being different from ours," Richard said. "Does that mean ours aren't really any good?"

"Of course not, darling." His mother sighed. Her baby was growing up. "It just means . . . When they're on duty they could be nearer to – well, to any gas that may have come out of a bomb, and need some extra protection. We can run away and hide, but if they're on duty, they can't."

That was the moment, Richard remembered all his life thereafter, when he first felt adult fear. And he remembered

25

too, with a touch of pride, that although it had been devastating he had been able to hide it. "They're very brave," he managed to say.

"We're all brave when we have our backs to the wall. You'll be brave too, darling, I know, and keep very quiet and calm when . . . if . . ."

She was giving him a pep talk, and at that point he stopped listening. He was thinking about the service gasmasks that made people look like elephants, and feeling a mixture of curiosity and fear at the thought of seeing his father and Uncle Freddy wearing theirs.

He should have been ready for Uncle Freddy. When they'd gone home and his mother opened the sitting-room door an elephant was awaiting them, waving its trunk, and Richard, who had imagined Uncle Freddy and his father in a slow metamorphosis, cried out in shock and to his immediate shame turned his face into his mother's skirt.

"For goodness' sake, Freddy!" his mother said crossly. "That isn't funny! It's all right, darling, it's just Uncle Freddy being silly," she said to Richard, softening her voice.

The boy had already moved away from her. "I know. I was just being silly, too." That was another key moment he was to remember, the moment of realising he would be able to look out for himself.

"Of course you were!" Uncle Freddy had taken off his mask and was beaming at Richard, allowing him the self-respect he'd made an instinctive grab for. That was what Richard liked about his uncle, he had no spite in him.

One thing nobody had been expecting was what history entitled the Phoney War: for the first year, while German troops invaded and subdued most of the countries of continental Europe, nothing happened in Britain. But in anticipation of immediate saturation bombing the sandbag piles grew

26

to the tops of the doorposts of government buildings, street lights were switched off, and drivers were forbidden to use headlights in case they guided enemy bombers to their targets. The hours of darkness started to be called the blackout rather than the night, and Richard's father and his Uncle Freddy went about the streets making sure people obeyed the new rules, even shouting up at windows where cracks of light escaped the statutory non-see-through blinds or curtains. They also took their turns to activate the wailing sirens that were to announce the beginning and the end of air raids, but only in practice. Large underground spaces, including the London tube stations, were earmarked for shelters, and a million and a half London back gardens were supplied with corrugated iron contraptions called Anderson shelters after the Home Secretary. Jagged metal stumps marked the crudely hasty removal of railings from the perimeters of old buildings for use in the construction of war weapons (but never used, since it was discovered after they had been cut off that they were the wrong kind of iron).

One of the worst fears was of poison gas: the tops of pillar boxes were given a special coat of paint which would change colour if any was around, and another new rule was that people had to carry their gasmasks wherever they went. Richard and his friends had to practise wearing theirs in school, and by the second session they were finding it amusing, with plenty of scope for the wags among them to act the fool.

When the Blitz eventually came, it came with a vengeance: the first bombs fell on London in September 1940, and the city was bombed every night for eleven weeks bar one (when bad weather prevented it). Londoners learned overnight that what had seemed like competent preparation was pitifully inadequate.

Richard's father and uncle were on duty almost every night and staggered filthy and sometimes bloodstained up to bed when they came home in the mornings. After a few nights Richard and his mother went straight to the cellar when it was bedtime, dragging themselves back upstairs at dawn in the hope of a couple of hours of normal sleep before it was time to get up and shrink from the details of another night's carnage. Everything was so chaotic that thieves and looters had a field day, and the Blitz was a couple of weeks old before one sinister piece of serial private enterprise began to be noticed and recorded.

When an ARP warden who lived not far from Richard got home one morning he saw that a bomb had destroyed part of his house. Not, though, the part where his claustrophobic wife had insisted on continuing to sleep, and he was shedding tears of relief as he ran in through the broken gate, so that (as he told the police) he didn't clearly see the man he almost bumped into who was running out. But he saw the gasmask the man was wearing, and struggled into his own as he stepped over the rubble that had been his front door. His wife was dead in bed in the undamaged room, and at first he thought it was gas that had suffocated her. But then he saw that the bedroom had been ransacked, as well as the other unscathed parts of his house. When he ran back into the street his shouts of outrage were lost in his gasmask but he could hear the outrage of the people out there because they weren't wearing theirs, and when he took his off he discovered that the air was contaminated by no more than the dust from the broken buildings. The other people were shouting because their loved ones had been blown to pieces by a bomb, and they were unable to take in that his wife had been suffocated by a pillow. So he went to the nearest police station, where a weary policeman took his statement down without seeming to take it in either. It was afternoon before a doctor, a couple of members of the local CID and a pathologist came to the remains of his house, and although

28

the doctor confirmed that his wife had been done to death, and the senior CID man said it was a very serious matter, it was clear to the bereaved husband that the seriousness that was really concerning them was the slaughter from the air they were expecting during the night to come.

It was only after the fourth murder with the same characteristics – entrance effected by first light and during enemy action, suffocation with a pillow, rough ransacking of drawers and cupboards, theft of small valuables, a man wearing a gasmask seen by neighbours or bystanders running away – that the local constabularies in the affected areas put their findings together, and that was by chance: a detective from one part of the Met telling a detective from another over a pint of ale about the bizarre murder that had been committed on his patch under cover of the current confusion. The evidence of the gasmask, which in normal circumstances would have been considered flimsy, was respected because to see a gasmask being worn at that time was the reddest of red alerts to the ultimate horror, and no one who had seen the runaway wearing one had any doubts that it might have been in his or her imagination.

But even when co-ordination had taken place, and the Metropolitan Police had sanctioned the addition of a new alert to the do's and don'ts they were posting about the capital each day, there was really nothing they could do. Bombs were still falling nightly over central London and over its inner and outer suburbs, and they could hardly anticipate which of the stricken areas the thief and murderer would select as dawn broke and the All Clear rang out. The police chiefs decided after the fifth murder that robbery was probably the prime motive and the murders had been committed merely to silence waking sleepers. Which could mean there had been other robberies by the same thief which had gone undetected in the general mayhem, particularly as more and more people were beginning to sleep the night through in public shelters and along the platforms of tube stations . . .

One night Richard and his mother heard a lot of noise even though they were in the cellar, and when the All Clear sounded and they went up into the house they found windows cracked and cups fallen from hooks. Richard's mother was frantic with worry about her husband and her brother-in-law and talked about going out to see where the bomb had fallen and if she could find them, but decided in the end that she would only be in the way of the professionals and that she as well as Richard should go to bed.

They had been back upstairs for about half an hour when Richard heard another noise. An awful sort of bubbly gasping that had him awake and upright in an instant, then running to his door and peering out, to see a man in a gasmask running out of his mother's bedroom and hurtling downstairs. He wanted to chase him, but he went of course to his mother. Most of the drawers in her room were pulled out, and their contents scattered about. One of her pillows was over her face, and she was dead.

So was the telephone, when Richard had given up his desperate attempts to revive her. He was stumbling out of the room when he heard the front door slam a second time, and he met his father on the stairs and fell sobbing into his arms.

When Richard had shown his father what had happened, and his father, too, had failed to bring his mother back to life, Richard made tea for them both and they sat downstairs in the ransacked sitting-room to drink it. Richard wished they would both cry but somehow he couldn't because everything was unreal, and his father just sat staring into space until Richard said he supposed they should go to the police. Then his father roused himself and said, "It's chaos out there because a bomb's fallen on The Maples, but yes, of course we must go."

Uncle Freddy came in when they were in the hall, shaking and sobbing because he had just helped dig a dead woman out of the remains of The Maples. When they told him about Richard's mother he broke down completely and Richard's father had to slap his face and give him a cup of very sweet tea before he felt it was safe for them to leave him. He begged to come with them, but Richard's father said someone should stay in the house and make sure there was no disturbance to anything before the police arrived, and at last he agreed. They left him slumped in an armchair, looking like someone Richard had never seen before.

At least, by now, the police knew what Richard and his father were talking about. Because Richard was under age his father had to be with him while they asked him questions, and they held hands.

Richard told them about the noise that had wakened him. Reluctantly, because he knew it would hurt his father, and as he spoke he felt his father's hand trembling in his.

"And then what happened, Richard?"

"Then I got out of bed and ran to the door and looked out towards Mum and Dad's bedroom."

"And what did you see?"

"I saw a man come out. He was running and he wore a gasmask."

"Did you see what else he was wearing?"

"Trousers . . . a jacket, I think . . . I only really saw the gasmask."

"I understand. So you didn't notice anything else about him?"

"I'm sorry . . ." And then he was realising he would never see his beautiful mother again and he was crying, great heaving

31

sobs that shook him to pieces and sent him twisting into his father's lap.

"I'm sorry," his father said, in his turn. "I questioned him when I got home and I don't think he's got anything more to tell you. He just watched the man head down the stairs and then he went in to his mother."

"Of course. We may get some more information about the man from the people who were in the street when he ran out."

But it turned out that this time the gasmasked intruder had got away unseen. There was one more murder the following week where he was spotted, and two reports by absentee householders of their homes being ransacked on the night of a nearby raid, and then the Blitz came to an end and the murders and robberies with it. The murderer was never caught.

Uncle Freddy returned within days to his own home, even though, as he himself told Richard, his wife wasn't coming back to him. Richard's father seemed relieved. He did his best to be both father and mother to his son, and life in the house and life in the street moved back slowly and in tandem towards normality.

It wasn't until the end of the war, when he was into his teens and beginning to learn the ways of the world, that Richard thought again about the reactions of his father and his mother to Uncle Freddy's long visit. Began to interpret, soon after he acquired his first real girlfriend, the looks he had seen pass between his uncle and his mother, the looks his father had given both of them when they were unaware. So that a picture began to form slowly and relentlessly before his mind's eye of the man in the gasmask, that horrendous night, slamming the front door from inside the house, hiding in the cupboard under the stairs, then slamming the front door again . . .

Masks and Faces

At sixteen Richard ran away from home and was never found and never contacted his father, although he had the occasional wild impulse to demand his mother's engagement ring with menaces. He didn't drift on to the streets because he knew how to look out for himself, and quite quickly he found a job with opportunities. He took them, and secured himself a well-heeled future and a loyal wife.

But he never told her, or anyone else, the answer to the question the police in their blitz-induced weariness had failed to ask him in 1940.

Oh, no, the gasmask didn't have a pig's snout, it had an elephant's trunk.

CHAPTER AND HEARSE

Catherine Aird

There are few more skilled exponents of the traditional English detective story than Catherine Aird. Her Calleshire-based series featuring Detective Inspector C D Sloan began in 1966 with The Religious Body *and is still going strong. Her gentle humour and adept plotting are seen to equal advantage in both the novel and the short story.* Chapter and Hearse *is an agreeable example of her style, which offers a refreshing slant on the theme of past crimes.*

"Sloan," barked Police Superintendent Leeyes down the telephone, "You're wanted, and quickly!"

"I'll be right over, sir." Detective Inspector Sloan didn't exactly click his heels together but he did get to his feet pretty smartly.

"No, not by me. Don't come to my office . . ."

"Sir?"

"It's the Assistant Chief Constable who's asking for you." The Superintendent didn't even try to keep his amazement at this unlikely event out of his voice. "Don't ask me why."

"Me, sir?" Detective Inspector Sloan did a rapid mental revision of his past week and work. As far as he knew he hadn't blotted his copy-book in any way but you never knew. With the Police and Criminal Evidence Act in operation even not offering a suspect a cup of tea was capable of being misconstrued by a defence solicitor.

"You, Sloan. He says," said Superintendent Leeyes, "that it's a sudden emergency."

"I'm on my way . . ."

The Assistant Chief Constable – a gentleman copper if ever there was one – received him with his customary courtesy.

"Ah, Sloan, there you are . . ." If there was anything urgent pending it certainly didn't show in his manner. "Take a seat . . ."

"Thank you, sir." It wasn't going to be a disciplinary matter then: rebukes were delivered to a man standing. On the carpet, if there was one.

"A little problem has cropped up this morning in connection with the Minster . . ."

Sloan sat down. That explained one thing anyway. Calleford Minster was not in Superintendent Leeyes' 'F' Division and the Superintendent took as narrow a view as did the Coroner as to what was and what was not within his jurisdiction.

"And," continued the Assistant Chief Constable unhurriedly, "it's got to be resolved before tonight."

"I see, sir."

"By half past seven, actually," said the Assistant Chief Constable.

"Time is of the essence, then, is it?" ventured Sloan.

"It was and it is," said his superior enigmatically.

"And the problem?"

"There are two problems," said the ACC, "and one of them was murder."

"Ah! And the victim, sir?" Every case had to begin

36

somewhere and every case – every murder case anyway – had a victim. "Do we know . . ."

"Oh, yes, Sloan. There's no doubt about that. The man's name was Lechlade. Walter Lechlade. Exact age unknown. Probably about forty."

"And his occupation?" If unemployment carried on on its present-day scale a man's occupation – or lack of it – would soon cease to be worth recording.

"Precentor and prebendary," said the ACC.

"So this Walter Lechlade was a clerical gentleman, then, was he, sir?" Sloan wasn't quite sure of his ground here but the words sounded ecclesiastical enough and they were talking about cathedrals.

"That's the whole trouble," said the ACC gently.

"The Church looking after its own?" suggested Sloan. It had, after all, been known to happen.

"Well," conceded the ACC, stroking his chin, "I must say it was all hushed up at the time. Nothing written down and so forth."

"People will always try . . ."

"Until Peter Quivel . . . he's the Bishop in the case . . . started making a fuss."

"Ah," said Sloan. "Truth will out."

"I'd very much like to think so, Sloan, but I'm afraid the Bishop had his own axe to grind."

"It happens," said Sloan without thinking. He pulled himself together and got down to business: he wasn't here to philosophise. "And the time of this murder, sir?" After all, the ACC had said himself that time was of the essence, hadn't he? "Is it known?"

The ACC looked down at a pile of notes on his desk. "Between one and two o'clock in the morning."

"And where exactly?" Detective Inspector Sloan opened his notebook from sheer force of habit.

37

"Between the Cathedral and Lechlade's own house nearby. That is, in the lane between the Bishop's Close and Canon de Derteford's house at the corner of Bear Lane."

"Not a very usual hour for a clergyman to be out and about, sir, if I may say so." Sloan tried not to sound at all censorious. Time was, when it would have been relatively safe to be abroad at that time of night but not these days. Small wonder, though, that someone had wanted the whole matter hushed up.

"Oh, yes, it was," said the ACC unexpectedly.

"Not a sensible hour even so, though," insisted Sloan.

"He was in the Cathedral Close," the ACC reminded him.

"But was it secure?" said Sloan, unimpressed.

"Well, no, it wasn't actually. That's the whole point. But it ought to have been, Sloan, and I must say you've got to the heart of the matter very quickly."

"Thank you, sir."

"You see, the gates to the Close should have been shut at curfew . . ."

"It's good that these old customs are kept up, sir, isn't it?" put in Sloan. "It's still done at eight o'clock every evening at the Minster, I believe."

"Yes," responded the ACC briskly. "But what happened the night Walter Lechlade was murdered, Sloan, was that not only was one of the gates – the Southgate – left open for his murderers to come in, but it was also left open for them to get out."

"Murderers?" Sloan sat up. "Was it a gang killing, sir, then?" They didn't have a lot of those in the mainly rural county of Calleshire, thank goodness, but the ways of the city were bound to reach them in the end.

"I suppose you could say that it was, Sloan," agreed the ACC thoughtfully. "I must say I hadn't thought of it in that light myself ... more of a conspiracy, you might say."

"And the gateman given something for his – er – forgetfulness?"

"He was indeed," said the ACC warmly, "and probably not what he expected either." He prodded the pile of papers in front of him. "He – the gateman, name of Stonyng, Richard Stonyng – said that the Mayor hadn't told him to shut the gate."

"What had it got to do with the Mayor, might I ask?" Criminal Investigation and Local Government usually met head-on over fraud and Planning Law, not murder.

"Quite a lot. The Cathedral had been in dispute with the civil authorities about their boundaries for years."

"It's not unknown, sir." It had always been a great relief to Sloan that property disputes were civil, not criminal, matters. He added, a trifle sententiously, "Good fences make good neighbours."

"Good neighbours the city and Cathedral weren't," said the ACC emphatically. "In the old days men on the run from the Mayor and Commonalty used to jump over St Peter's churchyard wall and take sanctuary in the Cathedral – much to the city's annoyance."

"Men have always tried to escape from justice," observed Sloan, who carried several scars on his person to prove it.

"I suppose," said the ACC, who had been at school at Eton, "that you could call it a sort of Wall Game. Anyway, it seems that the man on the gate ..."

Sloan glanced at his notebook. "Richard Stonyng ..."

"... took his orders from the Mayor that night."

"And the Mayor's name, sir?" prompted Sloan, his pen poised. Office holders always had recorded names.

"Alfred Duport."

"And where, sir, does he come in or don't we know?"

"Good question, Sloan. First and foremost he seems to have been in cahoots with the Dean against the Bishop."

"That's bad." It sounded an unholy alliance to Sloan.

"Very. But not unknown in English history," said the ACC grimly. "In this instance the *casus belli*—"

"Beg pardon, sir?"

"What? Oh, sorry, Sloan. The cause of their dispute was the appointment of John Pycot as Dean of the cathedral."

"Not popular?"

"Not with Bishop Peter Quivel, anyway. He said the election had been rigged."

"And as it was the Bishop who – er – blew the gaff, do I take it the Dean had something to do with the death of the pre— the other clerical gentleman, sir?" Rigged elections were not usually the province of a detective inspector but murder was.

"You've got it in one, Sloan," beamed the Assistant Chief Constable.

"Not a lot of brotherly love lost," observed Sloan. That, at least, could be safely said about most murders.

"None."

"But why should it have been Walter Lechlade who got killed then?" asked Sloan, anxious to get at least one thing clear.

"Pro-Bishop, anti-Dean," said the ACC succinctly.

"So where does the Mayor – Alfred Duport – come in, then?" asked Sloan for the second time.

"Friend of the Dean," said the ACC.

"But the Dean wasn't the murderer, surely, sir, was he?" ventured Sloan, although naturally prepared to concede that it wasn't what you knew that mattered but who . . .

"John Pycot didn't kill Walter Lechlade personally, if that's what you mean," said the ACC, "any more than Henry II

40

actually killed Thomas à Becket on an earlier and much more celebrated occasion."

"That, sir," observed Sloan, greatly daring, "is a fine point."

"Oh, he was morally guilty," conceded the ACC, who didn't have to deal with split hairs on a daily basis in court. "No doubt about that."

"And did penance," said Sloan. There had been a picture in his history book of a barefoot Henry, in sackcloth and ashes, making his way to Canterbury in the snow to be flogged, that had stayed in Sloan's mind since he was a small boy.

"The Dean did penance, too," said the ACC.

"For helping get rid of another turbulent priest?" asked Sloan, his memory stirred now.

"For getting rid of a priest," amended the ACC.

"Really, sir?" Sloan's mother, who was a great church-woman, was forever insisting that she didn't know what the Church was coming to. It was beginning to sound as if she might be right.

"From all accounts," said the ACC drily, "it was the Dean who was turbulent."

For reasons that Sloan had never enquired into, his mother always blamed any present-day trouble in a cathedral on Thomas Cranmer amd his Statutes – perhaps he should have listened to her more. Detection was a more arcane business than it seemed at first sight.

The ACC was still talking. "History, Sloan, says that Walter Lechlade was a peaceable enough fellow. Not that that saved him, of course."

Detective Inspector Sloan nodded. Being peaceable was no insurance against being murdered. "How was he killed?" he asked, the policeman in him taking over from the erstwhile schoolboy and the inattentive son. There had, he remembered, been another Archbishop of Canterbury as well as Thomas à

Becket who had been done to death in office. His name had stayed in Sloan's memory from his history lessons purely because of the manner of his murder.

The ACC consulted his papers again. "Two blows on the skull and the arm from knives, swords and Danish axes."

"Not a lot of those about, sir." With that other archbishop, St Alphege, it had been ox-bones.

"There were then, Sloan."

"Then?" Sloan's pen stayed suspended above his notebook, a suspicion confirmed. "Do I take it, sir, that we're not talking about the here and now?"

"Yes and no," said the ACC, quite unabashed. "More of the there and then, perhaps, than the here and now, but some of both."

"Might I ask where?"

"Exeter, Sloan."

"And when?"

"November 1283."

"When the Mayor and the Dean murdered this Walter Lechlade—"

"The Precentor . . ."

"With a Danish axe?" Their pastry must have come later.

"No, no, Sloan. The actual murder was done by others, orchestrated by three Vicars and a Canon."

With Thomas à Becket, thought Sloan, it had been four knights but the end result had still been the same spilling of brains.

"In fact," murmured the ACC, "one commentator called 'em Satellites of Satan."

Sloan said he wasn't at all surprised.

"Henry de Stanway, Clerk in Holy Orders, John de Wolrington, Vicar of Ottery St Mary, John de Christenstowe, Vicar of Heavitree, and Canon Reginald de Ercevesk," recited the ACC. "Almost the Four Horsemen of the Apocalypse, you might say."

"Caused a bit of a flutter in the dovecotes, that, I daresay, sir." There had been other clergymen who had hit the headlines but Sloan didn't think this was the moment to mention them.

"The Bishop appealed to the King for justice—"

"And which King would that have been, sir?"

"Edward I of blessed memory."

"The Hammer of the Scots?" More of those history lessons had stuck than Sloan had appreciated.

"He was known as the English Justinian," said the ACC, who had had a classical education.

"I didn't know that, sir."

"And he came down to Exeter at Christmas 1285."

"Two years later?" In Sloan's book justice delayed was justice denied.

"This is where it gets interesting, Sloan."

"Really, sir?" Interesting, he decided, it might be: urgent – today, this minute, urgent – he couldn't see how it could possibly be.

"The case was begun on Monday, December 24th—"

"Christmas Eve?"

"Christmas Eve – the judges were Roger de Loveday and Richard de Boyland – and then it was adjourned for Christmas."

" 'The hungry judges soon the sentences sign,' " Sloan quoted Alexander Pope, " 'And wretches hang that jurymen may dine.' " They had that piece in their speeches every year at the Berebury Magistrates' Dinner.

"It wasn't like that at all," said the ACC a trifle plaintively. "No, they all kept Christmas Day in high old style and then on St Stephen's Day—"

"Boxing Day."

43

"They found Richard Stonyng—"

"The gatekeeper."

"Guilty of murder."

"For not shutting the gate?" Sloan was sensitive about gates. There had been one terrible week in his schooldays when the boy who had been detailed to play brave Horatius, Captain of the Gate, had gone down with mumps. Sloan had been the unwilling understudy and anything to do with gates, fearful odds, ashes of his fathers and temples of his Gods still struck an unhappy chord.

"For opening the gate to let the felons in before the murder and for not shutting it after the deed was done to keep them in."

"I see, sir." Dereliction of duty or complicity he would have called that himself but apparently the judges had reckoned it murder. "An accessory before and after the fact," he said neatly.

"And as for 'Mr Mayor, sirrrr,' " baaa'd the ACC in the tones of Larry the Lamb.

"Alfred Duport," supplied Sloan. The ACC's literary background had obviously been broad enough to have included Toytown.

"Found guilty of consenting to and planning the felony and receiving and harbouring the felons."

"Aiding and abetting," translated Sloan.

"And then on Holy Innocents' Day . . ."

That, thought Sloan, couldn't have been judicial irony, surely?

". . . All those who had pleaded Benefit of Clergy—"

"That, sir," said Sloan, "was some sort of establishment cop-out, wasn't it?" He knew that, like sanctuary, they didn't have it anymore, although it was true to say that the only criminal clergymen to come his way officially had certainly been attempting – one way and another – something for their own benefit.

"A way of exculpation of men of the cloth grounded in a text in the First Book of Chronicles," said the ACC, admitting that he'd looked it up. "Chapter sixteen, verse twenty-two."

Sloan decided he really would have to pay more attention to his mother's interests in future.

The ACC shuffled the notes on his desk and read out, " 'Touch not mine anointed and do my prophets no harm.' And all they had to do to prove they were clerks in Holy Orders was to be able to read the first verse of psalm fifty-one. The Miserere."

"So the clerical conspirators got off?" concluded Sloan doggedly.

"Handed over to their bishops, except the Dean, who was sent to a monastery."

"And the actual murderers, sir?" Sloan knew who he meant – the ones with blood on their hands, which was as good a definition as any he knew.

"Escaped abroad."

Detective Inspector Sloan, currently coming to terms with the vagaries of the Crown Prosecution Service, sighed and said, "Not a very satisfactory outcome, sir."

"There was one more puzzle."

"Sir?"

"The records are a bit shaky but afterwards they wrote down that the Mayor had been hanged on St Stephen's Day."

"But," frowned Sloan, "surely that was before he was tried?"

"It has been known."

"Lynch Law." That was the only law the police were pledged not to uphold.

"Actually, Sloan, it was known as Lydford Law. Punish first and try afterwards."

Catherine Aird

Sloan said he thought 'Try first and don't punish afterwards' was more the vogue these days.

The ACC said, "What they meant was that the prisons were so awful that often those who were accused died from gaol fever before they could be brought to trial – which is rather different."

"Yes, sir." Sloan paused. "I take it that this has all been written up somewhere?"

"Admirably."[1] The ACC patted a thin square grey book on his desk. "I can't think why no one's made a play out of it."

What Detective Inspector Sloan couldn't think was how something that had happened in the year 1283 could suddenly become enough of an emergency this morning for him to have been summoned post haste from dealing with latter-day criminals who only ever pleaded broken homes and unhappy childhoods.

"You think it hangs together all right, Sloan, do you?" asked the ACC.

"Yes, sir."

"I've made myself quite clear, I hope?"

"Perfectly, sir."

"And you found it an interesting case?"

"Yes, sir." He ventured a modest pun. "What you might call a top brass rubbing out."

"The problem is," said the ACC, surreptitiously making a note of this, "that they have a Literary and Historical Society attached to Calleford Minster. I belong myself."

"Really, sir?"

"And they've got a bit of a problem."

"Sir?"

1 *Exeter Vignettes* by Frances Rose-Troup. (Manchester University Press, 1942)

"Yes, indeed." The ACC leaned back in his chair. "Their Secretary's just rung me to say that tonight's speaker has been taken ill and would I step into the breach with something suitable."

"I see, sir." The quotation 'Once more unto the breach, dear friends, once more,' could, Sloan felt, safely be left to the Chairman in his introduction.

"I thought I would tell them about this murder," said the ACC.

"The Cathedral interest," nodded Sloan.

"I'm calling my talk 'Another Exeter Riddle,' Sloan, because there were some famous medieval Exeter riddles . . ."

It all seemed quite open and shut to Sloan. He said restrainedly, "Should go down very well, sir."

"It was helpful to rehearse it with you," said the ACC unblushingly.

"Thank you, sir."

"I thought I would begin with a quotation."

"It's often done, I understand, sir." It was always done at the Berebury Magistrates' annual dinner.

"From Shakespeare."

"Naturally, sir."

"This one." The ACC squinted modestly down at his notes. " 'Some men are born great, some achieve greatness, and some have greatness thrust upon them . . .' "

WAR RATIONS

Martin Edwards

The initial impetus to write this story came one Sunday lunchtime a year or so ago when my mother was reminiscing about her life as a young teacher in Leeds at the time war broke out. (I hasten to add that she bears no resemblance to Amy Jessop!) I was fascinated by what she told me about the process of evacuation and also by her recollections of a place known locally as the Murder Woods – although the latter played no part in the final version of this story. War Rations *offers a brief glimpse into an extraordinary period of our history, a time when life sometimes seemed cheap. I enjoyed writing it and telling a story, for the first time, from a female character's point of view.*

One of the children was screaming. Amy Jessop scanned the crowd of youngsters, but she could guess who was making all the fuss. For most of the others, this was the most exciting day of their lives. It was seven o'clock on a bright September morning and they were being evacuated from their homes in Leeds, heading for safety before war

49

broke out. They were laughing, giggling, pulling faces and playing games outside the school gates. But Tom Harker always had to be different. Today he wasn't the centre of attention and he did not like that one little bit.

She hurried along the pavement to comfort the boy, only to find that a couple of the older girls already had their arms around the skinny six-year-old. With his blond curls and blue eyes, he never seemed to be short of people to cuddle him. Rather like his mother, Amy said to herself.

"He's heartbroken, Miss Jessop," one of the girls said.

"Come on, Tom. The trams will be here any minute. No one else is crying. Your mother would expect you to be brave."

The tear-stained face turned towards her. "I want my mummy!"

"You'll see her soon. I promise." Amy crossed her fingers behind her back. Elsie Harker had, so far as she could tell, always resented the burdens of motherhood. Now she would have the chance to spend even more time with that fancy man of hers. What on earth had John Harker ever seen in her? He was a decent respectable man who kept one of the shops on the little parade. Elsie came from the vast estate behind the parade which housed people who had once lived in the endless rows of back-to-backs in the centre of Leeds. She was the youngest of a family of ten; none of her brothers and sisters had ever done a hand's turn in their lives, so far as Amy could tell.

Tom muffled a sob. Amy gazed at the blond curls and eyes that, although puffy, still were beautiful. On second thoughts, it was all too easy to understand why John Harker had been smitten. Elsie Cornforth had, so Amy understood from Mary Brough, who also taught the infants, found herself a job behind John's counter when he was short-staffed. Within a short time, she'd also found herself pregnant and of course John had done the decent thing. That sort of man did.

Amy sighed. More fool him, for walking into the trap.

A cheer went up. "Miss! The tram's coming!" the girl said, letting go of Tom.

Although close on a thousand children and staff were waiting to travel to their unknown destination, they all crammed into a dozen of the double-decker trams. At City Square, everyone had to get out at the station and pile into the waiting trains. It was a complicated journey, with innumerable stops and, when they had reached the North Riding, another transfer, this time to a fleet of buses. Amy did not have a moment to herself; the children kept plying her with questions. She had few answers for them and concentrated on vague words of reassurance. At least the endless distractions saved her from having to speculate about what the future might hold.

At about midday they arrived in Helmsley. Amy knew it as a pretty market town with a large square and the ruins of an old castle. She and her parents had come here for days out in her own schooldays in the early thirties. Today, though, it had lost its charm. By now the children were tired of travelling and Tom Harker was not the only one who could not stop snivelling. But they had to march to the local school, along streets lined with onlookers.

"Poor mites!" she heard a woman say. "They'll never see their homes again!"

Everyone was fed with corned beef and given a brown paper carrier bag containing two days' rations: evaporated milk in a tin, cocoa, a few biscuits, more corned beef. Then it was time to assemble in the yard and divide into groups before the final stage of the journey. She and Mary were in charge of a couple of dozen small ones, including Tom. Another bus took them out to a village called Coldkirby where once again they gathered in the playground, waiting to be told where they would spend the night. A worried-looking man told them that there seemed to have been some mistake. The villagers had been expecting to take no more than half a dozen evacuees. It was evening before all the children were found a bed. The two teachers slept the night on rough made-up beds in the school hall.

The next day, a Saturday, was spent getting organised. A farmer's wife offered Amy a poky room with a window which commanded a view of the pigsty. That afternoon she wrote a letter to her widowed mother, who lived in Wakefield, to explain where she had finished up. '*This place is pretty enough,*' she wrote, '*but I bet in winter it's like the back of beyond. The sooner we are allowed home, the better. I could very easily get bored with corned beef! Perhaps even now it isn't too late. War may still not be inevitable.*'

In less than twenty-four hours, she knew better. She was with the farmer and his family, clustering around the wireless, when the Prime Minister announced that a state of war existed with Germany. There was a sick feeling in her stomach. So many people, she knew, would die senselessly. No one could tell what the future might hold. Amy resolved that she would return to Leeds as soon as she could. It might be less safe there, but she needed to be in a place where she felt she belonged. In a moment of self-awareness, she thought: *That's what I need, somewhere to belong. And, who knows, perhaps someone to belong to.*

Others felt much the same. Parents started to arrive to collect their children and take them back home. After three or four weeks she and Mary only had a handful of pupils to look after. It was agreed that Amy should return to the city. When she got back, the schools were closed, but she was given a series of jobs. Useful work to help the war effort. She checked census forms, and wrote out identity cards and ration books. Although some of the schools soon re-opened, Amy's was being used as a temporary barracks for newly called-up soldiers and so she helped out elsewhere until it was ready again and she returned to her digs with Mrs Garbutt in Ephraim Street.

One day, on her way home, she bumped into John Harker. He was just shutting up shop and in response to his greeting she asked how Tom was.

"All right, I think. I went up there a fortnight back. They seem to be looking after him, as far as I can judge. I miss him, of course, but he's in the safest place."

After that she often stopped and spoke to him. At first they merely passed the time of day for a few minutes, discussing the previous night's air raid and the people they knew who had been killed in the bombings. John was just too old for the call-up and she sensed that he felt it keenly that he was unable to fight for King and Country. He was a pleasant man, muscular but kind and softly-spoken. Gradually their conversation began to range more widely. He told her a little about his business, of how he had grown up in the seaside resort of Scarborough before his parents had moved to Leeds twenty-five years earlier. She told him about her own past, school in Ossett and teacher-training here at Beckett Park. She'd always loved children; teaching was all she had ever wanted to do. Increasingly, though, she felt as if she were just marking time, that there must be more to life than this.

"What about boyfriends?" he asked. "I bet you're not short of admirers."

She blushed and shook her head. She'd never considered herself pretty: she had a nice enough face, she thought, but her appearance was compromised by a tendency to put on weight if she so much as looked at a good meal. She liked her food too much, that was the trouble. The young men who had taken her out on dates had been amusing enough for a short time but soon the attractions of their company had palled. They seemed somehow callow, immature, embarrassingly incapable of taking their eyes away from her ample bosom. Of course, the war had taken them away from home and although the city was full of soldiers, Amy had resisted their wolf whistles and cheery invitations to the pub. When John Harker pressed her, she said something of this. His response startled her.

"You know, Amy, if I were a few years younger, I'd ask you out myself."

Again she felt herself colouring. "But . . . you . . ." she stammered.

"What, Amy?"

"I mean, you're married."

"She's left me, Amy. Run off with that chap of hers."

"Oh, I'm sorry. I didn't know."

She felt foolish, embarrassed, wholly unsure of herself. He bent his head closer to hers and she wondered whether he was about to kiss her. The thought alarmed her, but she realised that it excited her too. When he simply said, "I haven't gone around shouting it from the rooftops," she felt a rush of sympathy for him.

"No, no. Of course not."

"Look, would you like to have a drink with me this evening? We could walk over to Beeston, if you like. People won't know us there."

He was sensitive enough to realise how much that mattered, she thought. If they turned up together at the local pub, tongues would soon start wagging.

"That would be lovely."

"Seven thirty, then?"

"I'll meet you here, if you like."

"All right, but I make it a condition that I walk you home afterwards. You don't want to be hanging round these streets on your own in the blackout."

The evening they spent together was the most enjoyable

Amy had known since war broke out. John proved to be an agreeable companion, but when they said their farewells outside Mrs Garbutt's, he became hesitant again. After a brief pause, he gave her a peck on the cheek and asked if she would mind seeing him the following day.

"Mind? Of course not. I'd love to."

His craggy features lightened. His surprise and gratification were flattering, for during the past few hours, Amy had been appraising him quietly and deciding that, despite the age gap between them, he was really rather a handsome man. No Flash Harry, far from it, but strong and possessing, she felt sure, hidden depths. The grey touches in his hair simply added to his distinction. She realised that she would be counting the hours before their next date.

As the days and weeks passed, their relationship – she soon began to think of it as a relationship – deepened, even though John always behaved like a perfect gentleman. He wasn't one for dancing, but then neither was she. Once or twice they went to see a film and sometimes to a pub. More often, she would go over to his house after he had shut up shop and they would spend the evening together, just talking. He always cooked the evening meal; he really was very domesticated and steaks were his speciality. Running a shop was hard work, but there were compensations: it was usually possible to supplement basic rations. Neither he nor she had any time for the spivs who ran black market rackets, but making the most of the chance of something a bit special to eat was rather different.

She gladly allowed him to kiss her at the end of an evening, but she didn't want to rush things. For the first time in her life she had found someone whom she could, she told herself, depend upon in an uncertain and dangerous world. From odd things he let slip in conversation, she guessed that he bitterly regretted having let himself be swept off his feet by Elsie Cornforth. Much good had it done him, being dazzled by her brassy good looks.

He never talked at length about his wife, and Amy could understand why. She suspected that the marriage had been unhappy once the first infatuation had worn off. John must have realised the mistake he had made and Elsie would soon have become bored with such a sober, respectable husband. He had a certain dogged Yorkshireman's pride and must have felt humiliated by her desertion. Perhaps in the long run he would see it as a blessing in disguise. Yet Amy couldn't help being curious. He'd never mentioned the possibility of divorce. She wondered what he intended to do. Was it possible that he had lost all faith in the institution of marriage, that his motto was once bitten, twice shy? If so, did that matter?

Every now and then she asked after Tommy, but John's answers were monosyllabic. She did not doubt that he cared for the boy, but his attitude seemed dutiful rather than devoted. He had made occasional visits to Coldkirby since the evacuation, but they were few and far between. Perhaps there were understandable reasons for that: the boy's physical appearance and wilful temperament must have been constant reminders of Elsie. All the same, it struck her as odd, for she was sure that John Harker was, beneath his surface reserve, a man of intense feeling.

One evening, on their way back to Mrs Garbutt's, she was emboldened by an extra glass of port and lemon to ask if Elsie kept in touch with the boy. John paused in mid-stride. It was as if he were trying to choose his words with special care, knowing that a few drinks had dulled his judgement.

"Well – no, she doesn't."

"It's so sad."

"She was no good," he said roughly.

"Do you ever hear from her?"

"No, I don't."

They were turning into Ephraim Street. Amy knew that he would like to change the subject, but she could not let it go. "And she walked out on you – just like that?"

"Aye."

"It must have been just after the evacuation."

"Day after you and the other teachers took the kids off," he said grudgingly.

"She seized her chance as soon as her child was off her hands," Amy said, half to herself. It wasn't unknown. At school she'd heard several tales of parents who had not seen their children since their evacuation. Some of them hadn't even bothered to keep in touch. One couple had moved over the Pennines to somewhere in Lancashire and according to gossip their three youngsters, housed with a retired couple in Bawtry, did not have the faintest idea. The old woman at Coldkirby who had prophesied that the evacuees would not see their homes again might not have been so far off the mark after all.

"Don't worry about Elsie," he said. "She's not worth it."

"But it's so unfair! She's left you with all the responsibility for the child. But Tommy is hers as much as yours."

"More than that," he said grimly.

Now it was her turn to hesitate. "What do you mean?"

He sighed and faced her on the pavement. "You might as well know the truth. The evening she left, she told me that I wasn't Tommy's father."

"*What?*"

"It's the truth, I'm afraid. I'd suspected as much from the outset, but like an idiot I chose to believe what I wanted to believe. She owned up while she was telling me that she was off to make a new life with her fancy man, some travelling salesman who owned a car. Apparently she knew she was pregnant when she started giving me the glad eye. Needless to say, I fell for it. Then she broke the news that I'd got her pregnant and asked what I was going to do about it. The father was some lad off the estate who'd never have kept Elsie in the style she wanted to become accustomed to."

Amy gripped his arm. "You poor dear."

"I've treated the boy as my own for six years. I couldn't abandon him. I make sure he's all right, you can count on that."

"I know," she said. Shock was beginning to turn to anger, hatred almost, directed at the long-gone Elsie. "And that bloody woman never goes near him?"

He cleared his throat and said gruffly, "For a while after she'd gone, I was in a daze. Mortified. No, worse than that. It was a kind of madness, I reckon. When folk asked where she was, I said she'd gone to look after Tommy. A lot of mothers did, I knew that. But I suppose plenty of people started putting two and two together ages ago. The fact her fancy man disappeared at the same time made it easy for them to see through what I was saying. I don't encourage questions, but now when they do ask, I admit that she's run out on me. I've decided it's the best thing."

"And where is she now, have you any idea?"

He shrugged. "I don't think about that. It's over between her and me. I have to get on with my own life. Let's face it, I'm no spring chicken. Moping's a waste of precious time."

She touched his hand. "You're very brave."

He coloured. "I don't see it like that. But you've helped, Amy. You've really helped with putting the past behind me."

"I'd like to keep on helping."

"I'd like that too."

They paused, not knowing what to say next. She looked into his eyes and realised that he was making up his mind about her. The next moment, she was in his arms.

Some time later they were interrupted by the sound of Mrs Garbutt's front door opening.

"Are you going to be carrying on out there all night, Amy Jessop? Have you any idea what time it is?"

She pulled away from John. "Sorry, Mrs G. I'll come in now."

The landlady stared. "And you, John Harker. A married man! You ought to be ashamed of yourself."

He stood his ground. "My wife's left me, Mrs Garbutt. As far as I'm concerned, it's as if I'm divorced."

"And what if your Elsie turns up again, like a bad penny?"

"She won't. We'll not be seeing her or her boyfriend again, I'm sure of that."

Mrs Garbutt sniffed. "A right carry-on!"

"Don't worry, we won't be embarrassing you again after tonight," he said. "Amy's coming to live with me. Aren't you, Amy?"

His sudden boldness stunned her. It was as much as she could do to gasp her agreement. Mrs Garbutt tossed her head and went back inside.

He shook his head. "Sorry, love. I shouldn't have startled you like that. You don't have to move in, you know. I realise it might look bad, you being a teacher and all."

"I don't care!" she said. "As long as I can be with you . . ."

He considered her for a moment. She was acutely conscious of his eye settling on the ample curves of her figure, but somehow it did not displease her. "That's settled, then. How long will it take you to pack your things? Ten minutes, maybe? I'll wait out here, then we'll walk back to my place."

She went inside and raced up the stairs. Her mind was whirling. She was barely conscious of the sound of Mrs Garbutt's footsteps, padding up the stairs, of the old woman's sceptical expression as she peered into the tiny back bedroom where Amy was flinging clothes into a suitcase.

"And what do you do if Elsie Harker does come running back to him? She may be a trollop, but she has a way with men. They can never resist a pretty face. He may change his mind if she begs him for a second chance."

"She won't," Amy said calmly.

"You can't be certain. Neither can he. At first he gave out she'd gone off with the rest of the evacuees. Until you came back, you who knew better because you'd been with the boy all that time. Then he changed his tune."

"If he says he's sure, he's sure," Amy replied. The jealousy of an old woman was not about to rattle her. Her life was on the point of being transformed. She did not yet know John Harker well, not as well as she yearned to – and would do. But he had said with unshakeable authority that his wife was gone for ever and that assurance was good enough.

Mrs Garbutt grunted. "He's been downright shifty over it, if you ask me. Makes you wonder what's happened to her and that other fellow."

"I couldn't care less," Amy said brusquely. "Now, if you'll let me finish my packing, I'll be away inside ten minutes. I'm more than up to date with my rent, I think."

Mrs Garbutt allowed herself a parting shot. "And what a comedown! A young schoolteacher, gone to live under the brush with the local butcher! A fine way to behave."

"At least I'll eat better with John than I ever have done here," Amy said sharply.

And although it was nothing more than a small bonus to a woman in love, it was perfectly true. John said he still had a few choice cuts in his cold store. He reckoned it was the finest meat he'd ever eaten, a delicacy too good to fritter away on customers, so he kept it just for the two of them. Only last night he'd said he was afraid he had acquired a taste for it. When she'd asked why it was a worry, he'd explained that it was very hard to find. But perhaps he'd have the chance to get some more, one day. After all, these were strange times: there was a war on. And he'd gazed at her generous figure with an expression that had made her feel needed. She told herself happily that he had begun to hunger for her.

THE BURNING OF LONDON

Susanna Gregory

In recent years, a number of talented young writers have been attracted to the historical mystery. One of the most successful, both in the UK and the United States, has been Susanna Gregory. The name is a pseudonym for a Cambridge scientist who kindly wrote this story for the book before setting off for a lengthy Polar expedition. The Burning of London *illustrates her gift for crisp and vivid writing and is a good example of the way in which a talented author can tell us as much, if not more, about a real-life historical event than any learned textbook.*

Thomas Farrinor, baker to the king, ducked into the still-smoking ruins of St Paul's in a desperate attempt to escape the mob that was determined to lynch him. Heart thumping so hard it hurt, he scrambled over the blackened timbers and smashed masonry, his feet crunching on broken glass and fragments of charred tracery. Sheets of lead from the roof had formed white-hot lakes as they had melted in the inferno, and then set hard, so that they swathed the sad remains of what had been the grandest church in the country like a metal shroud.

"Come out, Farrinor!" one of his pursuers howled, the mere sight of the destroyed church fuelling his anger. "Don't think you can skulk here to escape justice. If you hadn't been careless with your bakery, the fire would never have started and we would still have a city!"

"And a hundred thousand people would still have their homes!" screamed another.

Farrinor wanted to shout back that he had not been careless, and that he was certain the oven at 25 Pudding Lane had been properly doused before he had gone to bed. He was not a fool – he knew the dangers of leaving a hot oven unattended, when the houses in all the streets around him were made of wood, and crammed so closely together that it was not possible to ride a horse down the spaces between some of them. But he knew no one would believe him.

He waited, crouched like a hunted animal under a fallen pillar, until the mob, despite its fury, began to lose interest and drifted away. And then he waited for dusk, when the darkness and a cloak with a hood would hide him from yet more vengeful attacks by shocked Londoners who had lost everything during the four days that the fire had raged. They were not the only victims: Farrinor, too, had lost his shop, his home and all his belongings.

The acrid stench of smoke stung his nose and made his eyes water, as he moved aimlessly through the rubble of houses that had been so completely destroyed it was impossible to tell where he was. Even in the gloom, people moved like ghosts through the wreckage, prodding and raking through the cinders for anything salvageable, their cries of despair and anger stabbing through him like knives.

Eventually, he sensed he was near where the whole horrible business had started – although nothing of Pudding Lane was recognisable. He scuffed idly at the ground, kicking up clouds of ash, and reflecting bitterly on what the future held for a man accused of starting the Great Fire of London.

"Have you heard?" A woman holding a whimpering baby was addressing a group of people who were digging in the ruins nearby. "A Huguenot has confessed to starting the fire! The baker was innocent after all!"

Farrinor gazed at her in surprise, forgetting to keep his face hidden in his hood.

"So, the Papists were behind all this!" exclaimed a man wearing a dirty red doublet, nodding in satisfaction. "I knew it!"

"A man called Robert Hubert said he put a fireball on a pole, and thrust it through the baker's window," the woman went on. "He started the fire deliberately!"

Farrinor continued to stare as their excited voices drew others towards them. Soon the city of ashes was buzzing with the news, and people joined angry little bands to march on Newgate Gaol, where the unfortunate Hubert was lodged to await his trial. But not everyone went: two other men had resisted the temptation to storm Newgate, to demand the Huguenot's instant execution. Farrinor knew them from court: William Rokeby, the king's physician, and Master Curll, one of the Abbey Deans.

"In time, Londoners might see this fire as a blessing," said Rokeby, speaking more to himself than to the priest. He was a handsome man who wore the foppish clothes of a courtier – long boots turned over at the tops and a ridiculously large hat with a feather in it. "It has burned away all the filthy places where the plague might erupt again, and perhaps saved the city from another outbreak. It has come too late for my family, though, all dead of that evil sickness."

Curll touched his arm sympathetically.

"Seventy thousand people died from the plague," Rokeby

went on. "It seems to me that Huguenot has done London a service by burning these old and disease-ridden buildings to the ground."

"Perhaps," said Curll. "But I'm not convinced of Hubert's guilt. Rumour has it that his mother swears he was with her the night the fire started, and that he never left the house."

"But why would Hubert confess to something he didn't do?" asked Rokeby.

Curll shrugged. "Who knows? But he'll hang for it, and that's certain."

Farrinor stared after them as they strolled away, a sick, sinking feeling in the pit of his stomach. Hubert would hang, and Farrinor knew the man was no more guilty of arson than he was: all the bakery windows had heavy oak shutters, and each had been firmly closed when the stench of smoke had woken him that fateful night. There was no earthly way Hubert could have pushed a fireball through one of them to start the fire.

During the days that followed, Hubert's plight worried at Farrinor's conscience. Keen though he was to be exonerated, he did not want it to be at the expense of an innocent man's death. Hubert's confession was the talk of the whole city, and, as the news spread, Farrinor could see that people were already convinced of his guilt. In fact, Hubert provided such an attractive scapegoat that Farrinor found he could walk openly in the streets again without fear of attack.

Hubert's trial started with great crowds gathered outside the courthouse. When he was brought from his cell, a wild roar went up, and everyone surged forward, so that the guards were hard pressed to prevent them from tearing the Huguenot limb from limb before the trial even began. Farrinor was called to give his evidence – that the oven was well-banked before he went to bed, and that he escaped with his family by climbing out of a window and along some guttering. While Farrinor spoke, Hubert stared down at his manacled hands as though the proceedings were nothing to do with him.

As Farrinor was dismissed, the small man finally looked up. For the first time, Farrinor saw his grey-white face and large, sad eyes. Their gazes locked for an instant, and Hubert gave what might have been a smile, before the bailiff prodded Farrinor in the back to move him on, and Hubert's head dropped again. The exchange bothered Farrinor, and he found he could not push Hubert's haunted features from his mind. He did not attend the remainder of the trial.

On the day the jury were due to give their verdict, Farrinor made his way to Cock Lane, a shabby little alleyway that had narrowly escaped the fire. His tentative knock was answered by Hubert's mother, a frail woman with wispy grey hair whom he recognised from the courtroom.

"I know Hubert didn't start the fire," he blurted out. "At least, not with a fireball on a pole as he claims. It would have been impossible!"

"But he *did* start the fire!" she said firmly. She started to close the door again, but Farrinor sprang forward and pushed his way inside the house. A sick woman lay in a bed near the fire, pale and thin from some disease of the lungs. Farrinor nodded to her and then turned to Hubert's mother.

"It was rumoured – when he was first arrested – that you claimed he was here with you all that night."

The woman shook her head. "That was just shock. You heard what I said in court."

"Are you bothering his good lady, Farrinor?" came a voice behind him. It was Rokeby, the king's physician. "She has been through enough these last few weeks. Show some compassion, and leave her alone!"

"What are you doing here?" asked Farrinor, surprised that

a man of Rokeby's standing should frequent a lowly place like Cock Lane.

Rokeby gestured to the white-faced woman on the bed. "I have come to attend my patient – not that it is any business of yours!"

Hubert's mother hustled Farrinor out of her home and slammed the door behind him. Dispirited, Farrinor was walking back through the rubble towards St Paul's when he sensed he was being followed. He ducked down a seedy runnel that was virtually an open sewer, and waited in the shadows, reaching out to seize a black-garbed figure as it slunk past.

"What do you want?" he demanded, shaking his captive like a dog with a rat. "Why are you following me?"

"Please!" squeaked the figure. "I am a man of God! Let me go!"

Startled, Farrinor recognised the voice of Master Curll. He quickly released the priest, and watched him brush himself down indignantly.

"I was only going to warn you," said the priest resentfully. "There is no need for violence!"

"Warn me about what?" demanded Farrinor.

"About meddling in Hubert's affairs. Suffice to say that a kind of justice has been done."

"But justice has not been done!" objected Farrinor. "An innocent man is going to hang."

The priest shook his head. "You don't understand. Leave everything well alone, or who knows what might happen to you!"

As he roamed the ash-strewn streets of Eastcheap, Farrinor asked himself again why a man would claim responsibility for a dreadful crime for which he would pay with his life. It made no sense. His aimless wandering took him back to his bakery, the splendid house with fine brick ovens and great trays filled with the best biscuits in London. Not for nothing was Farrinor baker to the king. Except that there was nothing left now, except a pile of charred timbers, and stones that had burned so fiercely during the inferno that they were white and crumbly.

Wincing, he turned away, stumbling through the drizzle until he came to the little church of St Mary, a sad shell after the fire, with its roof gone and all its fine stained-glass windows blown out. The tombstones in the graveyard had shattered in the heat, and were stained black from the pall of greasy smoke that had slouched over the city for days after.

Farrinor was about to enter when he became aware that someone else was also in the churchyard. Not wanting to be recognised and questioned about the fire, he ducked behind a pile of fallen masonry and watched. He was startled to see Rokeby push aside a door that hung crazily on half-melted hinges, and ease his way inside. Curiously, Farrinor crept up to one of the broken windows, and peered through.

A man knelt at the broken altar and Farrinor saw that it was Master Curll, the Abbey Dean. Farrinor watched as Rokeby strode up the shattered aisle towards him.

"Give me your blessing, Father."

Curll sketched a benediction at the physician. "How is she?"

Rokeby leaned against a pillar. "She died tonight. But have you heard the news? The jury has just found Hubert guilty of arson. He is to be hanged at Tyburn tomorrow at dawn."

Curll closed his eyes, and began to mutter prayers that whispered eerily around the hull of the church. Rokeby left him, moving away from the ruined part of the city and heading towards the wealthier streets that lay to the north. With nowhere to go, and nothing else to do, Farrinor began to follow him, careful to keep out of sight.

It was not easy to pursue the man without being seen – Rokeby moved furtively, and the streets were unusually dark because of the rainclouds. At times, Farrinor thought he had lost him, but he learned that all he needed to do was to wait, and eventually he would spot him again, moving in and out of the shadows in a way that made Farrinor certain he was up to no good. Of course, the same might be said of Farrinor, trailing a man he barely knew through the streets of London in the small hours of the morning.

Just as Farrinor was considering returning to his lodgings, the physician slipped down an alley between two rows of tall houses, and began fiddling with something on the ground. Curious, Farrinor inched closer, trying to see what he was doing.

Suddenly, there was a flare of light as a tinder was struck, and Farrinor saw exactly what was happening: Rokeby was lighting a fire! There was a pile of faggots stacked against one wall, packed with straw to help them burn. Farrinor glanced up. If the fire took hold, the flames would leap upwards and catch the wooden overhangs of the houses above. And then the blaze would spread to the buildings opposite, and then . . .

Farrinor ran forward with a yell of fury, kicking the tinder from Rokeby's hand and sending the kindling scattering. Startled, the physician jumped to his feet, and drew a small, wicked-looking knife.

"It was you!" Farrinor shouted, ignoring the weapon as realisation dawned on him. "You set a pile of faggots outside my bakery, just as you've done here, so that I'd be blamed for the fire!"

"So? What are you going to do about it?" said Rokeby carelessly, advancing on Farrinor and waving his dagger. "Hubert has already been tried and convicted of the crime, and no one will believe you if you accuse me now. And anyway, I'll certify you as insane if you try!"

"I'll see Hubert doesn't hang, but that you do!" yelled Farrinor, goaded into rashness by the magnitude of Rokeby's crime. "You won't get away with this."

"Why not? I've already succeeded in ridding this great city of most of its verminous buildings. Another conflagration like the one I started before will ensure that London will be free of outbreaks of the plague for ever!"

"Is that why you did it? To prevent the return of the plague?"

Rokeby nodded. "I did it for the common good. Seventy thousand people perished of that vile disease. Now the old city will be replaced by better, healthier buildings and we'll never be stricken by such a pestilence again."

"But Hubert . . ."

"Hubert is one man. I'm talking about saving thousands. But I cannot waste time on idle chatter."

He darted forward quickly, his sudden movement making Farrinor start backwards, so that he stumbled on one of the spilled faggots. Farrinor fell to his knees, and the knife flashed in the air above him. Helplessly, he closed his eyes, waiting for the searing pain that would end his life.

Rokeby's startled gasp and the clatter of the dagger on the cobbles made Farrinor open his eyes and glance up. For a moment, all he could see was the swaying shape of the physician in the dark. Then Rokeby pitched forwards, landing on the ground next to him. A long-handled knife protruded from his back, while behind him stood Curll, his hand stained red with blood.

"The mad physician is dead," said Curll, reaching out to help Farrinor to his feet. "The danger is over."

"You knew he was going to try again!" accused Farrinor

71

Susanna Gregory

in a shocked voice, pushing the proffered hand away and clutching at a wall for balance. "You knew all along!"

"I did not!" snapped Curll. "I thought he was satisfied with his handiwork. The old part of the city, where the plague raged the fiercest, has gone and he seemed content with that. It was the loss of his children that drove him to do this – his four daughters died in the plague. I knew he grieved deeply, but I didn't suspect it had unbalanced his mind."

"But what about Hubert?" demanded Farrinor angrily. "If you knew Rokeby was guilty, then you also know Hubert was innocent. You told me justice was being done – it is not!"

The commotion had woken the occupants of nearby houses, and one or two window shutters were thrown open as people tried to see what was happening. Neither Farrinor nor Curll wanted to be found with the murdered corpse of the king's physician, and they ran together along narrow alleys and across silent squares until they were certain they were safe. Dawn was beginning to break, shedding a soft grey light over the city, and lights gleamed here and there as Londoners prepared themselves for the new day.

"Well?" demanded Farrinor, when they had regained their breath.

"After the trial, I went to speak to Hubert," said Curll. "He could not lie to a priest and admitted his claim to have started the fire was false, but would say no more. And then I discovered that Hubert's wife is one of Rokeby's patients."

"The sickly woman confined to the bed at his mother's house?" asked Farrinor. "I saw her."

"Rokeby made some comments in court that suggested he thought the Great Fire was the best thing that could have happened to London," Curll went on. "I plied him with plenty of fine claret and the whole story came out in a drunken babble: Rokeby started the fire to prevent further outbreaks of the plague. Hubert, wandering the streets to

72

escape hearing the suffering of his sick wife, caught him red-handed and a deal was struck: Hubert would take the blame for the fire if Rokeby would cure his wife."

"I don't believe you! Why should Hubert go to such extremes, just to secure the services of a physician?"

"The king's physician," corrected Curll, "and one of the best in the country. Hubert is poor, and could never have afforded such treatment – and he loves his wife more than life itself."

"But you said justice was being done . . ."

"So it was. Rokeby was paying for his crime by healing a desperately sick woman, and Hubert was paying for keeping his silence over the truth by forfeiting his life – otherwise it would have been *you* who was tried and sentenced to death. The citizens were ready to hang you before Hubert made his confession."

"But Hubert's wife died, didn't she?" asked Farrinor, recalling the conversation in the church. "Perhaps Rokeby even killed her to escape the burden of trying to cure her."

Curll would not meet his eyes. "Perhaps he did – it seemed she died at about the time Hubert was sentenced to death."

"But we cannot stay silent about this now!" cried Farrinor. "Rokeby is dead, and Hubert's wife is dead. We must do all we can to tell the truth and save Hubert!"

The priest was about to answer, when the dismal tones of the Newgate bell began to toll. It was dawn, and it was announcing to the city that Hubert had been hanged for the crime of arson.

Historical note

The Great Fire of London started in a bakery owned by Thomas Farrinor at 25 Pudding Lane on 2 September 1666.

Farrinor escaped with his household through choking smoke out of an upper window and along a gutter, although one of his maids refused to leave and was burned to death. The fire raged for four days, after which 100,000 people were left homeless, 13,200 houses were destroyed, 89 parish churches were burned, and 400 streets and alleys were wiped out. Robert Hubert, a Huguenot watchmaker from Rouen, claimed to have put a fireball on a pole through Farrinor's window. Even Farrinor, keen to exonerate himself, found inconsistencies in Hubert's story, and it is generally believed today that Hubert was innocent. Nevertheless, he was tried for arson, found guilty and hanged at Tyburn on 29 October 1666.

TABLE FOR TWELVE

Tony Wilmot

Like Eileen Dewhurst, Tony Wilmot has set his contribution to this anthology in the Second World War – but there the resemblance ends. Table for Twelve *is a brisk thriller set in German-occupied France and I was especially glad to include it given Wilmot's long association with the CWA anthology during the years when the collection was edited by my predecessor Herbert Harris.*

K laus Werner hummed a Bavarian drinking song as he rode his motorcycle along the straight, poplar-lined road that led to the village. The Normandy countryside was at its best but Klaus Werner scarcely noticed. He had two things on his mind – gourmet food, and a girl with lustrous red hair and green eyes.

She was the daughter of the restaurant's owner, Marcel Dubois. For a month or so Werner had been eating there on his off-duty nights. The cuisine was excellent and the daughter, who waited at table, was nineteen and almost certainly a virgin.

He swung the bike into the next bend and was annoyed to find the road blocked by a herd of cows. He sounded the horn and shouted to the cowman to clear a passage.

He rode on. Like all of his ilk, Werner revelled in his new-found authority in Nazi-occupied France. Nothing pleased him more than seeing people flinch when he issued an order or threat. He had joined the Nazi party as a humble Black Forest shopkeeper in 1938. Now, in the autumn of 1942, he was a sergeant major in the SS – feared as much by his own men as by the local populace.

At the restaurant, he left his bike in the cobbled courtyard and strode into the house without knocking.

"*Guten tag*, it's me, Klaus."

In the kitchen Marcel Dubois and his daughter Marie were preparing for the evening menu. Marcel dropped what he was doing and cleared the chair by the stove for the SS man.

"I've brought you some fruit," said Klaus Werner, seating himself by the stove.

"Fine," the girl said, not looking up from the vegetables she was chopping. "I'll feed it to the neighbour's pigs."

"She doesn't mean it," Marcel said quickly.

"I do, Papa, every word."

Marcel dropped his eyes, knowing she despised him for fraternising. He despised himself, but it was a means of survival. Being a widower, he was solely responsible for her; and her happiness was all he cared about.

"Doesn't Klaus get just a little smile?" the Nazi said.

"We're prisoners in our own country, monsieur . . . is that a smiling matter?"

The SS man warmed his hands over the stove. He was a coarse-featured man in his mid-thirties. His pale eyes, framed by wire glasses, never left her. A spirited filly, he thought, not at all like the blousy tarts who hung around the base. He wanted her more than ever and, by God, he would have her.

He didn't wish her people any harm, he said, but in war one sometimes had to do unpleasant things. Her father would tell her the same, he was an old soldier.

"Does that," the girl said, blazing up, "include your concentration camps?"

"Lies and propaganda, put out by the Allies."

"It's true. I heard it from the . . . from someone at the market." Flushing, she looked away.

"You shouldn't listen to gossip. Or was it someone in the Resistance who told you?" But they should not quarrel. He was there for a happy reason, to book the restaurant for tomorrow night. A dinner party for his sergeants. There would be twelve of them, money no object. A nice change from the watery vegetables and stringy meat in their mess. Marcel must remember how awful army food was from the First World War, *ja*?

Indeed he did, said Marcel. Now, how many courses did the sergeant major have in mind?

"Five at least. My men eat like horses."

"Papa!" the girl cried. "How can you, when our own people are going hungry?" Blinking tears, she ran to the door. Her father started after her, but the Nazi restrained him. Let her be, he said; she was young, idealistic. She would cool off.

For a few minutes Klaus Werner talked about the menu, then said he must be going. "Here's a deposit of two hundred francs, Monsieur Dubois." The Frenchman took it, feeling wretched. "Get in plenty of that Calvados I like."

Outside, Werner looked around for Marie. Something was flapping in the breeze, just by the wall at the far end of the courtyard. Part of a girl's skirt, *her* skirt. On an impulse, he moved toward her, treading softly.

By the time he reached the wall, the impulse was a strong urge. She was just around the corner, sitting, back against the wall, eyes closed, enjoying the sun. Suddenly she was aware of him.

"What do you want? . . . What are you doing? . . . Get away from me . . . Let go!"

She was not to call for help, he said; he would shoot her father if he had to. It would be better if she stopped struggling. He would be gentle with her.

She would rather die first, she said.

Klaus Werner began tearing her clothing, frenziedly.

There was the sound of a gunshot. The Nazi uttered a strangulated gasp and fell forward.

In the house, after Werner had left, Marcel had felt suddenly cold, the coldness of fear. He had not liked the way the man had kept looking at Marie. Appreciative glances, wolf whistles, were one thing . . . but Werner's had been pure lust.

Also, Werner had not ridden off on his motorcycle. Quickly, Marcel went to the attic. His old service revolver was still there, hidden away. He checked the chambers. One bullet. It would have to be enough. He'd get no second chance.

Marie, he knew, had a favourite spot near the outhouse.

It had taken him less than a minute to get there. Marie was under the brute, trying to get free. The man was proving too strong for her.

His old army training had taken over. He'd aimed instinctively and pulled the trigger.

Now, as he dragged Werner's body into the outhouse, his mind was racing. The Maquis would know where to get rid of the motorcycle. He would dispose of the body later. There was a more pressing problem: how to explain Klaus Werner's disappearance. He would have told his men he was coming to book the restaurant. Tomorrow they would be asking questions. If they suspected foul play, they'd use torture until they got at the truth. He and Marie would be as good as dead. And some of the villagers too, as a further reprisal.

"We have to be brave," he told Marie. "We have to carry on preparing for his dinner party as though nothing's changed. I'm going to telephone the Maquis."

Two men, both middle-aged, arrived on foot an hour later. Briefly, Marcel told them what had happened. The motorcycle was child's play, they said when he'd finished. They knew a spot where the river was very deep. But Marcel's ploy, to make the SS believe their sergeant major was still alive – *Dieu*, it would be easier to dynamite an enemy supply line!

It could be done, Marcel said, must be done. The Maquis had an expert forger, brilliant at faking documentation. Klaus Werner's wallet contained everything the expert needed – service number, identity card, and so on.

The two pocketed Werner's effects and left.

Alone again, father and daughter said little, both still stunned from the swiftness of events.

"Can it really be done, Papa, your scheme?" Marie asked, putting into words what he had been asking himself.

Yes, it could. He tried to sound optimistic.

"You're no more convinced than I am, are you?" she said.

He threw her a reassuring smile. He had better do something about the body in the outhouse, he said.

"Do you want me to help you . . . bury it?"

No, he said. It was something he must do alone. Better she got some sleep. He would see her in the morning.

The next day, the SS arrived as Marcel had expected. She should just try to act normal, he told his daughter, and let him do the talking.

There were two of them: Staff Sergeant Schmidt, who said he was Klaus Werner's deputy, and a Sergeant Muller. No, they did not want coffee, no, nor a brandy; this wasn't a social call.

79

Marcel told them of the conversation he'd had with their sergeant major, of booking the restaurant, choosing the menu, army mess food, Calvados. As he talked, the one called Muller made notes.

Schmidt walked round, slowly, peering into simmering pans, poking at vegetables. "Did he say where he was going when he left?"

No, he hadn't; but Marcel had presumed he'd returned to HQ. Why, had something happened to the sergeant major?

They were not sure, yet. What they did know was that he had not spent last night in his quarters. His motorcycle was missing, but none of his personal things had gone. It was a bit of a mystery, but no doubt there was a simple explanation.

Muller, now, was lifting pan lids and sniffing. Smelled ten times more appetising than what their mess cook served up. Bit of an oaf, actually. Didn't know a sausage from his elbow.

"That's why Klaus raves about your cooking. Says he's never eaten better anywhere in Normandy."

"I'm flattered," said Marcel.

Muller had turned his attention to Marie. What was that she was chopping up so finely?

"Fresh herbs, monsieur. Parsley, tarragon, fennel . . . they enhance the flavour of the stews. Here, have a taste."

The two men of the SS had thawed somewhat. Yes, perhaps they would have a nip of brandy after all. And as for Klaus, well, there must be a rational explanation, a mistress somewhere probably. He'd turn up, looking sheepish, at the last moment. He wouldn't want to miss tonight. Talked of nothing else for days.

He'd paid a deposit, too, Marcel reminded them. For the Calvados, the apple-brandy they were drinking at that very moment.

That settled the matter, so far as Schmidt was concerned. No sense in cancelling: Klaus would never forgive them.

80

Table for Twelve

Marcel was to set the table for twelve, as arranged, and they would be there at seven o'clock.

A clicking of heels, a salute, and they were gone.

At six, Marie began setting the places on the long table that dominated the dining room. It was actually three trestle-type tables pushed up together and covered by a floral-patterned cloth. Beside the sets of wine glasses and cutlery she placed a folded napkin. The napkins were her father's idea. He thought there should be a bowl of fresh flowers, too.

Fineries were wasted on that uncouth lot, in her view, but if he insisted . . .

"It's important we make a good impression," Marcel told her. "Our reputation's at stake."

While his daughter selected the flowers from the garden, Marcel slaved away in the kitchen. He hadn't worked so hard on a dinner menu in years. Every cooking utensil – pots, pans, roasting-trays, casserole dishes, jugs, jambonnieres – was in use. The charcoal burners shimmered and sparked, ovens glowed, saucepan lids rattled, condensation covered the windowpanes.

While the various items were cooking, he brought up the wine from the cellar. They were going to need white for the mussels and fish, and bucketfuls of red for the meats.

His daughter wouldn't approve, of course; she would give them pigswill ('they wouldn't know the difference') and begrudge them even that.

Perhaps she was right, he thought. Maybe he was bending over backwards to please them. Then, he had his reasons.

That night, the dining room rang with ribald laughter. Four carafes of wine were drained before Marie served the first course – bowls of steaming mussels and shallots in cider.

Marcel took in a bowl himself. He was tense and

anxious. Was there any news of their sergeant major, he asked.

There was. He would not be coming tonight, nor any other night for that matter.

They resumed eating.

Could he ask why not, Marcel persisted.

Sorry, they said, but Werner's case was still being investigated.

What could it mean, wondered Marcel, back in his kitchen. Had they caught the Maquis with Werner's motorcycle? Were they interrogating them? No matter how brave a man was, SS torture would break him. Perhaps they already had . . .

Course after course was put away, with shouts of "More casserole, Mademoiselle Marie . . . more roast potatoes."

Finally, Marcel took in the cheeseboard. He was finding the suspense unbearable.

"It's a shame," he said, "your sergeant major has had to miss this evening, he was so looking forward to it."

The Calvados had loosened their tongues. Strictly speaking it was classified information, but they didn't see why Marcel shouldn't know, Werner being one of his regulars.

That afternoon, they said, they had received an unexpected communiqué from Berlin – unexpected because it had not come through the usual channels. It was Werner's posting to the Russian Front, with immediate effect, and signed by Heinrich Himmler himself. Usually, a Russian posting meant a man had blotted his copybook. That seemed unlikely, Werner being such a stickler for SS regulations, but he must have done something to put himself in Himmler's bad books. They were intrigued, of course; would love to know what Werner had done. But you did not ask the head of Hitler's SS for explanations!

Marcel acted surprised. "So," controlling his voice, "he is there now, at the Front?"

Table for Twelve

The one called Muller was sucking on a cigar in expansive fashion. Should be, he said, but none of their units had seen hair nor hide of him.

The others seemed to find this amusing. Marcel said he did not understand; what was the sergeant saying?

"It's obvious, man. He must have been tipped off that the posting was in the pipeline – and he's done a bunk."

"You mean, deserted?"

It was the worst thing an SS man could do, Muller said. In a way, they sympathised; everybody knew a Russian posting was as good as a death sentence.

Another sergeant, Braun, thought Werner was making for neutral Switzerland. They'd catch up with him, though, and he wouldn't want to be in Werner's shoes when they did.

Marcel went back to the kitchen, to tell Marie the ruse had worked, but she was in too much of a temper to listen. Never had she seen such gluttony, she fumed. They were like pigs.

He had wanted them to be, he said quietly.

"But, Papa, your skills as a chef have been wasted on them."

Oh no, Marcel replied, not wasted, quite the contrary, in fact.

His daughter stared. There was an odd inflection in his voice, a strange expression in his eye, too. "Papa, you can't mean . . . last night *you* . . . and now *they* have . . . ?"

Just as he was about to answer her, he realised the dining room had gone quiet. Schmidt was calling for him.

He hurried to the table. Was something wrong? One of the cheeses, perhaps it was stale?

Eleven pairs of accusing eyes were turned toward him. Nobody spoke, but they all seemed to be expecting something to happen.

Not the cheese, Marcel said lamely. Then what, pray?

Schmidt, he saw, was resting a lightly clenched hand on

the table. "Monsieur Dubois," he said, "how do you," his fingers slowly opened, "explain this?" In the middle of his palm was a small object. "Muller there found it in your otherwise excellent stew."

Muller was grinning, toothily. "*Ja*, lucky I didn't swallow it."

Schmidt looked Marcel in the eye. "Well, what have you got to say?"

Marcel tried to speak. His right hand began to shake uncontrollably. "I . . . I . . . don't . . . can't . . ." How could he have been so stupid as to overlook it, he thought, he of all people? His carelessness had ruined everything. At any moment the SS men would put two and two together and—

Suddenly, Muller got to his feet and put a reassuring hand on Marcel's shoulder. Marcel must not look so alarmed, he said, his restaurant wasn't about to be closed down. Every chef had the occasional mishap. They were always fishing foreign bodies from their mess food – elastic bands, stones, bootlaces, even cockroaches.

Schmidt was holding the small, grey object up to the light.

"It's been fired," he said, turning it between finger and thumb. "You can see where the end's been flattened on impact. A larger calibre than in use today. First World War, I'd say. Here," pressing it into Marcel's hand, "you might like to have it – as a souvenir."

Indeed he would, Marcel said.

Then, swaying a little, and belching, Staff Sergeant Schmidt went out after his men.

THE QUEEN'S MAGICIAN

Edward D Hoch

Ed Hoch is, quite simply, the world's leading writer of short mystery stories. His staggering output includes a number of tales with a historical setting and for his contribution to Past Crimes, *he chose to locate his contribution in Victorian England.* The Queen's Magician *is a typically lively, well-paced and entertaining story from the pen of an author who is himself something of a master illusionist. As we approach the Millennium, it is interesting to read this turn-of-century tale and reflect upon the changes that have taken place over the last hundred years.*

M adge Keene arrived for the audition wearing her best black skirt, carefully hemmed to reveal just enough of her shapely ankles. Madge considered those ankles one of her best features, and she was a bit disappointed when Dr Merlin gave them not even a glance.

"Do you understand what the position entails, Miss Keene?" he asked. He was a slender man with an almost sinister expression, made more so by the stage makeup he wore.

"I–I think so," she replied.

"We are just two weeks away from the beginning of the twentieth century. Here in London, so close to the Greenwich meridian, numerous special celebrations are planned. As the Queen's Magician I will offer a spectacular magic show exactly at midnight. This audition today is to find a new assistant for my act."

"I understand that. It won't be dangerous work, will it?"

He gave a snort of laughter. "No, no, my dear girl! Other than being bitten once or twice by the tiger you should be perfectly safe."

"Bitten!"

"I jest. Come, lift your skirts so I may see your legs. You understand you will be wearing tights and spangles on stage?"

"I – yes. I've seen your posters around the city. Are you really the Queen's Magician?"

He smiled at her, trying to present a friendlier image. "Victoria is a great fan of magic shows. There are many prestidigitators who have claimed over the years to be the Queen's Magician. As with Dr Holden and Dr Lynn, I have performed before Her Majesty for more than a decade. I have as much right to the title as they have. When I perform my famous Vanishing Lady illusion at midnight on December 31st, I hope to have Victoria in the audience."

"Some say she is near death," Madge said reverently. Her mother had always taught her to show respect for the Royal Family.

"Any person of eighty-one years is near death," Dr Merlin agreed. "Still, we can hope. You may lower your skirts now." After asking a few questions that established she lived alone in London, he said, "You have the job."

She was delighted to hear it. At nineteen, barely out of

school, she longed for a life in the theatre. "What will I be doing? Assisting with your illusions?"

"Young lady, exactly on the stroke of the twentieth century I intend to make you vanish from a cage and be replaced by a tiger."

"It sounds scary," she admitted, though she knew it was only a trick. Then, "You know, I celebrated the twentieth century a year ago, even though our government said it didn't start until 1901."

"That doesn't matter. It's an excuse to celebrate twice."

"Will you show me how the trick works?"

"Of course. I want to rehearse it this week, before the long Christmas weekend." The holiday was on Tuesday, followed by Boxing Day on Wednesday, and little real business would be transacted on Monday. "Suppose we meet the day after tomorrow and I'll introduce you to my tiger."

"All right," Madge Keene answered, just a bit apprehensive, wondering for the first time what she might be getting herself into.

That night she told her American friend Gregory about it. He was a merchant seaman, good with his fists, but as he told her, "I'm not much help against tigers."

On Wednesday afternoon Madge walked through slushy London streets to the small theatre near Soho Square where Dr Merlin would be performing. It was not an area for a young woman to walk alone, and she remembered her mother's frightening tales of people who vanished, never to be seen again. When she reached the theatre she was greeted enthusiastically by the magician, wearing black pants and a loose-fitting shirt of white silk, moving among a half-dozen male assistants who worked mainly backstage during his act. "Madge Keene! It is so good to see you! I feared all this talk of a tiger had turned you against us."

"No," she said. "I want to get into theatrical life."

"This is your perfect opportunity. Come and meet the beast!"

Madge approached the cage with some trepidation, eyeing the great Bengal tiger a bit uncertainly. "I have to be in the same cage with that?"

Dr Merlin chuckled. "Not this cage. Come, I'll show you the cage we use on stage. You see, the tiger represents the new century, while you will symbolise the follies of our youth."

"I will?"

He led her over to a larger cage on a wheeled platform. A separate staircase was rolled out by one of the assistants and Merlin himself hurried up the steps to open the cage door. He stepped inside, bending almost double to squeeze through. "This will be much easier for you," he assured her. "You will be inside and I will lower a curtain over the entire cage. Then—"

Madge gasped as the magician yanked at the rear of the cage, pulling it down after him as he dropped through a trapdoor in the floor. She realised that what appeared to be the cage's back was really a partition, hiding a space more than a foot deep. This now became the cage's floor, and a tiger hidden in that rear compartment would have the entire cage to himself.

"But what happens to you?" she asked Dr Merlin.

"Simple, my dear girl." He disappeared through another hidden door in the base of the staircase they'd wheeled out, and it was promptly rolled offstage. He returned immediately and said, "Now get into your costume so we can see how it fits."

Madge thought the spangled tights more appropriate to a dance hall performer than to a magician's assistant, but she donned them gamely and allowed the seamstress to take a few stitches. When she returned to the stage she could see at once that Dr Merlin approved. "Perfect, my dear! Now let's run through the trick from the start, but without the tiger."

She was a fast learner, and in no time she'd mastered the technique of entering the cage, waiting until the curtain dropped around it, and then exiting through the trapdoor while she pulled the false wall down to release the tiger. Then into the space beneath the stairs, to be wheeled off by the assistants. After a half-dozen run-throughs she was ready to try it with the real tiger. "Don't worry," the magician assured her. "Susie is quite tame. I've performed this illusion with her a dozen times." He brought the tiger out on a gold leash to introduce them to each other.

Still, it was with a trace of apprehension that Madge mounted the steps and entered the cage, knowing a live tiger waited just the other side of that false wall. She managed to slip most of the way through the trapdoor before pulling down the false wall and releasing the beast. Then she scurried into the staircase trapdoor and shut it. She felt the hiding place rolling away, pushed by Merlin's assistant. Once off stage he opened the door and helped her out. His name was George Jamel, a dark-haired man in his thirties with a ready smile and soft hands. "There! That wasn't so bad, was it?" he asked.

Madge glanced back at the cage, where Merlin had just whisked away the curtain to reveal the pacing, restless tiger whose name was Susie. A few of the stagehands applauded and the slender magician gave them a mocking bow. He walked over to Madge and told her, "We'll have a full dress rehearsal next Thursday, just after Boxing Day. Jamel will give you the time."

Madge left the theatre feeling as if she owned it. Even the wet chill of the December day could do nothing to dampen her spirits. She passed a news vendor's stand and saw headlines about the latest British victory over the Boers in South Africa. We are winning at last, she thought. Everything is going right today.

Edward D Hoch

Though still late afternoon, it was growing dark. The electric lights in shop windows, brighter in this area than the old gas-lamps that still lined the street, seemed to heighten the festive look of Christmas. She thought of taking a motor-cab home, but knew the new electric underground tube, the Central London Railway, ran only blocks from her flat. With the few pence saved she could stop for afternoon tea in one of the shops she was passing.

Without a second thought she entered the next doorway, hung up her coat and chose a small table off to the side, ordering scones and a pot of tea. Before they arrived a middle-aged gentleman wrapped in a heavy coat and scarf entered the shop and came up to her table. "I'd like to speak with you, Miss Keene. May I join you?"

Madge was momentarily taken aback. There were several empty tables in the place. "Do I know you?" she asked.

He unwrapped the scarf from his neck and showed his identification. "I'm Inspector Snell from New Scotland Yard. It's quite important."

"Have I done something?"

His smile put her momentarily at ease. "I certainly hope not." He was in his forties, about her father's age, with a small purple birthmark on his left cheek. He hung up his coat and sat down opposite her. "I hope you'll excuse me for following you. As you'll see, it's a matter of great importance."

"You followed me from the theatre?" she asked.

"I did. We've been looking into the activities of Dr Merlin."

"He's a magician. He performed before Queen Victoria."

"We know that."

"And he's going to change me into a tiger during his Twentieth Century Show on New Year's Eve."

Inspector Snell nodded. "I was in the audience when he

90

last performed the trick, back in the summer. Did he tell you what happened to the girl he used then?"

Madge frowned. "No. What happened?"

"We don't know, Miss Keene. She disappeared and has not been seen since that performance. As a matter of fact, he has performed the Vanishing Lady illusion seven times in the past three years. None of the girls who vanished has ever been seen again."

The sound of his words numbed her with their implication. Her first reaction was to brush them away as meaningless. "That's impossible," she said firmly. "People don't just disappear."

"I'm afraid they do, every day in a city the size of London. It's especially true of stage and music hall performers, young women like yourself who come here without family ties."

"And you believe Dr Merlin is responsible for the disappearance of his assistants?"

"Without doubt. We just don't know what he's doing to them."

Madge tried to make a joke of it. "Feeding them to the tiger, no doubt."

"We have considered that possibility," he answered in all seriousness.

"Did you question him about these disappearances?"

The waitress brought her tea and scones, along with a second cup and saucer for the inspector, and he waited until she was gone before he answered. "One problem is that we didn't realise anything was amiss until after the sixth disappearance. No one even reported the first five. But the sixth young woman was living with a roommate who notified the Metropolitan Police that she'd gone missing. Scotland Yard was called in, but then a seventh woman disappeared after vanishing from that tiger's cage. Dr Merlin – his real name is Burt Haggis – was questioned and denied any knowledge of their whereabouts. It was part of the act, he assured us. Since the young women vanish from the cage, he did not want them reappearing on stage at the next performance. To maintain the air of mystery, he claimed to pay them a hundred-pound bonus to leave London."

"Perhaps it's true," Madge murmured, already thinking about where she could go if Merlin offered her that much money.

"If it is, we've been unable to trace a single one of them. When I questioned him I requested a list of all the women he'd used in the tiger illusion. We've checked back to the towns and villages where they grew up and even talked to family members where there were any. Not one of them has been seen since they came to London and joined Merlin's act. We've checked every body pulled from the Thames and even done some extralegal digging in the vicinity of Merlin's country home. There's not a clue. The women have simply vanished. I don't want that to happen to you."

"It won't," she insisted. "Come on New Year's Eve and I'll prove it to you after the show."

The inspector sighed. "Miss Keene, last summer I called on your predecessor, a girl named Mary Regan, and told her what I'm telling you. Her attitude was much the same as yours. After the performance no one ever saw her again."

"You'll see me," Madge promised, finishing her tea.

In truth the conversation with the Scotland Yard inspector disturbed Madge more than she was willing to admit. After leaving him she did not return immediately to her apartment. Instead she walked along the Thames Embankment, opposite the Houses of Parliament, which had been lit by electricity for more than two years now. Often in the evening people still came to marvel at the large light globes on the decorative cast iron posts some fifteen feet tall. The bright Embankment lights made it a safe place to walk in a city that still remembered the outrages of Jack the Ripper. The very thought of those crimes made her momentarily doubt her ability to protect herself. Then she remembered she'd be seeing her friend Gregory at a Boxing Day party. Perhaps she could prevail on him to attend Dr Merlin's performance.

The party the following Wednesday was full of young people. Some were shop girls pleased that the Christmas buying season was over for another year. Others were would-be actors and actresses like herself, talking about the latest Gilbert and Sullivan revival at the Savoy. *Patience* had been substituted for a new comic opera by the collaborators when it became clear that Arthur Sullivan was mortally ill and unable to complete his final work. Sullivan had died in late November, just two weeks after the successful revival of *Patience*.

"I like working at the Savoy," one of the girls told her. She was in the opera's Chorus of Rapturous Maidens. "It's a lovely theatre. They've had electricity since it opened in 1881 with the original production of *Patience*. Most people in London saw their first light bulb at the Savoy. Mr D'Oyly Carte even broke a lighted bulb to show people how safe they were." But Madge knew from her mother's stories that a few busy London intersections had seen electric lights as early as the Savoy.

Madge's friend Gregory appeared then, making his way through the guests to her side. "I'm glad you're here," he said. "I wanted to tell you I have a ship. I sail on New Year's Eve."

Her heart sank. "I was going to invite you to the magic show I'm in."

"Sorry, babe."

She glanced around the room. "You're not going off to those awful brothels in Brussels again, are you? The ones with the young girls?"

He laughed at that. "No, no, those were for my youth. I've given up loose women and pub fighting."

"Is there somewhere we can talk?" she asked nervously.

"In here," he said, leading her to the kitchen. "What is it?"

She poured out the story of the job, and the conversation with Inspector Snell. "Do you believe that story?" he asked when she'd finished.

"Well, no. But if you were still going to be in London—"

He fished an oddly shaped piece of metal out of his pocket and handed it to her. "Take this. Use it if you have to."

"What is it?" she asked, examining the oblong shape that seemed to have four fingerholes in it.

"In America we call them brass knuckles. You slip them on like this and swing hard."

"God! I could never do that!"

"You could if your life depended on it. Consider it a gift."

"All right," she finally agreed. "Thank you."

She wondered how she was going to hide his gift beneath her brief costume.

On the following day Madge took the tube to the dress rehearsal. From backstage she watched Merlin perform a dozen dazzling illusions wearing formal clothes and a black opera cape with red lining. Then, as the time neared for the final scene, Jamel transferred the tiger to the cage she'd be using, hiding it behind the false wall. He seemed to sense her nervousness and walked over to her. "Don't worry, it'll all go well."

She smiled nervously. "I hope so."

And of course it did all go well. If anything was going to happen, it wouldn't be until the real performance next Monday night. She exited the cage with perfect timing and when Jamel pushed the staircase off stage she was hidden inside it.

"You did very well," he told her after the rehearsal was over.

"Thanks. I was a bit worried."

"No need. Susie is like a big kitten."

Merlin joined them, looking pleased with himself. "If it goes that well on Monday night we'll have the audience eating out of our hand."

After he'd gone Madge casually asked Jamel, "What happened to the girl who had this job ahead of me?"

He looked up from a little English-Flemish dictionary he'd been leafing through and smiled. "She retired from the business. Merlin was lucky to find you. She wasn't nearly so attractive."

"Someone told me that Merlin's assistants are never seen again after they appear in the Vanishing Lady illusion. They said he pays them to leave town."

The young man chuckled at that. "He likes to keep up the fiction that they vanish from the earth and are never seen again. It's just good showmanship. I've been with him since '97 and I know he treats his employees well. He has occasional reunions with all the girls. You'll get to meet them someday."

"But where—?"

"All in good time," Jamel told her.

Inspector Snell came by Madge's flat early on New Year's Eve. He sat down opposite her, looking solemn, and said, "Miss Keene, I must urge you once more not to go through with tonight's performance. I will be in the theatre with some of my men, but I cannot guarantee your safety in view of what has happened in the past. We are at our wits' end to explain these disappearances."

Edward D Hoch

"I'll be all right," she assured him. "I have to go through with it."

The special New Year's Eve show was scheduled to begin at ten o'clock and Merlin had instructed her to arrive an hour early. Feeling like a real actress, she peered out through the curtains. A few people were already in their seats for the performance. Then she went over to Susie's cage and reached through the bars to pet the tiger. They were right about that. She was a gentle creature.

"Are you ready?" Merlin asked, bustling in through the stage door as he removed his greatcoat. "Where's your costume?"

"I'll change in a minute." She hesitated, then said, "Someone told me you pay a bonus to the Vanishing Girl so she stays vanished after the performance."

He waved her away with his hand. "Jamel must have told you. He handles all that."

"I thought I was getting a permanent job."

"My dear, in this illusion you are a symbol of the dying century."

"Then is the tiger a symbol of the twentieth century?"

He shrugged. "Who knows? Hurry and change into your costume now."

"Will Queen Victoria be at tonight's performance?"

"The Queen is too ill to attend. Some think she will pass away with the century." He turned and walked quickly away, anxious to prepare for the performance.

In her dingy dressing room Madge slipped into the spangled tights, carefully cutting a seam near her waist. A mass of spangles hid the opening from view but it was large enough for her purpose. She used the costume's belt to hold the cool metal in place against her side.

Dr Merlin's performance began just after ten o'clock, with an intermission at eleven. Madge was on stage, mainly for decorative purposes, during some of the other illusions. She carried the linking rings out to him and brought him a small stand and tray for the fireworks effect. The audience cheered each time she appeared. They knew from the poster out front that she would vanish from the cage in the show's grand finale.

Following a twenty-minute intermission Merlin returned to the stage in a dazzling display of flash powder and smoke. Behind the curtains Jamel and Madge worked with the other stagehands to ensure that everything ran smoothly. During the floating scarf illusion Jamel controlled a black fishing line that passed through an overhead eyelet and gave the impression that the scarf floated free. Merlin controlled a second line to add variety to the scarf's movements.

Finally, as midnight approached, the tension grew. Merlin appeared on stage with one of his assistants, undraping the cage on its wheeled platform. Susie the tiger was already in place behind the false back, but could not be seen by the audience. Madge peeked out from the wings and saw Inspector Snell over at the far side of the theatre, leaning forward in his seat. He held a pair of opera glasses to his eyes, studying the stage.

Merlin strode purposefully to the side of the stage, holding out his hand for Madge. Then he led her forward to the portable steps, rolled into position by Jamel. She went up the steps, paused at the top for a final unrehearsed wave to the audience, and entered the cage. Merlin immediately dropped the curtain around it. Exactly as she'd rehearsed it, Madge opened the trapdoor in the floor and dropped through, pulling the false wall down behind her and releasing the tiger into the cage. Then, in a single fluid motion, she went through the door into the compartment beneath the steps. Just as she closed the door behind her she felt Jamel start to roll the steps offstage. The audience, eyes fixed on the covered cage, hardly noticed.

She heard the gasps and applause as the cage was uncovered and the tiger revealed in her stead. Merlin would be rolling the cage to the front of the stage now, showing there was no trickery, no mirrors, no place where she could be hidden. She heard him address the audience. "Thank you, ladies and gentlemen, and welcome to the twentieth century!"

The little door beneath the back of the staircase opened and Jamel reached a hand in to help her out. In that instant she was a child again, at the municipal hospital having her tonsils removed. With the suddenness of a lightning bolt she saw her future before her and reached through the open seam in her costume.

Applause still filled the house as Inspector Snell and his men burst through the stage door. He took one look at Madge, and the unconscious George Jamel at her feet, and asked, "What happened?"

"He tried to chloroform me. When I recognised the odour I hit him with a pair of brass knuckles."

"My God!"

"He wasn't paying the girls to leave London, as Merlin thought. He was kidnapping them and selling them to one of those brothels in Brussels."

"White slavery," the inspector muttered. "Is Merlin involved too?"

"I don't believe so. You said the girls have been disappearing for the past three years, and Jamel told me he joined the show in '97. Apparently there was no trouble till he came on the scene. I think he chloroformed them and left them under the stairway till the theatre closed. Then he returned and took them away."

"How do you know they're in Brussels?"

"A guess. Jamel was studying an English-Flemish dictionary the other day, and I know from a friend that brothels in

Brussels specialise in attractive young girls. You should find confirmation among his papers."

"You're quite a lady," Snell said with admiration. From the audience they could hear another burst of applause. "Shouldn't you be out there taking a bow?"

"That's a great idea."

Madge strode purposefully onto the stage as the applause grew, and Merlin turned to her. His surprise lasted only an instant. Then he grasped her hand and they bowed together to the audience.

A LURKING FEAR

H R F Keating

Harry Keating, a crime writer as versatile as he is distinguished, is no stranger to the historical mystery. A Lurking Fear *re-introduces Harriet Unwin, the governess who first appeared in three novels Keating wrote in the 1980s under the pen-name of Evelyn Hervey. The story is of particular interest because of the way in which Keating maintains reader interest from first to last without any reliance upon uncertainty as to the killer's identity. The focus is instead upon whether guilt can be proved and is a good illustration of the sheer professionalism of the author's writing.*

Miss Unwin knew at once who had killed young Jane. It was the boy whose governess she had been for the past three years, Newton Codrington, only son of Professor Julius Codrington, pillar of Cambridge University's renowned Cavendish Laboratory. But how was she to make that implacably logical physicist believe his only son, his pledge to the future, had within him the streak of primitive wildness she had detected almost as soon as she had become his governess? The buried uncivilised past which had now led him – she could not doubt it – to batter horribly to death the only one of the servants, the impudent tweeny Jane, not fifteen years of age, who had not had permission to go to the nearby Midsummer Fair.

Certain though she was that skinny little Jane had been killed by Newton – the circumstances led logically to only that conclusion – she was certain, too, of one other thing. When her widower employer came home and was told what had happened he would decline absolutely to accept her unsupported assertion. A woman, and one who had been already given her month's notice as being no longer able to instruct nine-year-old Newton in the logic of mathematics: he would dismiss her every word.

But, whatever her lack of acknowledged educational qualifications, she knew Newton a great deal better than his father did. He seldom saw the boy other than for the half hour each evening when Newton was summoned to the library. And there Professor Codrington did no more than put to him a stream of mathematical questions.

"Seven twelves? Fourteen eights? A hundred and twelve divided by seven?"

"If $6m$ minus 8 equals 10, what is the value of m?"

"Seven pounds, nine shillings and fourpence raised by thirteen-and-a-half per cent?"

"What is pi r squared?"

Over the three years of her employment the questions had grown progressively more difficult. Before long, anticipating what they might be, she had taken to carefully coaching Newton beforehand. In the early days there had been one or two outbreaks of frightening violence in the nursery after Newton had been impatiently upbraided for failing to produce a correct answer. It was these sudden eruptions of primitive rage that had set up in her a lurking fear of what might one day come.

So she had known she was right about Newton having battered to death, like a straw-stuffed doll, thin little Jane. Right from the moment when, returning to the kitchen the dishes of the cold supper that had been left for her, turning to close the door of the servants' WC, seemingly left open against the rules, she had come upon the girl's flailed body in a welter of dark blood on white-tiled floor, lime-washed walls. Despite the shower of glass shards from a smashed pane in the window above, one glinting fragment adhering grotesquely to the sticky blood on the nape of the child's pitifully thin neck, she had been certain there had been no intruder.

More than once in the past she had had to rebuke Jane for speaking teasingly to Master Newton. She had never – it was scarcely a possible matter to refer to – told the girl that Newton, if roused, had this appalling savage streak. But now, standing with the unpainted wooden door of the WC tight closed behind her, conscious of the blood-smelling draught wafting in from its wide-open window, she felt a sharp pang of regret at not having found some way of warning her.

Then an odour other than the sweetish smell of drying blood came to her nostrils. A sharp lemony tang. She looked up and down the short passageway, and at once saw in the direction of the kitchen a thin puddle of wet, with beside it a glass rolled over on to its side.

Yes, she thought, I see it all now. What precisely must have happened. Newton, just before the eight o'clock bedtime his father insists on, would have gone to the larder where always in summer there stands on the wide slate shelf a large jug of barley-water covered with a circle of muslin weighted with sewn-on beads. Carrying back his cooling glass, he must have met Jane just emerging from the WC, and she must have said something perhaps as innocuous as *Just off to beddy-byes then, Master Newton.* And it had been enough. Sturdy Newton, hardly the smaller, must have seized her bodily, hurled her onto the hard surface of the WC's tiled floor and, to judge by the dark blood spatterings reaching high up the walls, done so again and again.

But, she added to herself, for all that I have long known Newton – there was, worst of all, the business of the tortured cat – to be unable in the end to hold back the primitive violence within him, I never could bring myself fully to believe he would kill a fellow human being. Yet that is what he has done now. I know it. The fear I have felt is justified at the last.

But where is he, she thought suddenly. Is he here, in the house? Or . . . or has he run off into the evening? Scared by what he has done?

But, no, that night a year ago when he vented his rage, at long length, on a cat whose midnight yowling had woken him he had simply brazened it out. And had been believed by his father, for all that she herself had seen him, in his nightshirt, coming gleefully back from the stableyard when she in turn had been woken by the animal's ear-splitting shrieks.

So will I find Newton in his bed now? Feigning sleep? Almost certainly I will. But I must go and see, whatever risk may lie there. Perhaps, after all, I may be wrong. Perhaps those shining splinters of glass in that pool of dark-red blood really do mean someone tried to break in, that Jane came upon him. And was killed because she had.

But she knew this was not what had happened. No, Newton was clever, if not as much of a young mathematician as his ambitious father wished him to be. But he was quite capable, after he had sated his fury, of attempting to lay a false trail. Yes, he must have slipped round to the stableyard, put his fist or a stone through that windowpane and then lifted the latch and pushed the window open. Look at the way immediately after the business with the cat he had furnished himself with a glass of water to account for his presence out of bed.

So, first to peer in at Newton. And then to ask the only other person in the house, Mr Franklin Laming, the tutor recently appointed to remedy her own supposed deficiencies as a teacher, to go post-haste into Cambridge itself to summon the police. He had been, so Mrs Whitaker, the housekeeper, had told her, lying all evening under a sheet in his room prostrated by a heat headache, even declining her offer to bring him supper. But he would have to rouse himself now.

She found Newton, of course, in his bed. He was lying still under the covers, deeply breathing as if in sleep – too cunning to put on any imitation snores – though in the usual way he would have been awake and reading at this still light hour. She took one quick look at the clothes tumbled on the bedside chair. Newton might, in the heat of it all, have left his shirt there and, if the walls of the WC were anything to go by, it was bound to be blood-stained.

But there was no shirt in the heap on the chair. Nor were there any underclothes. So had Newton done what she had drummed into him he must do each night, put his soiled clothes into the washing basket on the landing outside? Softly she closed the door, and thought of Newton, lying there with the bedclothes right up to his chin, carefully opening one eye to make sure she had gone.

She tugged off the tight-fitting lid of the basket – it gave a sharp protesting squeak – and saw the handful of discarded clothing at the bottom. Newton's clothes. Not until much later at night would his father put in his own soiled garments, as on the floor above she herself, Mrs Whitaker and presumably the newcomer Franklin Laming would put theirs into the similar basket outside their rooms. So will there be here the blood-marked shirt that will convince Professor Codrington surely that his son has done this appalling thing?

She bent and extracted the bundle. Two stockings, a summer vest, a pair of drawers. And nothing else.

So Newton had not, bewildered in the aftermath of what he had done, simply thrust his shirt away with his other clothes. No, he must have seen the blood and hidden it.

If my suspicions were in need of any corroboration, she thought, here it is.

But what had Newton, with all the simple, untrammelled cunning a child can rise to – cunning she had noted and frequently circumvented in all of the pupils under her governess' eye – done with this blood-spattered garment that would provide, if she could find it, her proof?

Not the moment to challenge him now. His murderous rage could well flare up again. And in rage Newton could be even stronger than herself. There had been only one occasion, in her first days in the house, when a sharp and necessary rebuke of hers had produced that savage response. But she had not forgotten it. The solid, cannonball-like six-year-old body hurtling at her, sending her crashing to the nursery floor. The little digging hands going for her face, her eyes. Not for nothing had she adopted ever since the habit of never turning her back after she had had occasion to utter a correcting word, however mild.

Then from outside she heard the sound of a cab turning in at the gate. Newton's father back already? It was possible. Sometimes he chose to work in the evening in the private laboratory he had had built on at the side of the house. Or perhaps he had returned expecting supper, not remembering that this was the evening when each year all the servants from Mrs Whitaker down – all on this occasion but impudent Jane – had leave to go to the Midsummer Fair.

He was going to be disappointed.

Taking her courage in both hands – she felt it almost as

an object, a jewel-box held between them – she ran rapidly down the stairs.

"Sir ... Professor ... Sir, I am afraid I have some terrible news."

Tall, and made taller by his silk hat, sombrely dressed in black, long face cut deep by vertical creases, mouth a single prisoning line, pince-nez on their wide black ribbon firm on nose, he turned to her. And palpably sighed.

What is the fool of a woman trying to tell me now? He might have spoken the words out loud.

"I have to tell you, sir, that – that someone has killed the between-maid, Jane. Has brutally battered her to death."

So, no, she had not managed it. She had not brought herself to say *Sir, I have to tell you that your son, Newton, has brutally battered to death the between-maid Jane.*

"What? What are you saying? Are you telling me one of the servants has been murdered?"

"Yes, sir. I have only just found her body. She is in the servants' WC, sir."

"Tush. Some fainting fit. Girls are known to ... What nonsense is this about battering, brutal battering? Come, Miss Unwin, pull yourself together."

For a moment Miss Unwin saw again the sight she had begun to try to put out of her mind. Jane's thin, horribly savaged body, the showered glass all round it with the one glinting fragment adhering to the thin neck, the spattered blood reaching half-way up the little WC's lime-washed walls.

"Sir," she said, "I think you had better see for yourself. And in the meantime I will go and ascertain if Mr Laming, who is suffering from the headache, will be able to go to the police station."

"You will do nothing of the kind. When I have examined the girl I will decide whether it is the police or a medical man who should be summoned. If there is a need for anyone at all. And now, where is this – this place where you say the girl is to be found?"

Miss Unwin, letting herself think how little the master of the house knew about those within it and the conditions of their lives, told him where he could find the servants' WC. For a moment she considered telling him, too, to take note of the odour of barley-water in the passageway outside. But at once she thought better of it. To herself that sharp lemony smell had been a clear indication of what had taken place. But, she saw, anyone wishing to believe that what had happened had not occurred could easily enough invent a dozen seemingly logical reasons why lemonade or barley-water might have been spilt in the passage there.

So she said nothing but, as soon as Professor Codrington strode away, she went far enough up the stairs again to be able to keep Newton's door under observation. It was possible that the sound of his father's raised voice would make him decide after all to run away.

She did hear after a little what seemed to be faint noises in the soft interior darkness above. She listened intently. But before she could decide whether the sounds were coming from Newton's room or from Franklin Laming's one floor higher, Professor Codrington came stamping back. His colourless face had taken on a yet paler, dun shade.

"Laming? Where is the fellow? He'll have to take my horse and go to the police."

Then Franklin Laming came hurrying down, tugging on a worn woollen dressing-gown over shirt and trousers. Ferociously Professor Codrington gave him instructions.

"But, sir, I am not well. I fear I will hardly be able to saddle your horse."

"What— What the devil— Where's Rogers? He'll saddle Bucephalus. I suppose you can ride, Laming?"

"Rogers has gone to the Midsummer Fair with the other

servants," Miss Unwin put in quickly. "But Mr Laming has his bicycle. I suppose in view of the emergency he will be able to ride that into Cambridge."

"Very well. So go at once, man. Ask at the police station for Inspector Wood. He knows me. He'll see the fellow who did this is hunted down quickly enough."

Franklin Laming hurried back upstairs.

And Miss Unwin asked herself, once again, how she could possibly tell her coldly hostile employer that it was no *fellow* who had killed poor Jane and then made his escape.

But she must try.

"Sir," she said, "there is something I feel obliged to inform you of."

"Yes, yes. I dare say you may know something arising from this business that may be of some small assistance. But you can tell Wood anything you may know, or think you know. In the meantime we must take thought for Newton. Do you have any reason to suppose the disturbance may have woken him?"

Miss Unwin straightened her shoulders and took in a full breath.

"Sir, I believe in fact that Newton may have been awake and out of his room when Jane was killed."

"You mean he may have seen . . . But the harm that would do to him . . . Incalculable. Incalculable."

Now. Now I must say it. Otherwise he will go on not paying attention to anything I tell him. He listens little enough in the ordinary way. Now he must hear me.

"No, sir. It is worse than you think. Much worse. Sir, it is very possible that it is Newton himself who is responsible for what has been done."

"What are you saying? I don't understand. How can Newton be in any way responsible? Are you saying he left open the window the burglar entered by? Hardly a likely circumstance, Miss Unwin."

Into it once more. When will he ever understand? How can he understand?

"What I am saying, sir, is that—" No, she could not do it; not come out point-blank with the accusation. "Sir, I believe the pane in that window was smashed from the outside after – after Jane had been killed, sir. Perhaps you failed to notice, but there is a splinter of glass adhering to the poor girl's neck. The pane was broken and the window opened after she was killed."

"Woman, you're talking nonsense. All this business has affected you. Go to your room. I shall send Mrs Whitaker to you."

"Mrs Whitaker, like all the servants, is at the Midsummer Fair. Or, perhaps, now returning from it. Sir, it would be best if, before they come back, you are made fully aware of what may have happened. The fact is that no one was in the house all evening except for Mr Laming who, I understand, was in his room feeling unwell, and Jane, myself and Newton."

Now at least Professor Codrington was paying her attention. In his eyes behind the glinting pince-nez on their broad satin band there was a look of steely anger.

"Do I understand, Miss Unwin, that you are suggesting that there has been no intruder in the house? I trust you are not hinting that Mr Laming, whom I have appointed as my son's tutor, is in some way responsible for the death of that girl?"

For a moment Miss Unwin made herself consider it. But, no. She had Mrs Whitaker's word for it that the tutor was lying in bed ill, too ill to want to eat. And, studious, pale of face, unable even to contemplate saddling up a horse, it was hardly possible to see him as a savage murderer.

"No, sir, I am not suggesting that Mr Laming had anything whatsoever to do with this terrible business. What I am suggesting—"

Another sucked-in breath. The last.

"Sir, I am putting to you the possibility, or more than the possibility, that it is Newton himself who killed Jane."

There. Said. Done. Let the heavens fall.

"Woman, you have gone out of your mind."

"No, sir. Sir, I am sadly afraid that it is Newton who has gone out of his mind. Sir, I have every reason to believe, from my experience over the whole time I have been Newton's governess, that he has in him a deep-seated tendency to ungovernable rage. To a rage, sir, which I can only describe as akin to that of the savage. And, sir, I believe – I have to believe – that in just such a fit of rage this evening Newton battered that poor girl to death."

Professor Codrington did not move so much as a muscle. But from him there emanated a chill contempt that told Miss Unwin that she was never going to convince Newton's father that his son was capable of doing what she knew that he had.

Not unless she could face him with irrefutable proof.

She was in her room, sitting by the door from where she could see Newton's door on the floor below, with her window open on to the moon-soaked front lawn stretching down to the bank of laurels and the high brick wall beyond them, when she heard the rattle of a trap arriving at speed and, looking out, saw Inspector Wood and two caped and helmeted constables jumping down. Professor Codrington had told her eventually, with unceasing chill anger, that as soon as it was morning she was to leave the house. But she had done nothing towards packing her valises with the acquisitions of her three-year stay.

Instead she had sat and watched Newton's door on the landing below. True, he had had the opportunity between his eight o'clock bedtime and when she had gone to see him

111

there in his bed pretending to be asleep to have crept out and hidden that blood-stained shirt somewhere. But she thought it was unlikely that he had. Out of his room, he would have known he might at any moment have encountered herself or Franklin Laming, whom he did not know to be lying ill, or even Mrs Whitaker back from the fair.

So the likelihood was that the shirt had been stuffed out of sight in his room, to be disposed of by daylight next day. But Newton was perfectly capable, lying awake and listening to the voices coming up from the hall, to have thought that in the general disturbance it would be safe to sneak out and find somewhere better to hide the telltale evidence. So she had sat watching, and thinking what she ought to do and how to do it.

About ten o'clock, with the last light of the long day rapidly fading, she had gathered that the servants had returned. Below, she had heard Professor Codrington, his voice unwavering, tell Mrs Whitaker that Jane had been killed by an intruder and that she was to see that all of the servants, except for Rogers, went at once to their beds.

Still listening, leaning over the banister, Miss Unwin heard the groom being questioned. And one thing had emerged that had pleased her. Question and cross-question as he might, Professor Codrington did not succeed in budging Rogers from his assertion that on the long straight road leading past the house to the field where the fair was held he had seen no stranger in all the time since the party of servants had set out until in twos and threes they had begun to straggle back.

"Come, at the fair you must have been caught up in your amusements, whatever they may have been. You would have been quite unable to notice this thief creeping away. Isn't that so?"

"No, sir, begging your pardon. I never went in, seeing as I don't hold with such childishness. But Mrs Whitaker had

112

said I was to go along the road with the other servants and that I did. But I stood there at the gate, smoking a pipe or two all the while, and I can tell you, sir, no one came out of our house and went along the road one way or the other. Not one single soul."

"Very well, the fellow made off across the fields at the back."

"I doubt he could, sir. The rain we've had this past month and more, sir, the floods are mortal deep right across the fen as far as the Cam herself."

"Nonsense, man. There must be a path the fellow could have got away by."

"Yes, sir, there be a path right enough. But 'tis as deep under water as anywhere."

"Then you must be wrong about the depth of the flood. That's all there is to it."

But then Miss Unwin heard Mrs Whitaker, somewhat timorously, come to the groom's support.

"I really do not think Rogers is mistaken, sir. I have not been able to have vegetables from the kitchen garden for a fortnight or more. It is well under water."

"If you say so. If you say so. Then, Rogers, you must be mistaken about your watch on the road. I dare say you nodded off once or twice. That's the logical explanation."

Professor Codrington had told Rogers then not to go to bed but to wait until Inspector Wood arrived. Miss Unwin retreated to her post at her door, from where she could continue to keep Newton's one below under observation.

But had the boy already tried to run away, managed to get out of his window and down to the ground? No. Escape that way was impossible. Though a Virginia creeper ran up the wall there, its vines, not long planted, were too thin to bear any weight. She had even pointed out herself the progress they were making, how the leaves on them had not yet turned to

113

the deep, luminous red of autumn, when just a week before she had been giving Newton a nature lesson, restricted by the spreading flood waters to the immediate surrounds of the house.

Hearing Inspector Wood coming back from viewing Jane's body and speaking to Rogers in the kitchen, she stepped cautiously out on to the landing once more and descended a few steps. Perhaps an inspector of police, a supposedly logical male, would be able to convince Professor Codrington where she herself had so calamitously failed.

"Oh, we shall lay the fellow by the heels, sir," she heard the inspector's assertive voice floating up from the open library door. "Never you fear. He can't have got far. Not with the fields flooded the way they are."

"So you think, Inspector, he went that way and not out by the road?"

"Seems he must have done, sir. I know Jem Rogers myself. He's a canny fellow, and if he says he was looking along the road all the time that his fellow servants were at the fair, then I believe him."

"Very well. Then the sooner you set off across the fields the better. Your man certainly won't have got very far in the floods."

"Very good, sir. And I dare say you'll find me coming out here first thing tomorrow morning to tell you we've got the villain safely in a cell."

"I hope so, Inspector. I hope so. So I'll wish you good night. And good hunting."

But, Miss Unwin thought, I would rather take Rogers' word for the floods as well as for the road. There's no one out there for Inspector Wood and his constables to haul off to a cell. Jane's murderer is a strong young boy, though he's no more than nine, in that room just below.

But how am I to convince Newton's father of this? How am

I even to see Professor Codrington again? I know him. He will decline absolutely to have anything to do with the vexatious female he sees me as. In the morning he will breakfast in his room and then leave immediately for the Cavendish. He will expect, when tomorrow evening he comes back home, that the exasperating governess he mistakenly took into his house will have gone for ever. He will leave it to Mrs Whitaker to see to that.

So how can I catch him unawares?

For a few minutes she traced out the logical path of her employer's time until the hour she herself would be constrained to leave. Could I go into Cambridge, to the Cavendish? But he will have instructed the porters he is not to be disturbed. And the same will apply if he dines in college tomorrow evening.

No, trace back again. Back to this very moment. And then work forwards.

And, yes, I have it now.

She waited, ears cocked at her open door. She heard at last the professor come out of the library and begin to march with leaden legs up the stairs to bed. Was he thinking that perhaps after all the intrusive female he had been harbouring beneath his roof might be right about his precious, mathematically inclined Newton? If so, no doubt he would quickly be pushing the thought down.

She stood listening still.

Then from the floor below she heard the sound she had been waiting for. A quick little shriek of hardened reed on hardened reed. The lid of the washing basket on the landing being tugged from its seating, the sound she had heard earlier looking to see if Newton's shirt was there.

In a moment she had run in the dark down the flight of stairs and was confronting the boy's father, as formidable in long nightshirt as he had been in black tailcoat, in

115

one hand a bundle of underclothes, in the other his bed-candle.

"Miss Unwin," he said, lifting the candle-holder high, "what are you doing? Get back to your room at once."

"Professor Codrington, I am here to ask you what is there already in that basket whose lid you have just removed?"

"What – what do you mean?"

"I mean, sir, would you be good enough to look into the basket and see if Master Newton left his shirt there when he retired to bed?"

"His shirt? I suppose he did. Doesn't he always? What are you—"

"Sir, if you fail to find the boy's shirt, won't it be because it has got badly blood-stained?"

For an instant she thought Professor Codrington was going to turn on his heel and stride back into his bedroom.

But then, darting her a look that combined disdain and perhaps a substratum of pure fear, he dropped his own clothes down on to the floor and plunged his free hand deep into the basket.

Before he had fully withdrawn it Miss Unwin realised that, despite her conviction, he was after all clutching a shirt. A boy's plain cotton shirt.

Her heart plummeted.

"Now, Miss Unwin," Professor Codrington said, voice icy as the east wind, "will you once and for all abandon this extraordinary notion you seem to have embraced."

"No, sir."

She heard herself bring out the words almost before she knew what it was she had worked out she had to say.

"No?"

"No, sir. If you care to bring your candle closer to that shirt you will see that it was not worn earlier today. It will be fresh from the iron."

A Lurking Fear

She hardly let Professor Codrington look at the shirt and confirm what she had guessed.

"So, sir, don't you see that in simple logic this must mean that Newton, soon after I had looked into that basket and found no shirt in it, must have realised – he would have heard the squeak of the lid being lifted – that I had noticed what was lacking? And that he then attempted to rectify the omission? He had his opportunity. When I was telling you, attempting to tell you, what had happened."

She watched on the professor's face the train of thought she had gone through being repeated. And saw him come to the same *quod-erat-demonstrandum* conclusion.

"But then . . . Then are you saying that the shirt Newton was wearing this evening will be in his room somewhere. And that it will be stained with blood?"

"Yes, sir. I have taken care to keep a watch on the door since I spoke to you, and I have not heard it opened. Newton has not left his room."

Professor Codrington took three rapid steps along the landing, candle flame guttering, and thrust open his son's door.

Not waiting even to see whether he had woken the boy, he set the candle down and began flinging aside the garments on the chair. Nothing. He dropped to his knees like a felled oak and peered under the bed.

"No, sir," Miss Unwin said. "You will not find it anywhere in the room."

She had seen Newton sitting up now, bolt upright in his bed. In the flickering candlelight there was an expression of malicious glee on his face.

It was some comfort to her that his father, though still on his knees, was between herself and him.

"I have been asking myself what I should do with such a telltale garment if I had had to hide it," she said. "And it appeared to me that the logical thing would be somehow to get it out of the room."

"But you have said you had the door under your observation."

"There is a window, sir."

"He has thrown it out? Is that what you are claiming?" He ran to the window and flung up the lower sash.

"No, sir. It will not be on the ground below. It might easily be seen there."

Professor Codrington drew in his head. Miss Unwin crossed the room swiftly, at every step keeping her eyes on Newton.

She reached the window, leaned out and felt round about among the thin, clinging vines of the new-planted Virginia creeper.

"Well?"

"Nothing, sir."

Behind her Newton laughed.

"If," Miss Unwin said, "something has not been pushed in among the creeper below the window or to the side, there is but one explanation. It will have been pushed in above."

She twisted round, reached up. Touched cloth. Gripped it. Pulled. And turned to face Newton's father with in her hand a once-white shirt deep-stained with blood. Proof.

HEROES

Anne Perry

Almost a decade ago, I acquired a Victorian mystery novel called Silence in Hanover Close *by a writer then unknown to me, Anne Perry. The book introduced me to Inspector Thomas Pitt and a novelist – already highly successful in the United States but at that time less well-known in her native Britain – who clearly possessed a distinctive talent. Perhaps there is a clue to her particular gift in a comment she contributed to the* St James Guide to Crime and Mystery Writers: *'I see mysteries as stories of what happens to people and communities under the pressure of fear and suspicion, especially the violent changes in perceptions and relationships brought about by investigation.' Her skill at describing those people and communities is now internationally acclaimed. By a stroke of good fortune, I met her when starting to put together this anthology and was delighted by her enthusiastic response when I asked her to contribute.* Heroes *more than lived up to my expectations; life and death in the trenches are evoked with much emotional force. This story is the work of a major crime writer at the height of her powers.*

Nights were always the worst, and in winter they lasted from dusk at about four o'clock, until dawn again towards eight the following morning. Sometimes star shells lit the sky, showing the black zigzags of the trenches stretching as far as the eye could see to left and right. Apparently now they went right across France and Belgium all the way from the Alps to the Channel. But Joseph was only concerned with this short stretch of the Ypres Salient.

In the gloom near him someone coughed, a deep, hacking sound coming from down in the chest. They were in the support line, farthest from the front, the most complex of the three rows of trenches. Here were the kitchens, the latrines and the stores and mortar positions. Fifteen-foot shafts led to caves which were about five paces wide, and high enough for most men to stand upright. Joseph made his way in the half dark now, the wood slippery under his boots and his hands feeling the mud walls, held up by timber and wire. There was an awful lot of water. One of the sumps must be blocked.

There was a glow of light ahead and a moment later he was in the comparative warmth of the dugout. There were two candles burning and the brazier gave off heat, and a sharp smell of soot. The air was blue with tobacco smoke and a pile of boots and greatcoats steamed a little. Two officers sat on canvas chairs talking together. One of them recited a joke – gallows humour – and they both laughed. A gramophone sat silent on a camp table, and a small pile of records of the latest music hall songs was carefully protected in a tin box.

"Hello, Chaplain," one of them said cheerfully. "How's God these days?"

"Gone home on sick leave," the other answered quickly, before Joseph could reply. There was disgust in his voice, but no intended irreverence. Death was too close here for men to mock faith.

"Have a seat," the first offered, waving towards a third chair. "Morris got it today. Killed outright. That bloody sniper again."

"He's somewhere out there, just about opposite us," the second said grimly. "One of those blighters the other day claimed he'd got forty-three for sure."

"I can believe it," Joseph answered, accepting the seat. He knew better than most what the casualties were. It was his job to comfort the terrified, the dying, to carry stretchers, often to write letters to the bereaved. Sometimes he thought it was harder than actually fighting, but he refused to stay back in the comparative safety of the field hospitals and depots. This was where he was most needed.

"Thought about setting up a trench raid," the major said slowly, weighing his words and looking at Joseph. "Good for morale. Make it seem as if we were actually doing something. But our chances of getting the blighter are pretty small. Only lose a lot of men for nothing. Feel even worse afterwards."

The captain did not add anything. They all knew morale was sinking. Losses were high, the news bad. Word of terrible slaughter seeped through from the Somme and Verdun and all along the line right to the sea. Physical hardship took its toll, the dirt, the cold and the alternation between boredom and terror. The winter of 1916 lay ahead.

"Cigarette?" The major held out his pack to Joseph.

"No, thanks," Joseph declined with a smile. "Got any tea going?"

They poured him a mugful, strong and bitter, but hot. He drank it, and half an hour later made his way forward to the open air again and the travel trench. A star shell exploded high and bright. Automatically he ducked, keeping his head below the rim. They were about four feet deep, and in order not to provide a target, a man had to move in a half crouch. There was a rattle of machine-gun fire out ahead, and closer to, a thud as a rat was dislodged and fell into the mud beside the duckboards.

Other men were moving about close to him. The normal order of things was reversed here. Nothing much happened during the day. Trench repair work was done, munitions shifted, weapons cleaned, a little rest taken. Most of the activity was at night, most of the death.

" 'Lo, Chaplain," a voice whispered in the dark. "Say a prayer we get that bloody sniper, will you?"

"Maybe God's a Jerry?" someone suggested in the dark.

"Don't be stupid!" a third retorted derisively. "Everyone knows God's an Englishman! Didn't they teach you nothing at school?"

There was a burst of laughter. Joseph joined in. He promised to offer up the appropriate prayers and moved on forward. He had known many of the men all his life. They came from the same Northumbrian town as he did, or the surrounding villages. They had gone to school together, scrumped apples from the same trees, fished in the same rivers and walked the same lanes.

It was a little after six when he reached the firing trench beyond whose sandbag parapet lay no man's land, with its four or five hundred yards of mud, barbed wire and shell holes. Half a dozen burnt tree stumps looked in the sudden flares like men. Those grey wraiths could be fog, or gas.

Funny that in summer this blood and horror-soaked soil could still bloom with honeysuckle, forget-me-nots and wild larkspur, and most of all with poppies. You would think nothing would ever grow there again.

More star shells went up, lighting the ground, the jagged

scars of the trenches black, the men on the fire steps with rifles on their shoulders illuminated for a few, blinding moments. Sniper shots rang out.

Joseph stood still. He knew the terror of the night-watch out beyond the parapet, crawling around in the mud. Some of them would be at the head of saps out from the trench, most would be in shell holes, surrounded by heavy barricades of wire. Their purpose was to check enemy patrols for unusual movement, any signs of increased activity, as if there might be an attack planned.

More star shells lit the sky. It was beginning to rain. A crackle of machine-gun fire, and heavier artillery somewhere over to the left. Then the sharp whine of sniper fire, again and again.

Joseph shuddered. He thought of the men out there, beyond his vision, and prayed for strength to endure with them in their pain, not to try to deaden himself to it.

There were shouts somewhere ahead, heavy shells now, shrapnel bursting. There was a flurry of movement, flares, and a man came sliding over the parapet, shouting for help.

Joseph plunged forward, slipping in the mud, grabbing for the wooden props to hold himself up. Another flare of light. He saw quite clearly Captain Holt lurching towards him, another man over his shoulder, dead weight.

"He's hurt!" Holt gasped. "Pretty badly. One of the night patrol. Panicked. Just about got us all killed." He eased the man down into Joseph's arms and let his rifle fall forward, bayonet covered in an old sock to hide its gleam. His face was grotesque in the lanternlight, smeared with mud and a wide streak of blood over the burnt cork which blackened it, as all night patrol had.

Others were coming to help. There was still a terrible noise of fire going on and the occasional flare.

The man in Joseph's arms did not stir. His body was limp

and it was difficult to support him. Joseph felt the wetness and the smell of blood. Wordlessly others materialised out of the gloom and took the weight.

"Is he alive?" Holt said urgently. "There was a hell of a lot of shot up there." His voice was shaking, almost on the edge of control.

"Don't know," Joseph answered. "We'll get him back to the bunker and see. You've done all you can." He knew how desperate men felt when they risked their lives to save another man, and did not succeed. A kind of despair set in, a sense of very personal failure, almost a guilt for having survived themselves. "Are you hurt?"

"Not much," Holt answered. "Couple of grazes."

"Better have them dressed, before they get poisoned," Joseph advised, his feet slipping on the wet boards and banging his shoulder against a jutting post. The whole trench wall was crooked, giving way under the weight of mud. The founds had eroded.

The man helping him swore.

Awkwardly carrying the wounded man, they staggered back through the travel line to the support trench and into the light and shelter of a bunker.

Holt looked dreadful. Beneath the cork and blood his face was ashen. He was soaked with rain and mud and there were dark patches of blood across his back and shoulders.

Someone gave him a cigarette. Back here it was safe to strike a match. He drew in smoke deeply. "Thanks," he murmured, still staring at the wounded man.

Joseph looked down at him now. It was young Ashton. He knew him quite well. He had been at school with his older brother.

The soldier who had helped carry him in let out a cry of dismay, strangled in his throat. It was Mordaff, Ashton's closest friend, and he could see what Joseph now could also.

Ashton was dead, his chest torn open, the blood no longer pumping, and a bullet hole through his head.

"I'm sorry," Holt said quietly. "I did what I could. I can't have got to him in time. He panicked."

Mordaff jerked his head up. "He never would!" The cry was desperate, a shout of denial against a shame too great to be borne. "Not Will!"

Holt stiffened. "I'm sorry," he said hoarsely. "It happens."

"Not with Will Ashton, it don't!" Mordaff retorted, his eyes blazing, pupils circled with white in the candlelight, his face grey. He had been in the front line two weeks now, a long stretch without a break from the ceaseless tension, filth, cold and intermittent silence and noise. He was nineteen.

"You'd better go and get that arm dressed, and your side," Joseph said to Holt. He made his voice firm, as to a child.

Holt glanced again at the body of Ashton, then up at Joseph.

"Don't stand there bleeding," Joseph ordered. "You did all you could. There's nothing else. I'll look after Mordaff."

"I tried!" Holt repeated. "There's nothing but mud and darkness and wire, and bullets coming in all directions." There was a sharp thread of terror under his shell-thin veneer of control. He had seen too many men die. "It's enough to make any man lose his nerve."

"Not Will!" Mordaff said again, his voice choking off in a sob.

Holt looked at Joseph again, then staggered out.

Joseph turned to Mordaff. He had done this before, too many times, tried to comfort men who had just seen childhood friends blown to pieces, or killed by a sniper's bullet, looking as if they should still be alive, perfect except for the small, blue hole through the brain. There was little to say. Most men found talk of God meaningless at that moment. They

125

were shocked, fighting against belief and yet seeing all the terrible waste and loss of the truth in front of them. Usually it was best just to stay with them, let them speak about the past, what the friend had been like, times they had shared, as if he were only wounded and would be back, at the end of the war, in some world one could only imagine, in England, perhaps in a summer day with sunlight on the grass, birds singing, a quiet riverbank somewhere, the sound of laughter, and women's voices.

Mordaff refused to be comforted. He accepted Ashton's death, the physical reality of that was too clear to deny and he had seen too many other men he knew killed in the year and a half he had been in Belgium. But he could not, would not accept that Ashton had panicked. He knew what panic out there cost, how many other lives it jeopardised. It was the ultimate failure.

"How am I going to tell his mam?" he begged Joseph. "It'll be all I can do to tell her he's dead! His pa'll never get over it. That proud of him, they were. He's the only boy. Three sisters he had, Mary, Lizzie and Alice. Thought he was the greatest lad in the world. I can't tell 'em he panicked! He couldn't have, Chaplain! He just wouldn't!"

Joseph did not know what to say. How could people at home in England even begin to imagine what it was like in the mud and noise out here? But he knew how deep shame burned. A lifetime could be consumed by it.

"Maybe he just lost sense of direction," he said gently. "He wouldn't be the first." War changed men. People did panic. Mordaff knew that, and half his horror was because it could be true. But Joseph did not say so. "I'll write to his family," he went on. "There's a lot of good to say about him. I could send pages. I'll not need to tell them much about tonight."

"Will you?" Mordaff was eager. "Thanks . . . thanks, Chaplain. Can I stay with him . . . until they come for him?"

126

"Yes, of course," Joseph agreed. "I'm going forward anyway. Get yourself a hot cup of tea. See you in an hour or so."

He left Mordaff squatting on the earth floor beside Ashton's body, and fumbled his way back over the slimy duckboards towards the travel line, then forward again to the front and the crack of gunfire and the occasional high flare of a star shell.

He did not see Mordaff again, but he thought nothing of it. He could have passed twenty men he knew and not recognised them, muffled in greatcoats, heads bent as they moved, rattling along the duckboards, or stood on the firesteps, rifles to shoulder, trying to see in the gloom for something to aim at.

Now and again he heard a cough, or the scamper of rats' feet and the splash of rain and mud. He spent a little time with two men swapping jokes, joining in their laughter. It was black humour, self-mocking, but he did not miss the courage in it, or the fellowship, the need to release emotion in some sane and human way.

About midnight the rain stopped.

A little after five the night patrol came scrambling through the wire, whispered passwords to the sentries, then came tumbling over the parapet of sandbags down into the trench, shivering with cold, and relief. One of them had caught a shot in the arm.

Joseph went back with them to the support line. In one of the dugouts a gramophone was playing a music hall song. A couple of men sang along with it, one of them had a beautiful voice, a soft, lyric tenor. It was a silly song, trivial, but it sounded almost like a hymn out here, a praise of life.

A couple of hours and the day would begin, endless, methodical duties of housekeeping, mindless routine, but it was better than doing nothing.

There was still a sporadic crackle of machine-gun fire, and whine of sniper bullets.

An hour till dawn.

Joseph was sitting on an upturned ration case when Sergeant Renshaw came into the bunker, pulling the gas curtain aside to peer in.

"Chaplain?"

Joseph looked up. He could see bad news in the man's face.

"I'm afraid Mordaff got it tonight," he said, coming in and letting the curtain fall again. "Sorry. Don't really know what happened. Ashton's death seems to have . . . well, he lost his nerve. More or less went over the top all by himself. Suppose he was determined to go and give Fritz a bloody nose, on Ashton's account. Stupid bastard! Sorry, Chaplain."

He did not need to explain himself, or to apologise. Joseph knew exactly the fury and the grief he felt at such a futile waste. To this was added a sense of guilt that he had not stopped it. He should have realised Mordaff was so close to breaking. He should have seen it. That was his job.

He stood up slowly. "Thanks for telling me, Sergeant. Where is he?"

"He's gone, Chaplain." Renshaw remained near the doorway. "You can't help 'im now."

"I know that. I just want to . . . I don't know . . . apologise to him. I let him down. I didn't understand he was . . . so . . ."

"You can't be everybody's keeper," Renshaw said gently. "Too many of us. It's not been a bad night otherwise. Got a trench raid coming off soon. Just wish we could get that damn sniper across the way there." He scraped a match and lit his cigarette. "But morale's good. That was a brave thing Captain Holt did out there. Pity about Ashton, but that doesn't alter Holt's courage. Could see him, you know, by the star shells.

Right out there beyond the last wire, bent double, carrying Ashton on his back. Poor devil went crazy. Running around like a fool. Could have got the whole patrol killed if Holt hadn't gone after him. Hell of a job getting him back. Fell a couple of times. Reckon that's worth a mention in dispatches, at least. Heartens the men, knowing our officers have got that kind of spirit."

"Yes . . . I'm sure," Joseph agreed. He could only think of Ashton's white face, and Mordaff's desperate denial, and how Ashton's mother would feel, and the rest of his family. "I think I'll go and see Mordaff just the same."

"Right you are," Renshaw conceded reluctantly, standing aside for Joseph to pass.

Mordaff lay in the support trench just outside the bunker two hundred yards to the west. He looked even younger than he had in life, as if he were asleep. His face was oddly calm, even though it was smeared with mud. Someone had tried to clean most of it off in a kind of dignity, so that at least he was recognisable. There was a large wound in the left side of his forehead. It was bigger than most sniper wounds. He must have been a lot closer.

Joseph stood in the first paling of the darkness and looked at him by candlelight from the open bunker curtain. He had been so alive only a few hours ago, so full of anger and loyalty and dismay. What had made him throw his life away in a useless gesture? Joseph racked his mind for some sign that should have warned him Mordaff was so close to breaking, but he could not see it even now.

There was a cough a few feet away, and the tramp of boots on duckboards. The men were stood down, just one sentry per platoon left. They had returned for breakfast. He realised he could smell cooking.

129

Now would be the time to ask around and find out what had happened to Mordaff.

He made his way to the field kitchen. It was packed with men, some standing to be close to the stoves and catch a bit of their warmth, others choosing to sit, albeit further away. They had survived the night. They were laughing and telling stories, most of them unfit for delicate ears, but Joseph was too used to it to take any offence. Now and then someone new would apologise for such language in front of a chaplain, but most knew he understood too well.

"Yeah," one answered his question through a mouthful of bread and jam. "He came and asked me if I saw what happened to Ashton. Very cut up, he was."

"And what did you tell him?" Joseph asked.

The man swallowed. "Told him Ashton seemed fine to me when he went over. Just like anyone else, nervous . . . but then only a fool isn't scared to go over the top!"

Joseph thanked him and moved on. He needed to know who else was on the patrol.

"Captain Holt," the next man told him, a ring of pride in his voice. Word had got around about Holt's courage. Everyone stood a little taller because of it, felt a little braver, more confident. "We'll pay Fritz back for that," he added. "Next raid – you'll see."

There was a chorus of agreement.

"Who else?" Joseph pressed.

"Seagrove, Noakes, Willis," a thin man replied, standing up. "Want some breakfast, Chaplain? Anything you like, on the house – as long as it's bread and jam and half a cup of tea. But you're not particular, are you? Not one of those fussy eaters who'll only take kippers and toast?"

"What I wouldn't give for a fresh Craster kipper," another sighed, a faraway look in his eyes. "I can smell them in my dreams."

Someone told him good-naturedly to shut up.

"Went over the top beside me," Willis said when Joseph found him quarter of an hour later. "All blacked up like the rest of us. Seemed okay to me then. Lost him in no man's land. Had a hell of a job with the wire. As bloody usual, it wasn't where we'd been told. Got through all right, then Fritz opened up on us. Star shells all over the sky." He sniffed and then coughed violently. When he had control of himself again he continued. "Then I saw someone outlined against the flares, arms high, like a wild man, running around. He was going towards the German lines, shouting something. Couldn't hear what in the noise."

Joseph did not interrupt. It was now broad daylight and beginning to drizzle again. Around them men were starting the duties of the day: digging, filling sandbags, carrying ammunition, strengthening the wire, re-setting duckboards. Men took an hour's work, an hour's sentry duty, and an hour's rest.

Near them somebody was expending his entire vocabulary of curses against lice. Two more were planning elaborate schemes to hold the water at bay.

"Of course that lit us up like a target, didn't it!" Willis went on. "Sniper fire and machine-guns all over the place. Even a couple of shells. How none of us got hit I'll never know. Perhaps the row woke God up, and he came back on duty!" He laughed hollowly. "Sorry, Chaplain. Didn't mean it. I'm just so damn sorry poor Ashton got it. Holt just came out of nowhere and ran after him, floundering through the mud. If Ashton hadn't got caught in the wire he'd never have got him."

"Caught in the wire?" Joseph asked, memory pricking at him.

"Yeah. Ashton must have ran right into the wire, because he stopped sudden, teetering, like, and fell over. Probably saved his life, because there was a hell of a barrage came over just after that. We all threw ourselves down."

"What happened then?" Joseph said urgently, a slow, sick thought taking shape in his mind.

"When it died down I looked up again, and there was Holt staggering back with poor Ashton across his shoulders. Hell of a job he had carrying him, even though he's bigger than Ashton . . . well, taller, anyway. Up to his knees in mud, he was, shot and shell all over, sky lit up like a Christmas tree. Of course we gave him what covering fire we could. Maybe it helped." He coughed again. "Reckon he'll be mentioned in dispatches, Chaplain? He deserves it." There was admiration in his voice, a lift of hope.

Joseph forced himself to answer. "I should think so." The words were stiff.

"Well, if he isn't, the men'll want to know why!" Willis said fiercely. "Bloody hero, he is."

Joseph thanked him and went to find Seagrove and Noakes. They told him pretty much the same story.

"You going to have him recommended?" Noakes asked. "Mordaff came and we said just the same to him. Reckon he wanted the Captain given a medal. He made us say it over and over again, exactly what happened."

"That's right," Seagrove nodded, leaning on a sandbag.

"You told him the same?" Joseph asked. "About the wire, and Ashton getting caught in it?"

"Yes, of course. If he hadn't got caught by the legs he'd have gone straight on and landed up in Fritz's lap, poor devil."

"Thank you."

"Welcome, Chaplain. You going to write up Captain Holt?"

Joseph did not answer, but turned away, sick at heart.

He did not need to look again, but he trudged all the way back to the field hospital anyway. It would be his job to say the services for both Ashton and Mordaff. The graves would be already dug.

He looked at Ashton's body again, looked carefully at his trousers. They were stained with mud, but there were no tears in them, no marks of wire. The fabric was perfect.

He straightened up.

"I'm sorry," he said quietly to the dead man. "Rest in peace." And he turned and walked away.

He went back to where he had left Mordaff's body, but it had been removed. Half an hour more took him to where it also was laid out. He touched the cold hand, and looked at the brow. He would ask. He would be sure. But in his mind he already was. He needed time to know what he must do about it. The men would be going over the top on another trench raid soon. Today morale was high. They had a hero in their number, a man who would risk his own life to bring back a soldier who had lost his nerve and panicked. Led by someone like that, they were equal to Fritz any day. Was one pistol bullet, one family's shame, worth all that?

What were they fighting for anyway? The issues were so very big, and at the same time so very small and immediate.

He found Captain Holt alone just after dusk, standing on the duckboards below the parapet, near one of the firing steps.

"Oh, it's you, Chaplain. Ready for another night?"

"It'll come, whether I am or not," Joseph replied.

Holt gave a short bark of laughter. "That doesn't sound like you. Tired of the firing line, are you? You've been up here a couple of weeks, you should be in turn for a step back any day. Me too, thank God."

Joseph faced forward, peering through the gloom towards no man's land and the German lines beyond. He was shaking. He must control himself. This must be done in the silence,

Anne Perry

before the shooting started up again. Then he might not get
away with it.

"Pity about that sniper over there," he remarked. "He's
taken out a lot of our men."

"Damnable," Holt agreed. "Can't get a line on him, though.
Keeps his own head well down."

"Oh, yes," Joseph nodded. "We'd never get him from here.
It needs a man to go over in the dark and find him."

"Not a good idea, Chaplain. He'd not come back. Not
advocating suicide, are you?"

Joseph chose his words very carefully and kept his voice
as unemotional as he could.

"I wouldn't have put it like that," he answered. "But he
has cost us a lot of men. Mordaff today, you know?"

"Yes . . . I heard. Pity."

"Except that wasn't the sniper, of course. But the men
think it was, so it comes to the same thing, as far as morale
is concerned."

"Don't know what you mean, Chaplain." There was a
slight hesitation in Holt's voice in the darkness.

"Wasn't a rifle wound, it was a pistol," Joseph replied. "You
can tell the difference, if you're actually looking for it."

"Then he was a fool to be that close to German lines," Holt
said, facing forward over the parapet and the mud. "Lost his
nerve, I'm afraid."

"Like Ashton," Joseph said. "Can understand that, up
there in no man's land, mud everywhere, wire catching
hold of you, tearing at you, stopping you from moving.
Terrible thing to be caught in the wire with the star shells
lighting up the night. Makes you a sitting target. Takes an
exceptional man not to panic, in those circumstances . . .
a hero."

Holt did not answer.

There was silence ahead of them, only the dull thump of

134

feet and a squelch of duckboards in mud behind, and the trickle of water along the bottom of the trench.

"I expect you know what it feels like," Joseph went on. "I notice you have some pretty bad tears in your trousers, even one in your blouse. Haven't had time to mend them yet."

"I dare say I got caught in a bit of wire out there last night," Holt said stiffly. He shifted his weight from one foot to the other.

"I'm sure you did," Joseph agreed with him. "Ashton didn't. His clothes were muddy, but no wire tears."

There were several minutes of silence. A group of men passed by behind them, muttering words of greeting. When they were gone the darkness closed in again. Someone threw up a star shell and there was a crackle of machine-gun fire.

"I wouldn't repeat that, if I were you, Chaplain," Holt said at last. "You might make people think unpleasant things, doubts. And right at the moment morale is high. We need that. We've had a hard time recently. We're going over the top in a trench raid soon. Morale is important . . . trust. I'm sure you know that, maybe even better than I do. That's your job, isn't it? Morale, spiritual welfare of the men?"

"Yes . . . spiritual welfare is a good way of putting it. Remember what it is we are fighting for, and that it is worth all that it costs . . . even this." Joseph gestured in the dark to all that surrounded them.

More star shells went up, illuminating the night for a few garish moments, then a greater darkness closed in.

"We need our heroes," Holt said very clearly. "Any man who would tear them down would be very unpopular, even if he said he was doing it in the name of truth, or justice, or whatever it was he believed in. He would do a lot of harm, Chaplain. I expect you can see that . . ."

"Oh yes," Joseph agreed. "To have their hero shown to be a coward who laid the blame for his panic on another man,

135

and let him be buried in shame, and then committed murder to hide that, would devastate men who are already wretched and exhausted by war."

"You are perfectly right." Holt sounded as if he were smiling. "A very wise man, Chaplain. Good of the regiment first. The right sort of loyalty."

"I could prove it," Joseph said very carefully.

"But you won't. Think what it would do to the men."

Joseph turned a little to face the parapet. He stood up onto the firestep and looked forward over the dark expanse of mud and wire.

"We should take that sniper out. That would be a very heroic thing to do. Good thing to try, even if you didn't succeed. You'd deserve a mention in dispatches for that, possibly a medal."

"It would be posthumous!" Holt said bitterly.

"Possibly. But you might succeed, and come back. It would be so daring, Fritz would never expect it," Joseph pointed out.

"Then you do it, Chaplain!" Holt said sarcastically.

"It wouldn't help you, Captain. Even if I die, I have written a full account of what I have learned today, to be opened should anything happen to me. On the other hand, if you were to mount such a raid, whether you returned or not, I should destroy it."

There was silence again, except for the distant crack of sniper fire a thousand yards away, and the drip of mud.

"Do you understand me, Captain Holt?"

Holt turned slowly. A star shell lit his face for an instant. His voice was hoarse.

"You're sending me to my death!"

"I'm letting you be the hero you're pretending to be, and Ashton really was," Joseph answered. "The hero the men need. Thousands of us have died out here, no one knows how many more there will be. Others will be maimed or blinded. It isn't whether you die or not, it's how well."

A shell exploded a dozen yards from them. Both men ducked, crouching automatically.

Silence again.

Slowly Joseph unbent.

Holt lifted his head. "You're a hard man, Chaplain. I misjudged you."

"Spiritual care, Captain," Joseph said quietly. "You wanted the men to think you a hero. Now you're going to justify that, and become one."

Holt stood still, looking towards him in the gloom, then slowly he turned and began to walk away, his feet sliding on the wet duckboards. Then he climbed up the next firestep, and up over the parapet.

Joseph stood still and prayed.

NOT A MINUTE ON THE DAY

Mat Coward

Mat Coward is unusual amongst the new generation of crime writers in specialising in the short mystery. Coward's stories are notable for their diversity, wit and (in many cases) sharply anti-establishment tone. Not a Minute on the Day *reflects these characteristics and offers an intriguing tale of past crime based on a 'what if' premise.*

On the ninth day of the general strike, Winston Churchill died of a heart attack, quite without warning. Less than a week later, I found myself just as unexpectedly back in my old job.

Well, almost my old job. In 1919, I had been a bobby – now I took the oath as Detective Inspector Enoch Jones, of Gloucester CID. Advancement is there for the taking in times of great change, of course. Even so, I wonder if my loyalty to the trade union cause would have been so rapidly and extravagantly rewarded had it not been for the violent and potentially embarrassing death of a young undergraduate named Ernest Scott.

*   *   *

Mat Coward

Churchill! Will history ever show us an Englishman more universally loathed by his countrymen? Hated with a passion by the working people, for the divers cruelties and injustices he inflicted on them over many years, and in which he seemed to take such a wicked delight; and at the same time despised by his own class as an unprincipled and reflexively treacherous career-chaser.

Even so, he shall have his small place in history. With his death the heart went out of the government's fight. It was no secret that Prime Minister Baldwin and his allies in the Cabinet had all along favoured a peaceful settlement to the dispute, and that Churchill had been almost alone in raising the banner of victory at any cost.

Until his death, the 'class war', as the *Daily Mail* called it, had been going badly for the unions. The TUC was ill-prepared, ill-led and divided, and rumours of its imminent surrender circulated freely. But the removal from the scene of Winston, that unyielding militant, coincided with a devastating fire (which may or may not have been started deliberately) at the BBC's Savoy Hill studios. The wireless, which by now reached almost two million listeners, had committed itself enthusiastically to the bosses' cause.

These two events, along with an incident in Hyde Park in which soldiers, apparently fooled by fog into believing that they were under attack by armed Russians, had opened fire on a peaceful crowd of protesters, changed everything.

Baldwin, having lost his voice and his strong right arm, lost his nerve. 'The master manipulator,' as the miners' leader A J Cook put it, 'became the missing rudder of a rudderless administration.' He sued for peace, but by now it was too late; now it was the strikers who had nothing to gain by compromise. Their leaders knew that by the end of the week they would either rule the country – or be in prison awaiting the rope.

Not a Minute on the Day

On the eleventh day of the strike, units of soldiers began to defect to what the pro-government press called 'the rebels'. When Winston's body set sail for burial in his mother's native America, Baldwin and co sailed with it. Nothing was said, but it was understood that they would not be coming back.

Councils of the People (the unions were careful to avoid calling them *soviets*, the words of the Bolshevik litany still having power to horrify, since the time of the Zinoviev forgery) were being established throughout the industrialised areas of Britain. In a manner surprisingly straightforward – or should we say predictably British? – these swiftly took over the running of essential services.

At tea-time on the fourteenth day, J H Thomas, on behalf of the TUC, informed the nation that the emergency was at an end, ordered all trades unionists to report to their places of work, and announced that a general election would be held as soon as practicable. Meanwhile, delegates from each Council of the People would convene to elect the officers of a Council of Councils which would govern pro tem (along with various bishops and suchlike sympathetic respectables), in the name of 'New Labour'; a term carefully chosen to distance the new government in the minds of the people from the failures of the *old* Labour gang of 1924.

"A policeman, yes. But are you a proper policeman? Hmm? Or are you a plainclothes Bolshevist?"

"I'm afraid I don't understand the question, Sir Randolph," I lied. I kept my voice soft. A man who has lost his son deserves respectful treatment, whatever his class.

"Don't understand the question? I'm sure!" Randolph Scott stood at one end of the great fireplace in his large, dusty, drab, unmistakably wealthy drawing room (reception room? parlour? Not 'front room', I imagine). I stood at the other, hat in hands. He was a tall, thin, clean-shaven widower in his mid-fifties, with a full head of white hair. I was a tall, thin, clean-shaven bachelor in my mid-thirties, with a full head of dark hair. We made a fine pair of bookends, or firedogs.

Scott ruined the symmetry by walking up to me and staring right into my eyes. "How long have you been in the police force?" he demanded.

"I joined before the war, sir," I replied. It wasn't quite the whole truth. I had joined the Metropolitan Police in 1913, but I had been expelled from it in 1919, following the second of that year's two police strikes. I had been a die-hard union man, one of thousands 'cleansed' from the force when the government made it illegal for police officers to be members of independent trades unions. Those who stayed, who agreed to renounce their industrial freedom, had been rewarded with generous pay rises and a ten pound bonus. Such a huge lump sum had proved an irresistible temptation to most. Since then, I'd been unemployed, save for occasional casual work running errands for the railway unions.

My economic reply seemed to satisfy Randolph Scott (I was damned if I would refer to him as *Sir* Randolph in the privacy of my own thoughts).

"Very well," he said, inviting me to sit at last. "No offence, Jones, I hope. But in these terrible days one doesn't quite know that anyone is who he appears to be. Days when a *collier* gives orders to a king . . ."

"Quite, sir," I replied neutrally. "May I offer you my condolences on the tragic loss of your—"

"Yes, yes," he said, waving my words away with a busy hand.

"I believe your late son, Ernest, was a student?"

"He was up at Oxford, yes," Scott corrected me. "Final year."

"And what did he study there, sir?"

Scott gave me a look of scorn. Clearly, my question had

142

been a *faux pas* in some way which I could not fathom. "You're not a university man yourself, Inspector." This was not a question; though I had lived all over England since my schooldays, my country accent still told him all he needed to know about my upbringing. "You'll not find the answer to Ernest's death in Oxford, man!"

"No, sir?"

"No sir! Look to the Bolshevists, look to the rebels, look to the strikers!"

I wondered if Scott was one of those rich men who believed that the new government of workers was a temporary aberration, sent by God to test the faith of decent Englishmen for a few weeks or months before the natural order of things inevitably reasserted itself. From our brief acquaintance I thought it likely; more likely than that he was of the other type, those who were already adapting, learning to live with the changed circumstances, holding on to as much as they could, whilst quietly awaiting the next spin of the wheel of fortune.

"I understand, sir, that Ernest took an active part in the recent events?"

"He did his duty, Inspector, as Scotts have done for centuries. Sadly there are others of whom the same cannot be said, but Ernest did his best to defend his king and country against atheists and traitors."

"And what form did this duty take, specifically?"

"My son drove an omnibus in London, under the auspices of the Organisation for the Maintenance of Supplies. He did, Inspector, what any decent young man would do – he answered his country's call, and it cost him his life."

In the course of the great strike, there were very few instances of real violence committed by the men against their opponents

– to the disappointment, one must imagine, of some factions on either side.

I did hear of one disgraceful attack by shoeless malcontents upon the dignity of the state, though to describe it as violence would probably be to exaggerate it. A mounted troop of Special Constables – made up of young financiers and retired military fox-hunting gents, sworn in for the duration of the emergency and armed with sawn-off polo sticks – was tricked into entering a narrow and stinking back alley in Whitechapel, where the contents of several dozen chamberpots were emptied over their heads from the windows above.

It is said that one young wag, his steel helmet dripping with all manner of filth, which had been especially reserved for the purpose, turned to his companion and remarked: "The socialists are right, damn it: these people *should* have indoor plumbing!"

But murder, as an act of political revenge? No, I could not believe that.

For the most part, the strikers did not particularly resent the blackleg role played in the strike by their 'betters'. Rather, they took it as natural that the class which had most to lose from democracy and equality should do everything in its power to prevent the rise of organised labour. Besides which, even from the perspective of a hungry picket, there was something just a little enjoyable about watching one of one's betters struggling to control a bus or mail van, his (or indeed, her) face running with the sweat of unaccustomed work.

Nonetheless, someone had killed the Oxford undergraduate, Ernest Scott. If not an angry member of the lower orders, then who?

I travelled up to London in most pleasant fashion, in a first class railway carriage, which was empty of first class people. Or indeed, of any others: old habits die hard, and the guard, to

144

my amused surprise, questioned my right to place my plainly proletarian bum upon such plushness, until I scared him off with my papers of identification.

The Civil Service had destroyed thousands of documents relating to the strike once it had become clear that their old masters were on the losing side. All was not lost, however, as good luck and a lot of polite questioning led me along a trail of Old Etonians and Oxford graduates (there had been no purge of the Civil Service; this is England, don'cha know!), stretching from the Organisation for the Maintenance of Supplies (where hung a pencilled sign: 'Under new management'), via the Foreign Office, to the Ministry of War. There I met a short, plain, young woman, whose name I heard as Anna Hyphen-Hyphen, and whose brother's flatmate's cousin had been a hunting associate of the late Ernest Scott. A small world, these people had lived in.

Miss Hyphen-Hyphen furnished me with an introduction to the hunting associate himself, a red-haired young layabout named Piers. From his animated manner, I deduced that he was fonder of cocaine than was likely to be good for him. Not that it was any of my business.

"Ernie did the driving," Piers explained, as we sat in his Chelsea flat. The place was evidently too small to house a manservant, so the cup of tea I had hoped for did not materialise, and I had to make do with gin, served with Indian tonic water. I found it rather medicinal. An acquired taste, no doubt.

"And you were the conductor?"

"That's it, spot on. Piers the Clippie – that's me. Tremendous fun, best laugh we'd had in ages! They should throw one of these general strike thingies every year, if you ask me. Makes a change from slaving away in my old feller's place."

"Your old feller . . . ?"

"Stockbroker, you know. Dullest business on God's earth."

145

A stray thought blundered, almost visibly, into the young man's impressively empty head. "I say, don't get me wrong, the old feller's awfully good at it. Everyone says so. I can give you his card, if you like – he says there's never been a better time to invest. As soon as this lot's sorted out, prices are going to go through the roof."

I smiled. "I fear my salary doesn't run to much in the way of stocks and shares. The odd horse now and then, that's about my limit."

"Oh, really? Right you are." He grinned vacantly, rubbed his nose on his sleeve and gulped down about four inches of his cocktail.

"The bus you were assigned to – it ran from Hampstead to the West End, is that right?"

"Oh, absolutely. All the way. Broom-broom-broom. Splendid fun! I begged old Ernie to let me have a go behind the wheel, but you see, the thing is, I can't actually drive. So that was that. Not that I minded, as it turned out. Poor old driver misses out on all the pretty girls, you see!"

"Ernie was a good driver, was he?" According to some reports, more buses were put off the road by incompetent volunteer driving than by mass picketing.

"Rather, I should say." The ginger hair, thinning already, flapped as Piers nodded his bulb-shaped head. "At least, we didn't have any accidents. Didn't squash any pedestrians, you know."

"You were on this bus from Day Two through to Day Seven of the strike, is that right?"

"If you say so," said Piers. "I'm hopeless with details, but that sounds about right."

"And during that time did you meet with any trouble?"

"Trouble?" said Piers.

"I mean, did you run into much opposition? From the striking transport workers, or their supporters."

"Oh, right, see what you mean. Well, yes, actually, we did. The last trip we took, we were just coming up to Cambridge Circus, and suddenly we were surrounded by – God, I don't know – *hundreds* of working chaps. You know, all shouting and pushing up against the bus."

"The enemy within," I muttered, remembering a phrase of Churchill's from his propaganda rag, *The British Gazette*.

"Well, absolutely," said Piers, refilling his glass and emptying it again, virtually in the same movement. "I don't mind telling you it all looked a bit hairy for a mo. I mean to say, there were a lot of these chaps, and they were jolly determined. Still, fair's fair, they were perfectly decent about it as it turned out. One of them climbed up into the bus and told us, quite politely, that he'd really rather we didn't go any further. Well, of course, the way they had that old girl hemmed in, we couldn't have moved if we'd wanted to. I mean!"

"So what did you do?"

"Well, *moi*, I was all for abandoning ship. I mean, fun's fun, but no sense banging your head against a brick wall, is there? In any case, it was getting on for lunchtime, so I went up front to old Ernie and I said, 'Come on, old thing, let's see if the club's open.' "

"The club?"

"Oh, the Tiger Club. It's a sort of, you know, club thing. You probably wouldn't know it," he added unnecessarily, "it's more for the younger set, if you see what I mean."

"And was Ernest ready for lunch, too?"

Piers sniffed vigorously, hoping I suppose to inhale a few specks of powder left over from his last indulgence. "Well, no, not entirely. He took the whole thing rather seriously, you know, this bus driving lark. He seemed quite put out at the way we'd been brought to a halt. Said something about not being dictated to by a mob of stinking scarecrows. Well, as I say, *I* was most impressed by their good manners. Sort of chaps you'd be glad to have beating for you, if you see what I mean. But Ernie – well, he was a sound fellow, but he was rather the type who let people rub him up the wrong way."

"Was there a confrontation?"

"Wouldn't call it that, exactly. But old Ernie did get down from his cab. Wanted to speak to the chaps, I suppose."

"And did he? Speak to the chaps?"

"Dunno, really. He sort of disappeared from view, do you see? Into the crowd."

"Was there violence? Were blows exchanged?"

"No, good heavens, no. The chaps were rather taken by surprise, I think. They let him through. I saw Ernie put out a hand, to tap this one chap on the shoulder, sort of get his attention, but the fellow turned away, wouldn't speak to Ernie. And then I lost sight of him. Well, I wasn't going to sit around doing nothing for the rest of my life, so off I went to lunch. The old club was open for business as usual, which was nice."

"And did Ernest turn up for your next driving shift?"

"No, afraid not. Never saw him again." said Piers. "Probably went on strike, what?"

"The man that Ernest wanted to talk to," I asked, "was he one of the ringleaders?"

Piers shrugged. "Didn't seem to be. I didn't get a proper look at him, but I mean to say – ringleaders would be at the front of the crowd, wouldn't they? Bound to be, sort of thing."

As I took my leave of Piers he belatedly asked: "I say, do you happen to know? How did Ernie die?"

"Strangled. His body was found in ditch not far from his family home."

"Oh I say! Poor old Ernie. Strangled – not much fun, what?"

"No," I agreed. "Not much."

* * *

148

Not a Minute on the Day

I had one more call to make in London; at Scotland Yard.

George Lake had been my sergeant when I'd been in the force before, in Islington. Never a union man, I wasn't surprised to discover that he'd been transferred to the secretive, nameless unit of the Metropolitan Police which dealt with monitoring and undermining 'subversives' – the name people like him give to those who would rather fight than starve.

We had been on different sides in 1919, and we were on different sides now. The difference being that now I was a detective inspector, and a man in tune with his times. And poor old George was still a sergeant.

"Good to see you again, George," I said, as we shook hands in his tiny office.

"Likewise, Enoch," he replied, just as insincerely. I'd get no 'Sir' from him – men like George Lake wouldn't accept defeat even if you hanged them. In a way I admired him for that; better a principled enemy than a fair-weather friend.

"So," I said, looking around the broom cupboard. "What have they got you doing these days?" I am not a cruel man, but I couldn't resist asking that question.

"Administration," he said, his tone daring me to make something of it.

I took the dare. "Ah," I said. "The fast track to promotion, eh?"

My banter found no echo. "What do you want from me, Enoch?"

"I'm investigating a murder," I explained, "and I have reason to believe that one of the people involved might be known to you." I was guessing, more or less, but I wasn't going to say so to Sergeant Lake.

"Known to me? In administration?"

"Known to you," I said, "previously."

149

I gave him a name, and George smiled for the first time. Smiled the way a wolf might smile, to greet the scent of injured prey. "You want to watch it, Enoch. Take care. It's not friends in high places who count in the long run, you know – it's *enemies* in high places."

He told me what I needed to know, however.

The road from Gloucester city to Randolph Scott's stately pile passes through several small villages and hamlets known to me from my youth. They haven't changed much in three decades. Few of their inhabitants enjoy the benefits of mains electricity, gas, or even water. When they fall ill, they are more likely to see a priest than a doctor, since the clergy charge less. The success or failure of what New Labour calls 'this great project' will be judged by many of us according to how much transformation we see in places like this, amongst people like these.

"I need to speak to your son, Sir Randolph. Your *other* son." I was aware of how absurd that clarification sounded, but also aware that many of the rich were quite obsessed with spiritualism, and this was no time for misunderstandings.

"My – my other son?" Scott didn't sit, though his legs begged him to. "I have no other son."

"And yet you *had* another son, Sir Randolph. Didn't you? Harold. He'd be a few years older than Ernest. I remember his name appeared frequently in the local paper at one time – giving out Sunday school prizes, and so on. Don't hear much about him now, though. Why is that?"

"I tell you again," said Scott, rousing his blood for one last burst of *ancien regime* defiance, "I have no sons, sir! One is dead, and the other ought to be."

"Nevertheless, Sir Randolph. If you would be kind enough to fetch Harold – unless you'd rather I did?" I really didn't know whether or not the boy was at home, but hoped that my threat of tramping my working class boots around the House of Scott would bring a truthful reply, either way.

In the event it did better than that. Just as Randolph started to say, "Harold is in Europe," another voice joined us.

"If you truly wish me dead, Father," said Harold, stepping elegantly though one of the several doorways which led off from the Scott's front room, "then all you need do is wait, I'm sure, and let justice take its course." Tall, thin, he was a younger image of his father, as I could plainly see despite the bruises and healing scars which covered his face.

"Justice?" Randolph snarled. "They'll not hang one of their own!"

"As a matter of fact, Sir Randolph," I offered, "I have heard that the government plans to abolish capital punishment."

"Then they are fools as well as devils," he said, and turned his back on us.

I placed my hand on Harold's shoulder and said: "Harold Scott, I am arresting you in connection with the death of your brother, Ernest."

"*In connection?*" sneered Harold. "Inspector, I killed him."

One thing I'll say for the upper crust – they confess in style. "Because he saw you in the rebel crowd that stopped his bus, yes?" I'd assumed that Ernest had leapt from his driving seat to confront someone he recognised; if he'd merely wanted to remonstrate with an anonymous revolutionary, he wouldn't have needed to wade into the crowd. And when I'd asked Sergeant George Lake whether any of Ernest Scott's known associates had been suspected subversives, the name Scott itself had immediately rung a bell in George's memory.

"I wasn't happy to be spotted, I admit," said Harold. "But it needn't have been the end of the world. At least, as far as I was concerned. Sadly, Ernest never did have much of

151

a sense of proportion. When I came down here to visit dear old Pater – to tap him for some funds, if you must know – Ernest insisted we go for a walk, to talk things over. The conversation was not to his liking, I fear, for he attacked me, as you can see from my face, and in the ensuing struggle . . . well, he died, and I didn't. Self-defence, you see."

"That'll be for the court to decide," I said. There was still one thing I wished to get clear – as a trade unionist more than as a policeman. "Did the TUC know that Soviet agitators like you were—"

"Soviet?" Harold laughed, an affected, effete laugh. "My *dear* Inspector! Bolshevism is dying even as we speak, a Jew-raddled old whore. My allegiance is not to Moscow, but to Rome."

For a moment I wondered what the Catholics had to do with anything, and then I understood. "Mussolini?"

"You've heard the name, at least. Jolly well done, Inspector. And you shall hear it again. The Reds won't hold power for long – they lack the guts, you see, the guts and the breeding. While the old ruling élite is too decadent to reclaim its throne." He smiled, like a young man who knows everything and hears nothing. "Which only leaves us, d'you see? From chaos comes order. The future, Inspector, is fascist."

As I settled Harold Scott into the back of my official car, his father tapped me on the shoulder. He looked pathetic, as a man well might who has lost both sons in one moment.

"They're all Bolshevists," said Randolph Scott, "whatever they call themselves. But Ernest – Ernest was a good boy, a fine man. You'll see, Inspector, they'll build statues to that boy one day. He'll be remembered as a hero one day, you see if I'm not right."

That seemed unlikely to me, but it would have been cruel

to say so. Let the dinosaurs die in peace, I thought, as I drove my prisoner through the English countryside in spring. Let them die in peace, in a world they didn't make and cannot comprehend.

MURDER AND MIRACLES

Edward Marston

*Keith Miles has written with much success for television,
radio and the stage. His output also includes a critical
study of Guenter Grass, books about sport and children's
fiction, as well as history–mysteries which have appeared
under the name of Edward Marston. He writes two
distinct crime series, set in the eleventh and sixteenth
centuries, and over the past decade has won a legion
of fans on both sides of the Atlantic. He wrote* Murder
and Miracles *whilst coping with the many demands
upon his time as Chairman of the CWA and modestly
describes it as a 'midnight oil short story'. But the neat
plot and engaging style are characteristic of this skilled
and versatile entertainer.*

C all me Iddo. I'm a bad example of a Good Samaritan.
Indeed, there are those in Samaria who would be happy
to disown me and dispatch me into permanent exile. The
thorny problem for my detractors is that they need me. I'm
a merchant, you see. A highly successful one. I bring goods
into Samaria that nobody else could manage to buy and I

sell those that my rivals fail to unload. They are insanely jealous of me. I enjoy exciting such jealousy. It adds spice.

I own a house in Sebaste, a beautiful city built by Herod the Great of not-so-beautiful memory. My house is large and well-furnished. Its garden is the envy of my neighbours. It has everything a home should have but it also contains one glaring defect. My mother. Zilla. For a small woman, she bulks exceedingly large. In fact, there are moments when I feel that I do not so much have a house with a mother in it as a mother around whom four cowering walls have obediently arranged themselves.

Here she comes. Be warned.

"Iddo!"

"Yes, Mother?"

"When are you going to get married?"

"You ask me that every day."

"Then give me a reason not to ask it."

"I'm not ready for marriage yet."

"You've been ready for the last ten years," she says with a roll of her eyes, "but you refuse to commit yourself. Why? Samaritan girls make excellent wives. Look at me."

I stifle a waspish comment. "Yes, Mother."

"Your father snapped me up when I was fourteen. He called me the pick of the bunch. Our families agreed to the match. Your father was twenty at the time. When you came along, I was barely sixteen. A young, proud, loving, caring, Samaritan mother. Marriage is a duty and we were both dutiful, your father and I. Why must you be so different?" She pauses long enough for me to get in an apologetic shrug. "You're thirty, Iddo. Thirty! That's a lifetime for most people. Thirty years without even a betrothal to raise my hopes. I sometimes think you are doing it deliberately to vex me. Are you?"

"No, Mother."

"Then where is my daughter-in-law?"

156

"She will arrive one day."

"When?"

"In the fullness of time."

"Thirty years is full enough," she argues. "At my age, a woman is entitled to be a grandmother. To pass on her love and wisdom to a new generation. But you have no wife in sight, let alone any children. It's unnatural, Iddo. Thirty years of sleeping alone. It's indecent!" Her voice darkens. "Unless, of course, you've been sharing a bed with another kind of female."

"Mother!" I protest. I'm good at injured innocence.

"I've heard the rumours."

"Cruel lies!"

"Are they? I saw the way that prostitute looked at you in the street yesterday."

"Prostitutes look at every man in that way."

"She wouldn't have done it to your father. Or to any other respectable married man. And how did she know your name?"

"Everybody knows my name."

"Iddo the Wifeless!"

"The merchant, Mother. Iddo the Merchant."

"What kind of trade did you have with that prostitute?"

"No kind!" I say with controlled outrage. "How can you even suggest such a thing? It's humiliating. I honour my father and my mother. And you should trust your son."

My righteous indignation silences her for almost thirty seconds and gives me the opportunity to escape. Amok is waiting for me outside. Mother comes after me.

"Where are you going?" she demands.

"Galilee."

"But you've only just come back from there."

"I'm returning a barrel of fish. It was unacceptable."

Amok, my assistant and bodyguard, big, brawny, taciturn

Amok, is sitting astride his donkey. Two camels are loaded with goods and provisions. I mount my horse, Jubal. In a country where most people travel by donkey or camel, Jubal gets me noticed. He suggests wealth, distinction, individuality. I like that. More to the point, his gentle gait does not chafe my buttocks or make me queasy.

"Who sold you the fish?" asks Mother.

"Zebedee."

"Does he have any marriageable daughters?"

"What Jewish girl would look at a Samaritan?"

"She should be so lucky!" says Mother, defensively, then she taps the cargo on one of the camels. "This barrel of fish is unacceptable? Why?"

I give her a broad smile and a wave of farewell.

"It has a man's head in it!" I tell her.

The journey from Samaria to Galilee is as long and tedious as the one I have just made from Galilee to Samaria. In the interests of safety, Amok and I join a caravan as it wends its way along dusty roads in the blistering sun. Reflecting on my mother's exhortations to marry, I recall that Amok himself is recently betrothed. A phenomenal development. Not simply because he is so vast, hideous and unlovable but because such a close relationship as marriage presupposes speech.

Amok is frugal with words. I've known him go for a month without uttering one of them. Reserved with men, he is struck completely dumb by women. How, then, did this rock of silence induce an attractive young girl like Deborah to become his wife? What grotesque form did his wooing take? Did he expend a year's vocabulary on the enterprise?

As we bed down on the first night, I catch him unawares.

"When did you ask Deborah to marry you?" I probe.

The answer slips out before he can stop it.

"She asked me."

Three words from Amok are three thousand from anyone else. I will not get another syllable out of him now. She asked me. The first complete sentence I've heard from his lips in ages. The effort has exhausted him. He falls asleep.

We reach our destination by nightfall on the third day. Zebedee is still at the quayside, watching the last catch being unloaded by the light of torches. He never strays far from the Sea of Galilee. A misnomer, of course. It's not a sea at all but a deep lake with illusions of grandeur. Galilee itself is a densely-populated Jewish district, surrounded by Gentiles. Zebedee and his sons are encircled by enemies. Just like Amok and me. Two Samaritans among thousands of Jews. The Gentiles look down on the Jews and they on us. I choose to forget what Samaritans look down on.

While Amok unloads the barrel, I close in on Zebedee, a truculent old character with a white beard and a sparkling eye. A man of substance. With nine large townships around the lake itself and a further ten cities in the Decapolis, there is an immense demand for fresh fish. It's a thriving industry. Zebedee thrives as well as any. He knows how to charm the best fish out of the blue water and is proud of his skills.

"Iddo!" he says, identifying me in the gloom. "What are you doing back here so soon?"

"I have a complaint to make, Zebedee."

He bridles at once. "About my fish?"

"The fish were fine," I assure him.

"Then what is the problem?"

"He is," I say and point to the barrel.

Having prised open the lid, Amok extracts the object and holds it up by the hair. Zebedee recoils. It is a gruesome sight. When a man's head has been pickled and cured along with the fish, it loses all dignity and definition. Eyes, nose, ears, mouth and beard are all one, an amorphous mass of

159

flesh and bone. The hair is glutinous seaweed. The stink, unimaginable.

Zebedee recovers quickly. Fishermen are men of the world.

"It must be Matthias!" he says.

I'm astonished. "You *recognise* him?"

"His own mother would not recognise him, Iddo, but there is something about the hang of his lip and the droop of his nostrils. Besides, Matthias has been missing for several days. Where's the rest of him?"

"He wouldn't tell me," I joke. "He's even less of a conversationalist than Amok. But I could hazard a guess."

"What is it?"

"You won't like what you're about to hear, Zebedee."

"I'll hear it just the same."

"Brace yourself, then. I've been brooding on this for days now and I'm sure that I'm right."

"Where is Matthias's body?" he presses.

"Distributed among other barrels of fish."

"Contaminating my livelihood!" he erupts. "I'll not endure it. Why is he doing this to me? Matthias was one of my best fishermen. I paid him well. He has no cause for complaint."

"I'd say he has every cause for complaint," I argue with a gesture towards the decapitated head. "Matthias did not do this of his own volition. When a man wants to sleep with the fishes, he usually drowns. He doesn't cut himself up into pieces before jumping into a series of barrels."

"We're not certain that that's where he is."

"True, Zebedee. But my guesses are rarely wrong."

"Let's find out."

Zebedee leads me across to the warehouse where his fish are stored in barrels awaiting dispatch. He barks orders to a couple of men and they react with amazement. Open the barrels? Pour out the fish? Has their master taken leave of his senses? Zebedee repeats his command and they set to work, lifting the lid of the first barrel and sending its contents slithering across the floor.

No sign of Matthias in this or in three subsequent barrels and Zebedee grows sceptical. I urge him to try one more and my theory is proved correct. As another consignment cascades onto the floor, a human hand appears like a phantom starfish. It is enough to convince Zebedee, who is so enraged that he joins his men in the task of opening up the rest of the barrels.

Matthias is ubiquitous. Parts of him are scattered in a dozen different barrels, an arm here, a leg there, a foot, a toe, a kneecap, elsewhere. The torso itself is never found but all but a few of the appendages are soon laid out on the warehouse floor. The men goggle in horror. I preen myself. Zebedee is close to hysteria.

"Who has done this to me?" he wails.

"Matthias is the one who suffered," I point out.

"Only in order to hurt me. This is a direct attack on my business. What will happen to me if customers find human remains among their fish? My reputation will be ruined." He becomes vengeful. "I'll kill the man who did this. I'll flay him alive!" Reason takes over. "An investigation must be set in motion. I'll report this to the authorities."

"No," I say, firmly. "I have a better idea."

"This villain must be caught, Iddo."

"He will be. Trust me."

Our whole commercial relationship is based on trust and Zebedee has not found me wanting in the past. He agrees to hear me out. Having sworn his men to secrecy, we send them away so that we can talk in privacy. Only poor Matthias – whose pendulous ears lie a yard apart at our feet – eavesdrops.

"Let me solve this crime," I ask. "Discreetly. Contact the authorities and the whole of Galilee will know that you sell contaminated fish. Do you want that to happen?"

"No!"

"Then leave this to me, Zebedee. One of your enemies is behind this outrage. How many of them are there?"

"Hundreds. They hate my success."

"I'll need a full list of those enemies," I tell him. "And I must speak with your sons, James and John."

"They've gone, Iddo. They left home to follow The Healer."

"The Healer?"

"A man from Nazareth who performs miracles."

"What sort of miracles?"

"He makes the dumb speak, he feeds five thousand with a few loaves and fishes, and he raises men from the dead."

"Could he do anything for Matthias?" I wonder.

"Forget the Healer," he says. "Think of my fish. Some of these barrels were due to be sent off to the High Priest's Palace in Jerusalem tomorrow. My produce is held in high regard there. How long would that regard last if someone was served Matthias's Adam's apple at the next banquet?" He embraced me warmly. "Thanks to you, that danger has been averted. You stopped that shipment in time. If you can solve this crime, Iddo, I'll not only replace the barrel you returned to me. I'll give you thirty others as well."

That kind of deal is music to a merchant's ears.

"Done!" I confirm.

Then I realise that *I* must now perform miracles.

Amok and I begin our investigations at first light. Boats are already out on the water. The best fishing-grounds are near the mouth of the River Jordan at the north-east end of the lake. Fed by the melting snows of Mount Hermon, the river comes hurtling down into the lake with a mass of silt in its wake. The silt contains rich food for fish and shoals converge on it. Fishermen converge on shoals. Zebedee and his sons are among them, often working in partnership with Andrew and Peter, the brothers from Bethsaida. A strange coincidence. Andrew and Peter have also gone off to follow The Healer. This man from Nazareth must be something of a fisherman himself to land such an impressive catch.

By hanging around the wharves in Capernaum, I pick up every scrap of information I can about Matthias and his dispersed remains slowly merge into a whole man. He was an unappealing fellow, grumpy, outspoken and disliked by all for his grinding pessimism, which is why his disappearance has been noted with relief rather than alarm. Yet he was an able and conscientious fisherman whose job was to catch and land fish then load the very barrels in which he himself took up residence.

Did a discontented colleague hear one complaint too many from Matthias's whinging lips? Or was his death the result of a violent argument? Neither possibility seems likely. When a man takes up simultaneous lodgings in a dozen barrels of fish, calculation is patently at work. His accommodation has been carefully planned in advance so that horror can be scattered far and wide.

Galilee is a meeting-place of nations with trade routes crossing in all directions, from the Levant to Damascus, from Jerusalem to Antioch, from the Nile to the Euphrates. Zebedee exports to all these regions. Matthias would have provoked chaos across the whole of the known world. As barrels were unpacked, unkind remarks would have been made about Jews.

Am I searching for an anti-Semite?

I start with the men who gut and pickle the fish before leaving them to cure. It is a smelly occupation and the sheds in which they work make my stomach heave. But hours of patient watching eventually pay off. His name is Alphaeus. Alone of the men in the sheds, he has a real zest for his work, using his knife with the practised ease of an assassin and grinning vacantly as he grabs each new victim from a wooden box. Slit, gouge, slice. He is an expert.

Alphaeus is tall, thin and sinewy. There is brute strength in those long arms. Instinct is a vital part of my trade and my instinct tells me that this man makes a hobby of bearing grudges. The face has a deathly whiteness but there is deep darkness in the soul of Alphaeus.

When I finally catch him alone, he is not welcoming.

"Piss off, you Samaritan turd!" he hisses.

"I want to talk to you," I say.

"Come near me and I'll cut your tongue out," he warns, brandishing his knife. "Go back to Samaria while you can!"

"Did you know a man called Matthias?"

"No!"

"Everybody else did."

"Then sod off and talk to them."

"We need your help, Alphaeus."

"I don't help Samaritans."

"That will disappoint him."

"Him?"

"Amok," I say. "He's standing behind you."

Alphaeus swings around with his weapon at the ready but he has met his match in Amok. My bodyguard comes into his own on occasions like this. He stuns Alphaeus with a blow between the eyes, seizes the knife from his grasp then lifts him a foot from the floor. Alphaeus squirms impotently like a giant eel.

"Now will you talk to me?" I invite.

"No!" splutters the eel.

A nod is all that Amok requires. He has ways of making even the most reticent men speak. Alphaeus is tough but his resolve soon weakens when he has been held headfirst in a barrel of fish for two minutes. When Amok hauls him out again, he is gasping for air and begging for mercy.

"Now you know how Matthias felt," I suggest. "Tell me about him. While you still can."

"I've no idea where he is," he lies.

"Then go and search for him."

Amok plunges him deeper into the fish this time and all resistance vanishes. When Alphaeus is finally released, he looks as if he has been to hell and back in a basket. Amok holds him while I begin my interrogation.

"Why did you kill Matthias?"

"I didn't kill him," protests Alphaeus.

"You were involved somehow."

"Only afterwards," he bleats. "My job was to cut him into portions and share them out among the barrels. I never liked Matthias. It was a pleasure to slice him up. And I needed the money. Zebedee doesn't pay me enough."

"Did you want to ruin his business?"

"Yes, I did."

"Why?"

"Zebedee always criticises me."

"He'll have good reason when he hears about this."

"I didn't murder Matthias," insists the prisoner. "I did what I was paid to do and nothing more."

"And who paid you?"

"I don't know."

"Forgotten his name already?" I ask, jocularly. "Put him back in the barrel, Amok. It will jog his memory."

"No, no!" he implores. "Anything but that!"

"Who paid you?"

"I really don't know," he repeats in desperation. "We met

in an inn and he was in disguise. A big man, that is all I can tell you. And rich. He paid me extremely well."

"Did he bring the body himself?"

"Yes. One night. Matthias had been strangled to death. The man was so pleased with himself. He was giggling. Giggling with excitement at the way he'd killed his victim. He couldn't stop telling me how easy it'd been. Matthias was strapped to the back of a donkey."

"One donkey brought him to another," I muse.

"Eh?"

"Samaritan wit. Too subtle for you."

"Spare me!" he begs. "Spare me and I'll give you all the money I have." He grins hopefully. "What do you say?"

Amok answers for both of us. A mighty punch fells the wretch. Taking a leg apiece, we drag him off to Zebedee and hand him over. I have to move on to the next stage of the investigation on my own. Amok would never approve. Beneath that bear-like exterior, he has too many moral imperatives floating around.

They'd be a severe handicap in the house I'm visiting.

Naomi is unique. Tall, slim and sensuous, she moves with the grace of a dancer and the dignity of a queen. Naomi has fathomless beauty but she also has a dimension beyond the merely physical and emotional. Locked in her wondrous embrace, I attain true ecstasy. I actually forget my mother.

"It is wonderful to see you again so soon," she purrs.

"Have you missed me?"

"Painfully."

"That is what I like to hear."

"Are you happy in my arms, Iddo?"

"Blissfully."

"Do you like this?"

I moan in sheer delight.

Her fingers are magical. A saint would capitulate under her
delicate touch. Except that a saint could not afford to call on
Naomi. She is highly selective. Her clients are few in number
and chosen for their wealth or their personality. I prefer to
believe that it is the latter criterion which was applied to me.
My personality blossoms in Naomi's mansion.

I force myself to concentrate on the murderer.

"I need your help, Naomi."

"That's what I'm giving you."

"Information," I explain, trying to ignore the thrills of
delight shooting up through me from her tantalising digits.
"You consort with the great and the good in this city. You
know what goes on in Capernaum."

"Stop flattering me."

"I want the name of a murderer from you."

"No murderer is allowed in here," she protests, angrily.
"Is this some silly game of yours, Iddo? I thought you came
to me for pleasure."

"I did, my dove. And I received it."

"No more talk of murderers, then."

"But this is important," I say, softly.

And I slip some more coins into her hand. It buys me
five minutes to tell my tale. Naomi is inscrutable. A body
which can speak fluently in a hundred different languages
now lies stiff and unresponsive in my arms. She is deeply
upset. I suspect that I know why.

"Did he come to you that night, Naomi?"

"I never discuss one client with another."

"Then he was here?"

"I am saying nothing."

"He was a big man," I remind her. "Rich enough to afford
you and excited enough to need you. What better way to
celebrate his villainy than with the pride of Capernaum? He
could not stop boasting about it, Alphaeus said. I warrant

167

that you heard the whole story from him. You know him, don't you?"

"Close the door behind you, Iddo."

"You remember him. From that giggle of his."

"We will not be doing business again."

"Would you turn me away and harbour a killer?"

"I harbour nobody."

"Then give me his name."

"I have no notion what you are talking about."

"How much money would it take to give you a notion?"

"Far more than you have at your disposal."

"Do not underestimate my wealth."

"Do not overestimate my affection for you."

"How much?"

"I know nothing, I tell you."

"How much, Naomi?"

"Goodbye."

"I'll pay *any* price," I affirm.

Naomi gives me a curious look. Her body relaxes and she fondles me absentmindedly. Her expression is inscrutable but her mind is racing. She heaves a deep sigh.

"This is no life for me," she confesses. "Waiting on the whims of men. Pampering their passions. I deserve better. I was born for a life of leisured respectability."

"I could not agree more."

"You will pay *any* price, Iddo?"

"I give you my word."

"Then this is what it will cost."

She whispers in my ear and I give a slight shudder. Naomi drives a hard bargain. As merchants, we are well-matched.

When I collect Amok and go back to the wharf, chance contrives better than I could myself. The very man I am seeking is talking with Zebedee. I recognise him at once from Naomi's description. Big, dark, handsome and vain, with a beard that curls at the edges. He strokes his beard as I approach. A telltale giggle escapes him. I plunge straight in.

"Caleb the Fisherman?" I say, accosting him.

He frowns. "Who are you?" he snarls.

"My name is Iddo. I'm a friend of Zebedee."

"And a Samaritan!" The familiar note of contempt.

"That is immaterial. We must talk."

"I have nothing to say to you."

"Then say it to Zebedee instead," I encourage. "Tell him why you killed one of his men and had him carved up by that ghoul, Alphaeus. Why did you do it, Caleb?"

"Do what?" His coolness is breathtaking. "I have never heard of this – what did you call him – Alphaeus?"

"You paid him to do your grisly work for you."

"Is that what the fellow says?"

"Not exactly."

"Does he identify me by name?"

"No," I admit.

"Has he pointed the finger of blame at me?"

"Only indirectly."

"Then you are very bold," he says, black eyes ablaze. "Very bold and very stupid. I am wrongfully accused here and will call Zebedee as my witness. This is the grossest slander. You will answer for this, Iddo the Samaritan. I'm a keen rival of Zebedee, it's true, but that rivalry has always been friendly. Why on earth should I wish to kill one of his men?"

"To strike at the very heart of his reputation."

Zebedee intervenes. "But Caleb and I have known each other for years," he argues. "He would never do such a thing."

"Wouldn't he?" I challenge.

"No!" attests Caleb, stroking his beard.

"Not in a hundred years," adds Zebedee.

"So where is your proof, Iddo?"

Thinking he's safe, Caleb giggles with excitement.

"The lady took confession from you," I remind him and his giggle becomes a spluttering rage. "Murder aroused you, Caleb. You went to her in the exhilaration of your villainy and you could not resist bragging about your triumph. Naomi is my proof. I call upon her to unmask you."

"Who will listen to the word of a slut?" he sneers.

"Naomi is no slut," I retort with composure. "You speak of the lady who is about to become my wife."

Caleb is cornered. Even Zebedee is coming to see him in his true light now. Stout denial is no longer enough for the killer. We have him over a barrel of fish.

He is a powerful man. His fist catches me a glancing blow on the jaw and sends me reeling. It has the most remarkable effect on Amok. Springing into life, he not only pounds Caleb unmercifully until the fisherman crumples to the ground, he actually accompanies the beating with a stream of coherent, not to say, impassioned words.

"You attacked my master," he says with a reverence for me that I never expected to hear. "You hurt him. You'll have to account to me for that. If you murdered Matthias, you will pay at a latter date but I'll exact full payment right now for what you did to my master. Nobody touches him with impunity. You'll apologise to him, do you hear? On your knees, you'll grovel and apologise to Iddo the Merchant."

And Caleb does. Without even a trace of a giggle.

Three dusty days in the saddle take us home to Sebaste. A long train of camels is towed in our wake. Mother comes out of the house to welcome us. We dismount with relief.

"Where have you been?" she asks.

"In Capernaum, Mother."

"What were you doing there?"

"Competing with The Healer."

"Who?"

"The Healer," I explain. "Some clever Nazarene who does conjuring tricks to amuse the crowd."

"Conjuring tricks?"

"Yes, Mother. He makes the dumb speak. He feeds five thousand with a few loaves and fishes, and he raises men from the dead."

"These are not tricks, Iddo. They are miracles."

"I matched each one of them."

"How?"

"I, too, made the dumb speak," I announce, proudly. "At my prompting, Amok turned into a monster of garrulity. As for feeding the five thousand, look at these barrels of fish." I indicate the cargo on the camels. "I took one to Galilee and turned it into thirty at no extra cost. Nor was I defeated by the task of raising a man from the dead. I brought Matthias back to life again so that he could accuse his killer. Your son is a miracle-worker, Mother. Are you not impressed?"

She grimaced and gave her famous dismissive shrug.

"I'd be more impressed if you'd found yourself a wife."

"Ah, yes," I add, triumphantly, "I'd forgotten her. I'm betrothed at last, Mother. A delightful creature called Naomi. A lady in every sense of the word. I have the feeling that Naomi will be the ideal partner for me in life."

My mother fell silent for a whole day.

It was the biggest miracle of them all.

MURDER IN A TIME OF SIEGE

Marjorie Eccles

In seeking contributions for this book, I encouraged CWA members who seldom write short stories and do not set their books in the past to consider making a submission. Marjorie Eccles' books about Gil Mayo are far removed in time and place from this story about Mafeking, but I was delighted that, for the first time in her career, she decided to try her hand at a historical mystery.

They would soon be reduced to eating the horses. No one would like it, though they would do it, of course they would, if survival was in question. But it hadn't come to that, not yet.

The small township in the middle of nowhere lay sweltering on the unending, sun-scorched expanse of the African veld. A hitherto pleasant, orderly and uneventful place, now seething with fifteen hundred defending troops, surrounded by the enemy, Mafeking had suddenly found itself turned into a garrison by virtue of its strategic position on the borderland railway.

173

Three months of siege, but the morale of the Britishers stayed resolutely high. Though the bombardment had been heavy, loss of life and the numbers of wounded had been comparatively light so far, mostly confined to the military in their storming parties against the Boers. The first action of the enemy had been to cut through the telegraph wires, tear up two miles of railway and seize the waterworks outside the redoubts – though as to this last, they might have saved themselves the trouble: there remained an ample supply of water within the town from tanks, and wells drilled through the rock. After which, the Boers celebrated the first day of the new century by shelling the women's laager. This was the camp which housed the sisters of the Roman Catholic convent and the other women who had elected to stay and nurse the sick and wounded rather than seek the safety of Cape Town; later, the convent itself, now used as a convalescent home, had also been shelled, but only one of the helpers had been slightly wounded.

Relief was expected daily, but was not forthcoming. Belts were tightened further, while the overall commander, Colonel Baden-Powell, the idol and hero of the hour, continued to keep General Cronje and his Afrikaners busy, driving them back with his cavalry sorties and causing them considerable losses. His indefatigable, cheery confidence was immensely heartening to the beleagured townsfolk. Better than a pint of dry champagne, any day, good old BP!

Then, on the ninety-ninth day of the siege, Edward Carradine was arrested for murder.

'*Mafeking upon the hundredth day of siege sends loyal devotion to your Majesty, and assurances of continued resolve to maintain your Majesty's supremacy in this town.*'

Having dispatched his doughty telegram to the Queen, via a trooper valiant enough to risk breaking through the enemy lines and riding with it to Pretoria, the mayor of Mafeking, Mr Frank Whiteley, forsook his bicycle for once and made his way on foot down the main street. The town lay baking under the dry wind, red, gritty dust puffed out from under his boots at every step. An upright man with a clear and steady gaze, Whiteley was deeply tanned by his many years under the suns of Africa, thinner than he had been by reason of the privations to which they had all been subjected in recent months, here in Mafeking. He had followed the business of an interior trader and hunter, in partnership with a brother-in-law in Bulawayo, since he was seventeen, and no one was better acquainted with the territories and people of Bechuanaland and the country north of the Limpopo than he. He loved and understood Africa and the African people almost as much as he honoured England and the English. His hard years in this land had made him a man of foresight and courage. But at the moment, he was also a man beset by worries: the great loss to him of his company stores, recently reduced to rubble by heavy shelling, the longing for his absent wife and children, the continuing war, the continuing need to eke out food supplies. The responsibility – entirely his – of looking after the five hundred women and children in the women's laager. And not least, the troubling business of Edward Carradine, an all-consuming anxiety which almost eclipsed all the rest.

Carradine! That unfortunate young man who had arrived in Mafeking with such high hopes and was even now languishing in a makeshift gaol until he could be moved to prison in Pretoria.

Although he was of a good family, his people English immigrants who had interests in the diamond industry in Kimberley, and it was understood that he would, in time, come into a not inconsiderable inheritance, Edward Carradine was of that new breed which needed to prove that they could make their own way in the world, a young man of independence

175

who had chosen railway engineering as his special field. Due to this, he had been called to Mafeking to work on the Bechuanaland Railway. On the outbreak of hostilities he had immediately leaped, with characteristic enthusiasm and impetuosity, into the foray as a volunteer fighter in the amateur army, four hundred of them native Africans, who augmented the forces drawn from the ranks of the British South Africa police and the five-hundred-strong force of Colonel Hore's irregular cavalry. Since the township was bursting at the seams with police, the mayor should have felt able to leave Edward Carradine to them, despite their somewhat backward methods of detection, but he could not. It was a damnable business, but he could not simply wash his hands of this rash young man, a friend, a fellow-Britisher, tiresome and foolhardy though he had turned out to be.

Nor could he push the problem aside in his homeward progress; at every step he was greeted by friends and acquaintances wanting to discuss Carradine and the whys and wherefores of his incarceration. And when eventually he thought he had spoken to the very last of them, coming towards him was that prince of good fellows, Baden-Powell himself, but having other things on his mind, thank God, than Carradine.

"Never fear, Frank," he greeted the mayor, "we shall win through, come what may, and no small thanks to you and your calmness in the face of adversity. We are fortunate indeed in having such a stout fellow to maintain and support us in our efforts!"

Frank was uneasy with such compliments. A man of action, he preferred deeds to words. He was a notable game-shot and had had desperate adventures, had escaped being trampled by a rogue elephant and had saved a companion from a rhinoceros by great personal daring, and still his only comment on being congratulated

176

on his bravery had been: "It was to be done, and I did it."

He waved the flies away and sought an answer now as BP clasped his shoulder and made further congratulatory remarks on his capable administration.

"I said at the beginning I would sit tight and keep my hair on, and that's all I have done," he replied at last with a smile, taking off his hat and wiping his face with a bandanna.

The mayor's noble brow, compensated for by his luxuriant, drooping moustache, attested to the fact that this was not to be taken literally, and the twinkle in BP's eye showed he appreciated the joke. He replied with similar jocularity. "That's the ticket! It'll take more than brother Boer to prevent us Britishers from holding aloft the flag, eh? *Nil desperandum*, Frank, *nil desperandum* has always been my motto!" And with the parting shot that Lord Roberts had promised relief within a few weeks and he had therefore placed the garrison on full rations again, the intrepid commander went on his way down the street, whistling and cheerful as though he had no cares in the world.

Frank accepted most of these last comments with reservations, having more knowledge of the stubbornness of the Boer character than most of the British commanders. He was not alone in having the greatest admiration for Baden-Powell's leadership qualities, but it was with growing alarm that he thought of the colonel's last rash statement, relative to his own rapidly dwindling stores of provisions, hitherto so carefully husbanded. When the events of war began moving to a crisis, he had foreseen the strong possibility that Mafeking might fall under siege, and its people be forced to capitulate, not to the Boers, but to starvation. Planning for survival was second nature to him and, prepared for the worst, he had collected enormous stores of staple foods and medical supplies. The resulting diet was monotonous, to be sure, with no fresh meat other than that obtained through forages by the soldiery into the local African villages – something which the mayor strongly deplored. But it was a diet which kept hunger at bay. It was in no small part due to his native Yorkshire prudence that the story of the resistance of the gallant little garrison, which had not been expected to last out a month, had already become the stuff of legend back home in England.

If he had been vouchsafed the knowledge that Mafeking's ordeal had but reached the half-way mark, he would have been even less sanguine.

Leaving behind the cricket ground and the racecourse, a now ruined hotel, and several private houses turned into hospitals, he approached his own residence, about a mile distant. This was a smart bungalow with a pitched gabled roof, surrounded by trees, a low wall and iron railings, with a striped awning to keep out the sun, and draped lace curtains at the windows. The most English home, the most hospitable rendezvous for British friends in Mafeking. At the corner of the garden, the flagpole defiantly flew the Union Jack. It was in this house, at one of Sarah's 'at homes', that Edward Carradine had first met Kitty Rampling.

With this sombre reminder of happier times in his mind, he entered his now cheerless house, empty of all but servants, for Sarah, his wife, and his little boy and girl, were six thousand miles away, at home in England. But safe from the perils of war and starvation, thank God.

Sarah had not wanted to return home. She had stayed with him throughout all the anxious period when peace hung in the balance, while the gathering clouds of war began to darken the sky, and many other women fled. "My place as your wife is surely here by your side!" she declared, willing to enrol herself in the band of women who had stayed to nurse the wounded, at which duties she would no doubt have excelled, as she did in most things . . . During the eight years they had been married, Sarah had proved herself to be everything a man could want in a wife, handsome, smiling and good-humoured, a woman of cultivated tastes and true Yorkshire grit. He counted himself a lucky man.

"Do you not think, my dearest," he had answered in a low voice, "that you would not be the greatest support and comfort to me, the best friend a man might have at his side at such a time? But I should be a lesser man had I so little regard for your safety – or the safety of our children."

It was only this last persuasion which had induced her to travel with the children the nine hundred miles to Cape Town, on the last train before the line was blown up, and thence to take ship for the long journey to England. Now, her piano stayed as a silent reminder of her presence, the inexorable dry dust of the plains which insinuated itself everywhere collecting upon its keys, her books gathered more dust as they stood unopened on the shelves, her sketchbook and watercolours were put away, her sewing laid aside. Only her precious garden remained as she would have wished it. Frank tended it himself and would not leave it to the boys. He missed her as a man might miss his right arm, but he had no regrets as to his decision.

How was he to answer her, when he wrote to her about Edward Carradine?

Carradine had been a favourite of Sarah's, a popular adjunct to Mafeking society, agreeable, amusing and clever, if too outspoken in his extraordinary opinions, which he was wont to state with no little vehemence and less tact, and with no expectation in the world of being disbelieved. He had lately aired his view, for instance, after one glass of wine too many at Frank's table, that it was a barbarity to hunt the ostrich and the elephant, not pausing to reflect that this happened to be the basis of Frank's livelihood. Ostrich feathers for fans, boas, and hats, and for debutantes to wear in their hair. Elephant ivory for piano keys, billiard balls, oriental carvings and jewellery, for every decorative use that could be imagined. His was a luxury trade which had made him, if not rich, then comfortably off.

"With respect, sir," Carradine had continued heatedly, "you do not realise the significance of what you are doing! Mark my words, these magnificent animals will one day be hunted to extinction and disappear from the face of the earth! You hunters resemble the ostrich you hunt – you run away and hide your heads in the sand!"

Frank had managed to conceal his anger and lighten the embarrassment at this rash and ill-considered statement – for Africa was vast, the bounty of her wildlife inexhaustible, was it not? Culling was necessary to keep the elephant population down, to preserve the trees and vegetation they destroyed. He made some humorous remark about the ugly, bald and manifestly un-magnificent ostrich which occasioned smiles and passed the moment off. He would not take issue with one who was a guest in his house, and moreover, despite his brashness was, for the most part, a very likeable fellow. His greatest fault lay in his youth, which time would overcome. His heart was in the right place. And to do him justice, Carradine had later apologised.

It was Sarah who had warned Frank of what was happening between Carradine and Mrs Rampling, and the gossip it was causing. A certain coolness was always evinced by the female section of the community towards this lady, if not by their husbands, but it was impossible for someone of Sarah's warm-hearted and generous nature to follow suit, and she had been at special pains to be agreeable to her.

Kitty Rampling was pretty, lively, engaging and thirty-five

if she was a day. She had made an unfortunate and apparently disappointing marriage. Her husband, George, was considerably older than she was, a brute of a man, a sullen individual with a great propensity for quarrelling, one with whom Carradine, for one, had recently had a violent argument. He was said to owe money all around the town – as he certainly did to the mayor. Too busy, it was rumoured in the racecourse bar, drinking and losing on the horses what money remained to him to be any more suspicious of her affair with the handsome railway engineer than he had been of countless others. His wife held him in the hollow of her cool little hand – or under her thumb, depending on which way you regarded Kitty Rampling. She was small and feminine, wore pretty frocks rather than the fashionable, mannish coats and skirts, the shirtwaists and the ties which the other ladies favoured at the moment, and had huge, innocent brown eyes.

Foolish and infatuated as Edward Carradine might be, however, Frank could not believe that he was the sort of man to shoot another, and in the back, too.

There was no getting away from the circumstances, unfortunately. He had been discovered one evening outside the Rampling bungalow, kneeling over Rampling's body, blood on his hands. It was popularly supposed that Rampling had come home unexpectedly and discovered Carradine and his wife *in flagrante delicto*, and a furtherance of their quarrel had ensued, though why the shooting had occurred in the street remained a mystery. Nor had the gun ever been found.

Carradine denied he had been with Mrs Rampling. His story, not necessarily believed, was that he had been walking homewards along the street when a shot had rung out and the man walking in front of him had collapsed. He had run forward, discovered the injured man to be Rampling and supported him in his arms, only to find him already dead.

181

It was thus that the next man on the scene, the mayor, who had been working late and was bumping homewards on his bicycle, awkwardly carrying a Gladstone bag full of papers, came round the corner and found him.

His arrival was followed in but a few moments by others, including the ever-present police. Everyone was shocked, but no one had liked Rampling and no one wanted to believe in young Carradine's guilt, and it was at once suggested that Rampling had been killed by some sniper's bullet, regardless of the fact that the scene of the shooting was almost in the centre of the town. Other equally baseless suggestions followed – that one of Rampling's creditors had come after him, or, with more support, that due to the inadvisability of arming the natives, one of them had run amok. Or maybe drunken soldiers had been involved: the troops were not all disciplined regulars, and unruly incidents were not uncommon. However, Carradine's presence outside the Rampling bungalow and the gossip about his association with Kitty Rampling, together with that recent angry clash in the racecourse bar between himself and her husband, witnessed by many, made him a prime suspect.

The mayor, sitting in his empty house, could find no answer to his own pressing problem of what was to be done about the matter.

The siege continued, Mafeking still miraculously holding out after more than six months. But the fortified trenches encircling the town were not proof against Cronje's onslaughts, and casualties grew, despite the warning horn blown from the lookout whenever the Boer's twelve-pounders were being loaded. Small acts of heroism and courage were reported daily from the loyalist civilians, the women and children, the native servants. The townspeople buried their dead and began to eat the horses.

However, with the letters and despatches which still got through came news to stiffen the sinews: Ladysmith, another beleaguered town, an important railway junction in Natal, had been relieved after a hundred and twenty days. It was reported that the Boers were losing heart. It was also reported, once again, that relief troops were within five miles of Mafeking and BP promptly earmarked several more horses for a celebration dinner for the whole town, cheerfully urging everyone to bolster their courage, reminding them that their sacrifices for Queen and Country would not be in vain. The relief forces, unfortunately, were driven back with heavy losses.

Mrs Rampling, recovered from her prostration at the death of her husband, had refused to move out of her house into the women's laager and stayed where she was, retrimming her pretty hats and entertaining off-duty officers at afternoon soirées. She had grown noticeably thinner, her skin was transparent, but it only enhanced her looks and increased the lustre of her big brown eyes.

Carradine was still imprisoned, half-forgotten in the troubles of the moment, and allowed no visitors, and the mayor was looking, and feeling, ever more anxious. Problems, other than the exigencies of the moment, weighed heavily on his mind. Carradine had once accused him of burying his head in the sand, but he knew he could not do so for ever.

He thought of his last letter from Sarah, and felt worse. "If Colonel Baden-Powell is the most popular man in England – as there is no doubt he is," she had written, "then the most popular man here in all Yorkshire is the Mayor of Mafeking. News of his courage and the tireless work he is doing there has travelled across the continents and has made his wife and children very proud."

What would she think of him now, if she knew?

The Bechuanaland dusks were short, the nights cold and,

183

after cycling briskly home one evening the mayor, shaken by what he had heard that morning, was promising himself a tot of carefully-hoarded brandy before the scanty meal – dried biltong again, no doubt – which was all his servant would be able to provide, as he walked into his sitting room.

There he found Edward Carradine, sitting in his own favourite chair in an attitude of great melancholy, twisting round and round in his hands an object which had previously been standing on one of the small tables in the room – an ostrich egg, mounted upon ebony, and painted with a charming, delicate depiction of flowers of the veld. He was regarding it intently. Perhaps his time in prison had taught him to abandon his scruples.

Frank's greeting could not have been more heartfelt. "Carradine, how extremely glad I am to see you!"

Carradine was very pale from his incarceration, his ruddy good looks diminished, with lines drawn about his mouth. Frank looked at him with pity and saw that he had lost his youth.

"They have let me go, Frank," he said. "I had become nothing more than an embarrassment to them, they had to release me."

"I have never doubted they would do so, my dear fellow – in fact, I have expected it, daily! I have spared nothing in arguing with the officer in charge for your release, given him every assurance that a man of your character could have done no such thing!"

Carradine maintained silence at this until finally he said, "There is still no trace of the weapon, and they inform me they have better things to do at the moment than search for it. So there is nothing to prove my guilt, and she – Mrs Rampling – supports my story that I was not with her that night." An inscrutable expression crossed his face. "She even submitted to her house being searched, but of course no gun was found there. No doubt some unknown native with a grudge against Rampling will be the convenient scapegoat," he finished bitterly.

"The scapegoat?"

Carradine did not answer the question, looking down at the ostrich egg once more. "*She* painted this, did she not?" he remarked at last.

Frank regarded him gravely. "Mrs Rampling did indeed, and gave it to my wife on the occasion of her birthday. She is not untalented in that direction."

"In other directions, too."

The pretty trifle in Carradine's hands trembled. Frank reached out and removed it from him.

Suddenly, the young man sprang up, almost knocking over the lamp on the table beside him. "We must talk – but outside! I have for some reason developed a strange aversion to being inside four walls!" He laughed harshly and strode to the door.

Frank followed him into the cold dusk. The light was fading fast and the sky was the colour of the brandy Frank had been denied, shot with rose and gold, the garden smelling of the jasmine Sarah had planted around the door. He sank on to a seat, still warm from the heat of the day, under the jacaranda tree, while Carradine paced about. Suddenly, he turned and faced the mayor.

"I did not fire that shot, Frank."

Frank moved the toe of his boot about in the red earth, deflecting a column of ants. He moved his toe away and the ants regrouped themselves and went on. He busied himself with his pipe. In the light of the match, a column of fireflies whirled. The rich aroma of tobacco overpowered the scent of the jasmine.

"I know that for an indisputable fact."

Carradine stood very still and upright, his hands clasped

behind his back, looking down at the mayor. "Do you, Frank?" he said at last. "Do you, indeed?"

Frank saw the young man struggling to come to terms with something which he now recognised, and perhaps had subconsciously known all along. "It was not I who shot him either, my young friend."

"Then who?"

The sound of the look-out horn suddenly rang out from the redoubts, echoing throughout the town, signalling that the Boers were mustering for another bombardment, a warning to take cover while there was still time. A distant noise and confusion broke out as the townspeople ran for shelter. Civilians were ordered to stay indoors as far as possible during an attack so as not to hamper the trained volunteers, competent to deal with such a situation. Hooves clattered down the street, wagon wheels rumbled, a few shouts were heard, but presently the ominous waiting silence they had all become accustomed to fell, the lull before the shelling, and retaliatory mortar fire, began. The interruption might have been a mere rumble of thunder for all the attention the two men paid to it.

"If I did not shoot him, and you did not, then who did?" Carradine repeated tensely. "If—" He could not go on.

Frank decided to help him. "It was the blue diamond that started it, was it not?"

Carradine started. "How in the world do you know of the blue diamond?"

"My wife had the story of it from Mrs Rampling herself. I fear," he said carefully, looking directly at the young man, "that the lady is one of some – acquisitiveness. Sarah told me how you had procured the diamond for her—"

"How I did so in the hopes that it would buy her love, though I knew I could never marry her?" Carradine was suddenly in a passion. "How I beggared myself to procure

186

it? No, I wager she would not have told Mrs Whiteley that! I was – infatuated, there is no other word for it, I have had time to come to my senses and see that, at least. Infatuation that I thought was love. Through my brother's good offices, I was able to obtain the diamond at a fair price, though its value was staggering and it cost me all I possessed in the world, and though my expectations for the future are not nearly as high as many suppose." Carradine came to a wretched halt, and then said, "I see I must tell you everything . . . Between us, we may arrive at the truth."

Frank, who already knew the truth, said nothing, looking at the brilliant stars pricking the darkening sky. Every sound was exaggerated in the expectant stillness, the shrill of the cicadas, the *croo-crooing* of sleepy doves, a shouted command from the defences.

Carradine sank on to the seat beside Frank. "She knew I had bought the diamond. I had had it set into a ring for her, but it took me some months to pluck up enough courage to put it on her finger, with all that such an extravagant gesture implied. Though there could have been no marriage between us, our friendship had not yet reached . . ." He faltered, a deep and painful flush mantling his pale cheek. "However, she had given me to understand that, on that very evening, she would accept the ring from me, and thereafter our relations would be somewhat different. She allowed me to put it on her finger before we dined. Rampling came home unexpectedly, just as we had finished our meal. He was drunk, but not so drunk that he did not immediately see how it was between us. He burst into a vile stream of abuse and Kitty became very – excited, I think, is the only word which serves." Carradine passed a hand across his brow. "How can I explain this? Her husband's abuse did not appear to distress her – indeed, those big eyes of hers softened and sparkled, colour came to her cheeks when he actually raised his hand to her – it was almost as though – as though she was *enjoying* it! As if there was some strange complicity between them . . . Maybe, even, a kind of love. I think I began to see my folly, how I had been deceived, even then."

The desperate young man buried his face in his hands. When he raised his head, his face was wet with tears. "Nevertheless, I squared up to Rampling. I could scarcely tell him to get out of his own house, but I warned him that he must not lay a finger on his wife. Whereupon he laughed insolently and swaggered outside. 'Are you going to leave it at that, Edward?' she asked. 'No, by God, I am not,' said I, and rushed out after him, intending to knock the fellow down. But I had not reached him before . . . before the shot rang out and he fell down dead. And that, I swear, is the truth of what happened."

Into the silence erupted the loud *crump* of the first mortar shell, followed by another. A horse whickered in fright, and the night became hideous with noise and flames. Within the little garden, Edward Carradine sat as though turned to stone.

"How could I have been such a fool? Seen with hindsight, it is so obvious – Rampling coming home, apparently unexpectedly, finding me in intimate circumstances with his wife, strutting out like that . . . Either she had arranged matters so, or she seized her chance. In any case, she had estimated my nature well. She knew I would go after him, prompted by her." He said, his voice hard and dry as pebbles, "She would have shot me, like a dog—"

"Had you not stumbled. By the merest chance, or Divine intervention, just as the fatal shot was being fired. So that the wrong man received the bullet."

"She would have shot me," Carradine repeated bleakly. "But why? In God's name, why?"

"For love of money, Edward, for this." From his pocket, Frank pulled forth a small soft leather pouch and from that withdrew the costly blue diamond ring, its radiance undimmed in the starlit darkness. "For greed, the life of one young man less important than the glitter of a diamond she could not resist . . ." Having obtained the diamond, she had had no more use for him. "An ugly thought, is it not?"

"Supposing I had indeed been the victim? Rampling would have been the first to be suspected. Did she think of that? And what of the revolver – what did she do with it?"

"There is a well, not six yards away."

"But beyond where Rampling fell. She did not pass me, Frank."

Frank saw again the moonlit street as he had come upon it – Carradine kneeling over the dead man, the revolver lying between him and the Ramplings' door, heard again the running feet which heralded the arrival of others on the scene in moments. What else could he have done, but conceal the weapon in his Gladstone bag? A pity he could not have swallowed it, he had thought afterwards, as the ostrich swallows large stones, bricks or even chunks of metal to aid the process of digestion in its gizzard. It had lain on his conscience just as heavily ever since.

"She threw the gun towards me, purposely to incriminate me. And you picked it up, did you not? Frank, I owe you my life."

Frank did not say that it was Sarah to whom Carradine owed his life, prompting him as if she had been beside him, telling him that this man could not be capable of murder. "I could not let an innocent man hang," he said, and added words he had used once before, "It was to be done, and I did it."

Yet he had paid for his action with the sleepless nights which had followed. For the first time in his life, he had trifled with the law, and the burden of it had been heavy.

Until he had remembered the diamond.

189

He held the sparkling jewel out once more to Carradine, but Carradine shrank from it as though it had been a snake. "She may keep it, for all I care!"

"Don't be a fool, Edward. It is yours by right."

"How did you come by it?"

"She asked me to return it to you."

Carradine laughed bitterly. "Once I might have believed that!"

"It is true. When I saw that gun lying there on the ground, I picked it up with scarcely a thought, but when I took it out of the bag, at home, I recognised it as one I myself had sold to Rampling twelve months ago. It was one of several I wished to dispose of, and he insisted on taking it on trial. If he was satisfied with its performance, he would pay me – which, I might add, he never did! When I recognised what was once mine, I took it to Mrs Rampling and confronted her with it. Our conversation was – interesting. She subsequently asked me to return the diamond to you."

"In exchange for your silence? Am I expected to believe that?"

Frank said gravely, "There was no need to ask for it."

"I don't understand! Why did you not take the gun to the police when you knew to whom it belonged? I would have been released immediately! Instead, a guilty woman has gone free! You call that justice?"

Justice was a slippery notion, as Frank had discovered since coming to this land, not as clear-cut and unequivocal as it seemed in Britain. Sometimes, the Africans did it better. "Free? I think not."

He had known native tribesmen who had decided to die, and did so. Through shame or dishonour, loss of face. Had the knowledge that she had accidentally shot the husband she had in some curious way loved, worked upon Kitty Rampling so that she had lost the will to live? Maybe that was too fanciful,

190

but he could not forget his meeting with her three months ago – that hectic flush on her cheekbones, the cough, the feverish brightness of her eyes. The loss of spirit, the fun of playing dangerous games at last over for her. "She was ill, very ill, Edward. She knew that she had not long to live."

"What? Kitty?" Carradine sat in stunned disbelief, his complexion becoming, if possible, even paler than before. Then he leaped up, all that he had suffered on her account instantly forgiven. "I must go to her!"

Frank placed a hand on his arm. "Too late, my friend, too late. She died this morning."

With a groan, Carradine sank back, covering his eyes with his hand.

Frank had obtained her written confession, on his promise that he would wait until after her death before handing it over. He had immediately done so that morning, after hearing the news that she had died. His action in retaining the gun had not been viewed very gravely by the Chief of Police – he had, after all, himself known and been entranced by Mrs Rampling – it had been humanely prompted, he thought, and in any case, without her admission, her guilt or otherwise would have been difficult to establish. The authorities would have been bound to release Carradine after a time, and it was his opinion that the spell in gaol cooling his heels had done the hot-headed young fellow no harm at all, rubbed a few corners off, in fact.

The shelling had, for the moment, stopped. There would be no more that night. People were emerging from shelter, and a growing noise and confusion travelled across the night, from perhaps a mile away. Carradine raised himself and the two men walked out of the garden and stood looking out across the darkness, lit by flames soaring skywards. Not a house remained standing in the street where Kitty Rampling had lived. A pall of smoke rose like a funeral pyre over the area of flattened buildings. A Red Cross ambulance could be distinguished standing by.

Mafeking's siege was nearing its end. Victory or capitulation, one of them must come soon. Its story was played out.

"Come," said Carradine, beginning to walk rapidly down the road, "let us see what we can do to help."

WHO KILLED ADONIS?

Amy Myers

Although she is best known for her historical mysteries about the master chef Auguste Didier, Amy Myers has recently tried her hand at a variety of short stories set in the past, including a Sherlock Holmes pastiche and a Shakespearian whodunit based on The Winter's Tale. *Here is something quite different, a breezy comedy set in the world of Greek mythology which gives Aphrodite the unexpected role of detective.*

"**B**y the way, Aphrodite –" My darling Adonis lounged back against the grassy knoll preening himself in the afterglow of our yearly tryst. Though he is officially dead, the Underworld grudgingly allows him to return to earth for a few measly months of summer, in accordance with the terms of the Zeus–Hades custody order "– it wasn't you who murdered me, was it?"

"*What?*" I screeched, sitting bolt upright, partly in shock, and partly because flowery bowers tend to have by-products of uncomfortable thorns and thistles. (This one is allotted for our use alone, but since Adonis is – or was – mortal, I have to put up with such inconveniences). Handsome he might be, but my darling Adonis is none too bright at times, and his memory is not what it used to be. Murdered indeed! And I, the goddess of love, the chief suspect. I was extremely annoyed, but not wishing to mar the celebration of our reunion at least twice more I spoke to him gently. "You were killed by a wild boar, darling. Everyone knows that."

Certainly I was only too well aware of the fact. On that fateful day four years earlier I had driven down from Mount Olympus for a delightful rendezvous with the handsomest man on earth only to find him full of holes and blood, and the undergrowth heavily trampled by some wild animal. In the midst of my grief, however, it had occurred to me that I, as the laughter-loving queen of delight, should consider my reputation. I had instantly summoned Iris, the gods' messenger, to get a divine order signed for any tears I shed to be turned into anemones when they hit the ground, and sweet Adonis's red blood into red roses. In a trice our bower was sprouting flowers everywhere, and all traces of nasty blood had disappeared. Only the merest speck on one wrist remained as a delicate reminder of the kiss of death. Tenderly I wiped it off as one last service to my love.

Having prettied up the scene, I had then departed back to Olympus to plead with my father, Mighty Zeus, that I needed Adonis more than King Hades of the Underworld. (I'd long suspected Proserpina, his queen, had her eye on nabbing Adonis as soon as she could.) Even Father couldn't completely sway Hades on this occasion, however, and a time-share arrangement had been worked out.

Now, enjoying its fruits on our third tryst since that terrible day, I suddenly found myself accused of murder. How could he be so horrid? He'd never mentioned murder before. How did this horrible idea come to plant itself in his head, which is adorable despite his limitations in the brain department?

Who Killed Adonis?

And why, oh why, accuse *me*? Tears filled my eyes, and the thick mass of anemones all round me prepared to squeeze up to allow a few more in. (Father, Dread Son of Cronos, had never rescinded the order for flowers.)

"No." Adonis's long curls shook vigorously. "I've travelled across the Styx and drunk from the River Lethe of Forgetfulness so many times, I've forgotten who did kill me now, but I know it wasn't a boar. The murderer set it on me to hide the traces of the poisoned arrow."

"But even if you're right, whatever gave you the idea it was me?" I wailed. "If it hadn't been for me, you wouldn't be here now. I pleaded for your life. Remember?"

He blushed. "It's just that one of our sex games is Me Little Deer, You Mighty Huntress. I thought your foreplay might have gone wrong – by accident, of course," he added hastily.

"No," I replied coldly.

"Then find who did it. Then I can sue in the Low Court of Hades."

This was most unpleasant. My reputation now was in severe danger, and so – as I looked longingly at that handsome body – was my love life. No one wants to expose their most tender organs to someone suspected of having a penchant for poisoned darts. My tears began to fall, and a fresh crop of anemones sprang up. It was time for firmness. "You have a lot of lady friends. Naturally they are jealous of me."

"Then why kill *me*?" he muttered.

"Because I'm immortal, so they couldn't murder me." I told you he was none too bright.

Adonis sulked. "King Zeus was threatening to expel you from Olympus to Hades. That would make you mortal."

"Threatened, perhaps." I was highly indignant. "But of course he never would." He'd wipe out not only his own love life, but that of all the gods and goddesses with any ichor in their veins on Olympus. Try telling them their love lives were at an end because Aphrodite had been sent packing to Hades, and taken her magic girdle with her. It suddenly occurred to me to wonder *how* Adonis had discovered such Top Secret Information, for I would never confide in a mere mortal. Department OI6, the Olympus Intelligence service, makes us all sign the Immortal Secrets Act, and as the proceedings to which Adonis referred were held *in camera* it had to be someone present at my so-called 'trial'.

Unwillingly I was forced to think back to the terrible day of Adonis's death. Only the day before it took place I had been in a very good mood indeed. That charming young man Paris, prince of Troy, during his apprenticeship year as a shepherd on Mount Ida, had awarded me the Golden Apple for being the fairest goddess of all. I admit that considering the competition this was no great surprise: this consisted of Ox-eyed Hera, Mighty Queen of Zeus's Humping Bed, wallowing in transparent gauzes in the belief they make her look thinner, and six-foot Pallas Athene clomping along in a full suit of armour. How could they compare with *me*, clad with the help of the Three Graces in a blue silk *chiton* girdled with my magic *cestus*, and a cunning little arrangement of blue forget-me-nots and love-in-a-mist in my hair?

When Paris naughtily suggested we all strip off so that he could judge us better, I knew he had already made his decision. Hera, built like an ox, couldn't wait to get her clothes off, and six-foot Athene blushed virginally as she struggled to whip off breastplates and helmet provocatively. She couldn't provoke a Centaur who'd been deprived of nymphs for a year. (She'd tried hard not to remove a single item, on the grounds that Paris had used the words 'strip to your birthday suits', and armour *was* her birthday suit. She had sprung fully armed from Father's head instead of taking the more usual roundabout route via a mother.)

Who Killed Adonis?

Paris made a thorough job of looking us up and down, but just to be on the safe side I took the precaution of whispering in his ear: "Choose me and you shall have the fairest woman on earth for your own."

"Oh."

He had been momentarily distracted from eyeing parts of goddesses rarely seen by mortal men, and pressed the Golden Apple warmly into my hand. (On the way back to Olympus, I decided I'd give him Helen of Greece. Unfortunately I didn't realise this would begin the ten-year Trojan War when Paris changed her surname to 'of Troy' but omitted to inform her husband first. It's Father Zeus's fault; he's supposed to be the all-knowing one with the direct line to Destiny.)

My two mountainous naked rivals have sharp ears and had overheard my private remark to Paris. When they saw the Apple in my hand, all Hades was let loose.

"You've cheated," Hera roared.

"You're perfectly horrid." Athene burst into tears. So much for the goddess of wisdom and mighty warriors. "I'll tell Father of you."

She did too. The very next day just as I was stepping out of my shell-bath in pleasant anticipation of the afternoon ahead with Adonis, Hermes flew in to summon me to an extraordinary session of the Olympus Assizes. This is called whenever Father gets bored with Olympus; he orders an ambrosia picnic and takes the court down to his temple on Mount Ida on the pretext that a mortal witness has been called. Paris had been superpoenaed to give evidence and Father said he wasn't going to have any clod-hopping shepherds trampling sheep's muck over the Hall of the Golden Floor, and expecting to stay on for a nectar lunch.

So poor Paris (*almost* as good-looking as Adonis), peacefully snoozing on Ida while his dog did all the work, had woken up to find himself surrounded by all the senior gods of Olympus, perching on rocks to avoid all the animal dung. Ox-eyed Hera had landed on a sheep just as she was materialising and Aesculapius, the gods' doctor, had to do some hasty work to prevent its being shipped down to adorn Hades' lunchtable.

"I accuse Aphrodite of cheating," shrilled darling Athene to the jury. Everyone not personally involved in the case was on the jury, but Father never listens to a word they say, on the grounds that he is All-Seeing and All-Knowing, and they aren't. You might think therefore that he would know whether I'd cheated, and incidentally who killed my poor Adonis. The trouble with Father is that he never does. He always has some excuse, usually that he was 'asleep' (in other words, either preparing for, indulging in or recovering from his multitudinous erotic entanglements). The only time he's wide awake is when he's trying to avoid his legal wife.

"She always cheats," piped up an 'impartial' juryman, my darling sister Artemis, goddess of the chase.

"That's right. She wouldn't let me catch up with Daphne," whined Apollo. Not that he'd have known what to do if he had snared her, in my opinion. To be changed into a laurel tree was a merciful release for the poor girl.

"What say you, O Queen?" enquired Zeus cautiously.

Hera's broad hips wobbled indignantly. "She *must* have cheated, O Mighty Son of Cronos. I revealed myself in all my wondrous naked beauty and Paris still chose her."

"Hum." Father studiously avoided looking at me. *Hum* meant he was trying to get out of that one. Being Father, he did.

"I call Paris," he thundered, so loudly that several desert tribes cheered up and rushed buckets to their nearest oasis. "And if he bears out this accusation, Aphrodite, you can get your fare ready for Charon. It will be Hades for you."

Paris, I decided, even as I trembled with fear, had his

198

points. At any other time I might have ... I dragged my libido away and reminded myself that I'd allotted Helen to him. Anyway, his head was getting far too big for his calf boots. He winked at me, and then humbly fell on his knees before Father – always a good ploy. Mighty Zeus swelled with power and pride.

"Did Aphrodite cheat to win this Golden Apple?"

"No, Mighty Son of Cronos. I was blinded by the beauty of all three goddesses – who would not be? I, a mere mortal, was offered Power, Wisdom or Love – and what man would not choose love?"

Quite a few in my experience, but it was prettily spoken, and Paris won a round of applause led by me. Zeus, no doubt bearing in mind he needed my magic *cestus* that afternoon, brought in a not guilty verdict. "What do you say, Aphrodite?" He beamed graciously.

Meekness was the best policy. "Thank you, Father. Love does indeed rule all. This afternoon, my beloved Adonis is restored to my arms thanks to your mighty victory over Hades, and I therefore declare in his honour that my *cestus* is available to anyone who requires it."

There was a sharp intake of breath from someone. I'd forgotten my husband (Hephaestus, god of the forge) and my lover Ares (god of war) were present, and I briefly wondered whether I had been entirely wise to mention Adonis. The very thought of him and our forthcoming reunion made my legs tremble, not to mention their effect on other parts of my body, and I forgot all about Hephaestus and Ares, as I swept out triumphantly, singing a little ditty I had just composed:

"Goddesses three to Ida went ..." For some reason this seemed to upset my two mighty rivals in the Golden Apple contest, and they snarled their resentment of me. "You wait, Aphrodite, I'll get you," Athene shouted, brandishing a mailed fist, and Hera glowered.

I had won. I dressed carefully, then danced into luncheon to build up stamina for the afternoon ahead with Adonis. The *chiton* was exceptionally pretty, Doric style with one of those fashionable new metal pins to hold it up. Not that that would be necessary for long. Adonis might be My Little Deer, but he was a Tiger when it came to ripping off silk *chitons*.

Thus it was that I had set off to our bower full of the happiest expectations, only to find not the amorous lover I had so confidently expected, but my beloved's dead and bloody body.

Now, three yearly trysts later, he was accusing me of *murdering* him. Having delivered his Parthian shot, Adonis dozed off, looking more handsome than ever. Hades had made a good job of patching up the holes, I'll say that for him. I pondered whether to wake my beloved up immediately for another round of lovemaking, but reluctantly decided it would be prudent to clear myself of suspicion and deduce who this murderer could be.

Hera and Athene had to be top of the scroll. But which? Perhaps I needed Adonis's help. I shook him rather abruptly, and with a sigh he reached out his hand.

"Not yet," I said uncharacteristically. "Do any of these names jog your memory as having murdered you? Hera, Athene."

He gaped. "No."

I produced a trump card. "Artemis." My darling sister is very jealous of me, for all she stomps around proclaiming what fun it is to be virgin.

"She'd tackle you, not me. She can wound you, even if she can't kill you." We gods can certainly be wounded and *ichor* running from your veins, believe me, is every bit as painful as blood. However, I was quite sure he was wrong.

"Artemis," I informed him, "has a record of killing young men with arrows. It makes a change from chasing animals.

She'd have shot you just for your temerity in preferring me to her."

Once such a remark would instantly have called forth tender assurances that there was indeed no comparison between us. Now, all Adonis replied was: "Who else knew you were coming to see me?"

Typical male. They always want to take the whole show over. It was I who was supposed to be asking the questions.

"Father, everyone on Olympus, Paris of Troy."

"What about him?" Adonis asked eagerly.

None too bright, as I said. "I gave Paris Helen. He's got nothing to complain about."

"Your husband?"

I gave a short laugh. "Plenty to complain about, but impotent to do so." To do anything in fact.

"Apollo?"

"Possible. He was very annoyed with me over that nymph, and he does like playing with bows and arrows."

"Ares?"

"No." You've heard of a bull in a glazed pottery emporium? That's Ares. Thunders around as if he's Father. No fiddly arrows for him.

"It has to be one of you lot, if it's not you."

You lot? Hardly respectful. Keeping company with Queen Proserpina of the Underworld was giving Adonis ideas above his station, and he still had a distinctly suspicious note in his voice. I briefly considered whether Proserpina could have emerged to kill Adonis, but dismissed the idea. A breath of fresh air and she'd faint.

Then I had a bright idea. I'd look at the Olympus Meal Register, for whoever did it must have missed lunch on that day in order to arrive at the bower before me. The Register had been one of Father's worst ideas, but suddenly I saw its advantages. Father had got it into his head we were all one big happy family, and therefore ought to eat family meals round the table, and not grab a bite on the way to our next temple, or curled up in front of Earthvision, a hole specially cut in the clouds to give us a running peepshow on to earth. (*Such* fun at times, a real situation comedy.) We have to sign out if we are going to miss a meal, and state our reason. Even Mighty Queen Flat-Feet Hera has to toe the line.

"Wait, darling," I commanded, dematerialising rapidly, and leaping into my carriage. Swans are far too slow for emergencies, I'll hire the communal horses next time I vowed as I dashed into the Hall of the Golden Floor to study the register. It was an immortal register luckily, so the records were still there. I quickly swept through the book to the fated day and saw that my four suspects, Hera, Athene, Artemis and Apollo, had all been 'out to lunch' that day. Sulking over my acquittal, I expect. The excuses made fine reading.

Hera: gone to see Mother Rhea. The oldest excuse under the sun and only she could get away with it. Her Titan mother-in-law hasn't had a visit in years. Athene: chasing a rainbow – my foot. She might have been chasing her chum Iris, goddess of the rainbow. If you could find the end of a rainbow, there'd be no crock of gold, merely Athene, flat out after her love exertions. Apollo: bringing sunshine to Norway. Funny name for a nymph! Artemis: chasing wild boar. She always comes striding back with a bloody carcase over her shoulder – so unpleasant.

My mouth fell open. People say that without meaning it, but mine really did. I must have looked momentarily quite ugly, but I didn't care. I *knew* who had murdered Adonis, and I performed a little dance of victory. Then, highly pleased with myself, I debated my next move . . .

*　　*　　*

Who Killed Adonis?

I tracked Paris down in Troy where he was in bed making love to Helen while all his brothers fought the Greeks. He didn't even notice me when I materialised, although I coughed politely.

There was a shriek from Helen, clearly thinking she was about to incur immortal wrath. "We were only playing knuckle-bones."

"Get out, Helen," I ordered, a little unfairly.

She vanished, her peerless white body swathed in a sheet, as if I cared. Even Paris temporarily lost interest.

"I'm glad you're pleased with my choice," I said to him furiously.

"Your choice?" Paris looked startled, but gathered his wits instantly. "Of course, great goddess. You promised me the fairest woman on earth."

"Yes, and you assumed, you miserable mortal, I meant myself. Naturally," I added more gently, "I didn't tell you on Mount Ida whom I would allot to you, and as I was standing on earth at the time, you had every right to think it was me. So when next morning I said I was off to see Adonis, you were jealous."

He looked down at his feet, remembered his nakedness and rather to my regret, popped on his tunic. "Yes," he admitted sulkily.

"So you *murdered* him," I shrieked. He cowered in a corner.

"For you, Great Goddess," he gabbled. "Helen is but second best."

"She's not bad-looking." I decided to be gracious. It was, after all, very flattering. I just couldn't be too cross, as I gently removed the tunic again.

Later I had to explain to Father why I had done nothing to punish naughty Paris. I could manage Adonis, but Father was more tricky. I decided to show I was his daughter in wisdom.

"I applied logic, Father, like you always do."

He looked interested.

"After your gracious order to turn Adonis's blood into red roses," I continued, "there was a single speck of blood left. As it was still there, I knew it must be the murderer's blood. Perhaps he pricked himself on a thorn when checking the pulse to see his victim was indeed dead."

"And how did you know the murderer was Paris?"

I smiled. "It was *blood*, Father, not *ichor*, and Paris was the only mortal who could have known where Adonis was."

"Very clever. But," Father wasn't letting me off lightly, "you realise what you've done by not slaying him, especially as you were so careless in letting him have Helen?"

"Please, Father, don't kill him. He's such a *handsome* young man." Paris would make a most interesting mortal lover.

He sighed. "I'll have a word with Destiny."

Father came back from the Room of the Future downcast. "I'm afraid the Trojan War is still going to have to last its full term, and Paris is doomed to die. However, for your sake, Aphrodite, I won't kill Paris till right near the end."

"Oh *good*." I was so pleased. "I can have Paris till then? It's not a lot to ask, during all those winter months when Adonis is away."

Father looked cunning. "Yes, but I want that girdle of yours. Those Greeks are fine-looking women."

It was a small favour to grant, and I did so, for I was in Seventh Olympus. I had my Troy-boy.

PLUMAGE

Alison White

Although Alison White is best known as the prolific author of short stories for women's magazines, she has also enjoyed considerable success recently in writing for radio and in the mystery genre. At present she is working on a crime novel, but she took time off to contribute this gripping and distinctive story, which is very different from any of her other work.

France, 1587

"Did she really lose her head, Papa? Was she bald and twitching on the block?"

Detail after grisly, bloody detail. The boy Louis's words carry to me, even though I left them by the fireside when they began again with stories of the death of Mary Queen of Scots. I cannot bear to hear the truth. For me, it is another dream broken.

They call her a murderess, but if so, then unlike me, she did so only for the good of her people. The plumage of royalty weighed heavy on her shoulders. The plumage of a fool weighs on mine.

Much was expected of the young Mary. A queen at six days old. Yet as a child, little was expected of me. It was even doubted that I would live.

"He is mute," they said. And for a long time I did not understand, then all at once I did, when my father tried to cure me, hoping to beat words out of me. I bled, blistered and watched my skin rise red raw in weals, but still was mute.

"Why did God take Jacques, woman, and leave us with him? Cursed boy, even the plague would spare him," Father spat in disgust and slammed out of the house, leaving my mother watching sadly after him.

We lost my brother Jacques to a fever he had lain in for three days and nights. Until then he had spoken from morn till night and worked with my father on the fields. I would be no use there, Father said, and as he hated me I did not argue, so instead of being coloured by the sun like him and Jacques, I stayed lily white.

"More like a woman every day," Father muttered, loathing me all the more. I had two sisters, but they died in infancy. He forgave me for surviving the girls, but would never forgive me for surviving Jacques.

That morning we woke and Jacques had no fever on his brow but no breath on his lips either, was the only time I had seen my father cry. Alone, as he thought, his heart gave way and I crept up beside him to offer comfort, only to receive another beating.

"By God, I'll make you speak," he said, with spittle on his lips and a look in his eye I could not fathom as he seized me by the throat and shook me.

And that was when the treatments began. The potions. Old crones in neighbouring villages would mix an evil-smelling phial of a brew that no apothecary would trust. With this

206

forced down my throat, I would be tied to my bed for its magic to work overnight. The men of the village watched over me for fear of my bursting from the bonds to murder my family in their beds. I heard the crone whisper this possibility to my mother, who crossed herself with fright and held a rosary over me before the midnight blue liquid was administered.

They spoke about me then, as they often do now, as though I cannot hear and do not understand. Yet I do.

It would not be madness, then, that caused me to commit murder, but rather the effect of the potions – giving fevers and sweats worse than even Jacques had suffered, enough to make me seek death myself as a blessed release from the agonies of the night.

But perhaps the crone had second sight and her talk of murder was prophetic. Possibly her potions even gave rise to my own gift. For it was during one such fever that I had my first vision. I saw myself flying.

Men and women watched me. Yet these were not the rough, worn and reddened faces I was familiar with, but smooth-skinned and joyous, looking up at me and laughing. The light bounced and sparkled upon the jewels of the women as though they wore pieces of the moon itself.

In the morning I woke suddenly, to see my mother leaning over me, my father beside her.

"Wake up, my son," Mother whispered, before Father roughly pushed her out of the way and me half to my feet, tearing at the bonds that still secured me.

"Speak, boy!"

But of course, I said nothing.

The blow to my head sent me spinning across the room and I crashed against the table. Mother rushed to my aid but received a blow herself, then busied herself with food while I cried silently.

207

"They say there is another woman—" she began.

"No!" With a roar, Father swept his arm across the wooden table and cleared it of its dishes and food. "Enough of hags with their magic and chants. Have you not learned that it does not work, woman?"

After that vision, though, I knew there was another destiny for me. I was to fly away, before, in his desperation to make me speak, my father wrung the very last breath from me in the hope that a word would join it. Even my death would restore his pride if I managed to speak just once. But how could I fly? And where to?

The answer came just days later, when Mother took me to a nearby village, supposedly in search of another crone and cure.

"Shoo, Henri. Play!" she chided me, turning back to her toothless and pox-marked friend. The village had until recently been damned by plague. Perhaps she hoped any lingering remnants of the disease would attack my already weakened body and kill me. Then my father could blame her for my affliction no more.

I followed the children, who were laughing and excited. And then I heard singing! Not the raucous ale-fired songs I knew, but first merry and gay, then mournful and sad.

Around the corner they came, the travelling players, in clothes of colours so vivid they almost hurt my eyes. The colours of fruits, bright and sweet about their bodies as they sang and played their music with the beat of drums and a lute. One man dressed in red and yellow, his suit in patterns that split his body in half, a cap of velvet and feathers on his head.

Acrobats tumbled and jumped along, the children of the village scattered and parted a way for them to travel through. They had two carts pulled by horses and filled with even more laughing folk. Right at the back was a boy about my own age.

Plumage

Two of the acrobats threw him from one to the other. He started as a curled up ball, then reaching his target, flailed out his arms. Flying.

And then I was flying too. Tearing off my ill fitting tunic so I was bare chested, I ran and tumbled with them. They laughed with delight, encouraging me. As we left the village, I leapt on the cart with them. I had flown my nest.

The players did not question my decision to join them. Provided I worked for my passage, they did not care whether I spoke or not. Many were escaping from something.

Arlon, the other boy, had been born into the group. His father and uncles had been throwing him through the air since babyhood and he knew much more than I.

"I will teach you," he said. And at first he did, though he grew bored with a wordless playmate who evoked much sympathy from the womenfolk. A friendship is short-lived once jealousy sets in.

"Well done," he called as I mastered a complicated tumble. "Father, come and see what the mute has learned now!" For nobody called me Henri anymore – how could they when I had no means of telling my name? I had shed it as easily as down-feathers.

But as his father came to see my new trick, Arlon spitefully moved so that I fell and twisted my foot.

"It will come, boy," said his father, ruffling my hair. But his voice was a sigh and I knew he was disappointed. Arlon's eyes were smiling.

"Tell him, mute," he whispered at me. Then laughed.

It was summer and the days were long and hot, the nights not much better. Arlon's breathing grew heavy at night, and by day he sneezed and his eyes itched. Sometimes his chest would rattle like the string on a lute worked loose.

The woman who cared for us crossed herself at night as he rattled on. "Pray 'tis not the plague."

209

The men mocked, but I could see as his night ills grew worse that they were worried. Had we not travelled through villages which once had been made barren by those poxes which swept our land? Hadn't his mother died young?

"If 'tis God's will to take a boy, then so be it," I heard one man say. "Do we not find it a struggle feeding two?" But he was hushed by the woman, who knew that although I did not speak, I always understood.

And I was scared then, seeing why she had gone without food to allow Arlon more. Feeding two growing boys cost them dearly. And while Arlon was ill the players had not attempted the more spectacular stunts, feeling that I could not perform like him. If food was scarce – I feared they might abandon me.

That night I dreamed again. Of Arlon's corpse. Then of myself, in the plumage of brightly coloured costumes and hats, flying through the air like a bird, doing all the tumbles that Arlon did. Another vision. And hadn't I found the power to make the last come true?

Arlon worsened. The woman slept a little herself that night, unable to keep to her vigil of mopping Arlon's head, so exhausted was she from little food, little sleep and his demands of the day. Her breast rose and fell as she gave a gentle snore some distance from us. Arlon's chest was rattling, but he was in a deep sleep. If he should wake as I crept by, his panic could be dismissed as a fever, I thought, but he did not. Just minutes after I had blocked his nose and mouth with my clothes, the rattle in his chest stopped.

I slept soundly after that. I woke to the sound of the woman crying. Arlon was dead. And my position with the players was secure.

I may not have been given the gift of a voice. But I had the gift of visions which showed me a way of survival. A gift I would readily accept.

Plumage

I almost forgot this skill for a while, so busy was I learning the tricks of my new trade. Though I grew taller, my agility was strong and I could flex and bend to shapes that would make those who came to see us gasp. Around the fire at night I learned the lute, plucking out a melancholy song I would never sing as the flames cracked and hissed. And I learned the art of conveying much by saying little. My face could express any emotion.

I learned not only of my trade, but also of life. For people speak to those who cannot speak back, when your face tells them what they wish and no harsh words can spoil it. And did I have a conscience? Even if I had, I could not tell.

The news that the child Queen had arrived in France was on the lips of every peasant. Much responsibility lay on her shoulders. Her husband chosen for her, she was to unite countries and how we gambolled at the thought of performing at the French Court when we were invited by the Royal Governor.

I dreamed of a laughing lion that night. At first I thought the beast was advancing to kill me, as its huge jaws opened and the slavering teeth came at me, but instead, his lips furled back and the roar was a joyous one. I awoke, remembering my previous visions, and tried to interpret this. It seemed clear. If I performed well, then the King would like me.

So I made it possible and gave the performance of a lifetime. Tumbling and playing, admiring the beauty of the King's mistress, Diane de Poitiers, and trying to catch the stars from the sky to give to her.

The King laughed just as I had seen and I was asked to stay a while.

When I first saw the young Queen I could almost sympathise with my father who had preferred my brother Jacques over me. For here was Marie, robust and healthy, with a regal dignity yet even now, she was promised to the sickly milksop Dauphin. Water and wine.

Even then, her royal responsibility allowed her to be gracious and she opened her heart to the weakling like no other would. I felt humbled by her dignity and acceptance of her fate.

The Royal Governor sought many groups of travelling players in search of new entertainment and I could fit in with most, such were the variety of my skills. Then I was asked to attend at Anet, where the Dauphin, Princesses and the little Queen were travelling by barge.

It was an honour. Much had been said of the beautiful chateau of the King's mistress, fashioned in her favoured colours of black and white. And how the royal children enjoyed their time spent there, drawn to her beauty and the palatial surroundings of the chaste marble statues and memorial chapel.

Such fine clothes the children wore, velvets and damasks, embroidered caps and ribbons that twirled as they danced in the morning sun. All this, I marvelled that day we entertained them in the gardens, was like one of my dreams, with the exquisite richness of colour and sound. There were bears and wild animals too, but none impressed the little Queen so much as the proud peacock that strutted through the gardens.

"That bird wears skirts like mine," she declared, when its tail opened to reveal its exquisite feathers.

In the distance I played the lute, while she was told that the peacock was the male, and the peahen, the female, rather more ordinary and plain. Her answer was bright and quick.

"There must be a reason," she declared. "The peacock wears the plumage with dignity. It is the royalty of birds and has been chosen for the plumage."

"Yet the peacock has a dreadful cry," she was told by her governess.

Plumage

"Then the plumage weighs heavy," the Queen answered. "But when you have been given a path that is different from the rest, you must follow it," she informed the surprised woman. "Though at times it may hurt." She sighed heavily, and pointed at me. "He too has been chosen. Without the plumage, the peacock is a dull bird. Without the crown, I am just a female. Without the mute, this group has no voice."

She could see what I had always known. I bent my head down over my lute so no one could see the tears in my eyes. I was unused to the sensation now. And it was at that moment that I fell in love.

Whilst cosseted in luxury, the young Queen still had her enemies. Ordinary, dull-looking creatures who sought to use her for their own ends and to gain power and privilege. Rumours of treachery and attempts to poison her reached even ears like mine, in the different households of the Royal court. How reckless people can be in earshot of a mute.

And then I had a vision that left me breathless in the night. In this, the children of the court were being entertained by wild beasts. Wolves, with great jaws that would howl and three bears. But as the bears came closer, striking out with their huge fat paws and ripping at whatever was nearby, I saw there were only two. The third bear with the bloodiest mouth was no bear at all. It was a man.

Searching for the meaning desperately, within days I found it. I heard two men of the household in grave discussion of the damage the wild bears had caused and the bills that would have to be paid.

"They must be sent away before any more harm is done," one insisted.

The second looked across the gardens, towards where the Queen played, and smiled. "But no real harm has come to anyone." His smile like the bloody mouth from my dream made me shiver. And I knew what I must do.

213

Alison White

The gardens were large and in parts lonely at that household, and when a man chances upon a fool, he expects foolishness.

"Away," he growled as I leapt at him as he walked alone beneath the trees. "Go!"

With his own sword, I killed him. The brown velvet cloak of that bear was stained with his own blood.

The children were sent to another chateau without delay and the death not spoken of publicly. The bears were removed too and the bills settled for their rampaging. My gift had served me well once more. My Queen would not die at the paws of that bear.

I entertained many more times at court. Although I never spent time alone with the young Queen, nor bore witness to her friendship, I felt a bond still. She had an understanding I had not encountered before or since. She and I both victims of the plumage God chose for us. Committing what would be crimes in the eyes of some along our life's path. And yet they were our destiny, there was no other way.

Now she is free of that in death and will be a Queen forever. My plumage fades too. I can no longer bend and fly as I used to – the years have not been kind to my body. Although my face will still entertain, I am not as valued a player as I once was. And my spirit too has gone.

Her death has made me sad. It was another vision broken, the saddest one of all. I was walking amongst long grass and singing. Yes – in this dream, I had a voice, low and sad. First, I came upon the corpse of Arlon, my first victim. In fear I turned round the other way, only to find another corpse – that treacherous villain whom I killed by his own sword. I fled and sought an old crone in the woods to whom I handed gold and mimicked a death by poisoning. With greedy claws grasping the gold, she handed me a small bottle and we laughed. Back on the hills, I took shelter by a tree and slept as though at peace,

Plumage

yet woke to the sound of a peacock's scream. I leapt to my feet and ran, looking to where the dreadful sound came.

And then I saw it. The body of the regal bird, lying bloodied there on the lawns, its tail ripped out and spread beside it, blood-spattered and spoiled. The beauty gone, colour seeming to drain from the rest of the body of the bird. A death scream as its plumage was lost.

I waited to interpret it, yet knew it was prophetic. And now the tales that have crossed the seas about the manner of the Queen's passing have proved it so, reaching even little Louis. In paying for supposed crimes, stripped of even her hair in death. Yet never of her royal dignity.

But let me not forget the poison. For it too was in my dream and I too have a price to pay.

"Papa! Papa! The mute – I think he is dead."

His father roughly pushed past him, to see where the fool lay, mouth open and slack, eyes closed and skin cold as ice.

"Ah, well. That is the way, boy. Do not cry for him, he had a good life." Unseen by Louis, he fingered the small bottle at the side of the fool. He had been so sad of late. If this was his choice, then so be it.

"Papa!" The boy turned tear-stained cheeks upwards at his father. "Those groans in the night – would they be his? I was woken by them and thought it was drunken men outside but could see nothing when I looked out."

His father, who had heard the noises too, said nothing for a moment, watching the dead fool sadly.

"Was it him, Papa? The mute fool? Crying in death?"

The man ruffled his son's hair. "We must prepare him, Louis. Maybe he did speak at last. Who knows? But he is no longer mute. Nor a fool. In death, everything is stripped away. Now, he might find a voice."

"It was screams I heard last night," Louis insisted.

"A new voice needs training," his father said gently. "And perhaps now he will learn to sing." Deftly, he pocketed the empty bottle and took his weeping son from the room. And left the man at peace.

THE WOMAN WHO
LOVED ELIZABETH DAVID

Andrew Taylor

*One of the attractions of a book of fresh crime stories is
that the contributors have the chance to try something a
little different. Many of the writers whose work appears
in this collection relished the invitation to write a story
far removed in place and time from their main mystery
series.* The Woman Who Loved Elizabeth David, *however, sees Andrew Taylor broadening yet further the canvas of his Lydmouth chronicles. The result is thoroughly
enjoyable and will, I hope, tempt even more readers to
try Taylor's excellent books about the fictional town on
the border between England and Wales.*

O n the evening that Charles died I actually heard the
ambulance, the one that Edith Thornhill called. I was
putting out the milk bottles in the porch. I didn't take much
notice. Our house was on Chepstow Road and so was the
hospital; we often heard ambulances.

He died on the evening of the day the rat-catcher came –

the last Thursday in October. Our house was modern, built just before the war, but in the garden was a crumbling stone stable. Charles planned to convert it into a garage if we ever bought a car, which was about as likely as his agreeing to install a telephone. In the meantime we used it as a sort of garden shed and apple store. Almost all the apples had been ruined by rats in the space of a week. Hence the rat-catcher.

Charles was late but I had not begun to get worried. After he closed the shop, he often dropped into the Bull Hotel for a drink. Then the doorbell rang and I found Dr Bayswater and Mrs Thornhill on the doorstep. I know Edith from church, and Dr Bayswater is our doctor.

"I'm sorry, Anne," Edith said. "It's bad news. May we come in?"

I took them into the lounge. Edith suggested I sit down.

"Charles? It's Charles, isn't it?"

"I'm afraid he's dead," Edith said.

I stared at her. I did not know what to say.

The doctor cleared his throat. "Coronary thrombosis."

"A coronary? Do you mean a heart attack? But he was only forty-eight."

"It does happen."

"But he doesn't have a weak heart. Surely there'd have been some—"

"I'd seen him three times in the last month." Bayswater examined his fingernails. "Didn't he tell you?"

"Of course he did. But that was indigestion."

"Angina. Some of the symptoms can be similar to indigestion."

The doctor and Edith went on talking to me. I didn't listen very much. All I could think of was the fact that Charles hadn't told me the truth. Instead of grieving that he was gone, I felt angry with him.

My memory of the next few weeks is patchy, as if a heavy

fog lies over that part of my mind. Certain events rear out of it like icebergs from a cold ocean. The funeral was at St John's and the church was full of people wearing black clothes, like crows. Marina Harper was there, which surprised me because she wasn't a churchgoer. Charles had an obituary in the *Lydmouth Gazette*. It was not a very long one. It said that he came of a well-respected local family and referred in passing to Nigel.

It was unfortunate that Nigel, Charles's younger brother, was in Tanganyika, looking at some sawmills he was thinking of buying. I never really understood what Nigel did for a living. Whatever it was, it seemed to bring him a good deal of money. Once I asked him and he said, "I just buy things when they're cheap, and sell things when they're expensive. Nothing to it, really."

I sent a telegram to Dar es Salaam. Nigel cabled back, saying he would be home as soon as possible. He and Charles had always been very close, though Nigel was my age, a good ten years younger than his brother. He was also Charles's executor.

Everything was in limbo. Until Nigel came home, I could have very little idea of what the future held for me. I did not even know whether I would be able to stay in the house. In the meantime, the shop – Butter's, the men's outfitters in the High Street – was left in the charge of the manager, a man who had worked for Charles and his father for many years.

What struck me most was the silence. In the evenings, when I sat by the fire in the lounge, there was a quietness that I could not drive away by turning on the wireless. After a while, I stopped trying. I would sit in my chair, with a book unopened on my lap, and stare at the familiar room which had grown suddenly unfamiliar: at my mother-in-law's dark oak sideboard, which I had always loathed; at the collected edition of Kipling, which Charles and Nigel had

Andrew Taylor

laboriously assembled when they were boys; at the patch on the hearthrug where Charles had left a cigarette burning one Christmas-time.

I don't know when I realised something was wrong. I think the first thing that struck me was the key. When the hospital sent back Charles's belongings, the contents of his pockets had been put in a separate bag. There was nothing unexpected except for the key. Charles had other keys in a leather pouch with a buttoned flap – keys for the house, for the shop. This key, however, was loose – a Yale, made of brass and obviously quite new. I tried it unsuccessfully in our only Yale lock, the one on the old stable. I took it down to the shop, but it didn't fit any of the locks there, either.

On the same morning, I went to the bank to draw some cash – something I had to do for myself now Charles wasn't here. The cashier said the manager would like a word. Our account was overdrawn. The manager suggested that I transfer some money from the deposit account.

As I was walking down the High Street on my way from the bank to the bus stop, Mr Quale was sweeping the doorstep of the Bull Hotel.

"Morning, ma'am. Sorry to hear about Mr Butter."

"Thank you."

"Very nice gentleman. I saw him just before it happened."

"How did he seem?"

"Right as rain. He'd been in for a quick drink – left a bit earlier than usual. Thought he must be in a hurry for his supper."

"Earlier?" Charles had collapsed on the pavement outside the Thornhills' house in Victoria Road a little after seven-thirty. "Surely you mean later?"

Quale shook his head. "It was about a quarter past six."

"I expect he looked in at the shop on the way home."

The Woman who Loved Elizabeth David

I said goodbye and joined the queue at the bus stop. Charles had never worked in the evening. I was standing there, turning over in my mind what Quale had said, when there was a loud tooting from the other side of the road. It was Marina Harper in her little two-seater. She drove across the road and pulled up at the bus stop.

"Hop in, Anne. I'll give you a lift."

I was tired, and it was beginning to rain. Otherwise I might have tried to find an excuse. I never knew quite what to make of Marina. She had fair, coarse hair and a high-coloured face with small, pale eyes. She was comfortably off – her father used to own the local bus company. We had known each other since we were children but we weren't particular friends. And I was old-fashioned enough to feel that a wife should live with her husband.

Marina talked unceasingly as she drove me home. "I've just had a couple of days in town," Her husband worked in London. He and Marina had a semi-detached marriage: his job kept him in London while she preferred to live in Lydmouth, "... and you'll never guess who we met at a party last night. Elizabeth David – yes, *really!* Absolutely wonderful. Such style. She looks how she writes, if you know what I mean."

"Elizabeth who?"

Marina raised plucked eyebrows. "Elizabeth David. The cookery writer. You know, she's always in *Vogue*. And she's written this super book about Mediterranean food. Why don't you come to lunch tomorrow? We can try one of the recipes."

Marina dropped me in Chepstow Road. After lunch, I went into the dining room. Charles kept cheque books and other documents relating to money in the top drawer of the bureau. I settled down and tried to work out how the money ebbed and flowed and ebbed again in our lives. I found the

221

most recent bank statement among the pile of business letters which I had left on the hall table for Nigel. I wished he were here now.

At the date of the statement, our personal account had not been overdrawn, but it now was. In the week before his death Charles had made out a cheque for one hundred and eighty-nine pounds, nineteen shillings and eleven pence.

I leafed through the cancelled cheques enclosed with the statement. The cheque in question had been made out to H R Caterford Ltd and paid into a branch of Barclays Bank in Cardiff.

Feeling like a detective, I put on my hat and coat, walked to the telephone box on the corner of Victoria Road and consulted the telephone directory. H R Caterford Ltd was a jeweller's in the Royal Arcade. Suddenly the solution came to me: Charles must have bought me a present. The dear man knew I had been a little low since coming out of hospital in September. (Knowing one will never have children *is* a little depressing.) But in that case, where was the present? Christmas was two months away. He would hardly keep it until then.

On impulse I dialled the number in the directory. The phone was answered on the second ring, which was just as well as I was beginning to get cold feet about the whole business.

"Good afternoon," I said. "May I speak to Mr Caterford?"

"Speaking."

"This is Mrs Butter, from Lydmouth. Mrs Charles Butter. I believe my husband—"

"Mrs Butter. How pleasant to hear from you. You're well, I hope?"

"Yes, thank you. I was wondering—"

"Oddly enough, I was just thinking of you. Only yesterday afternoon the lady who sold us the brooch came in with the matching ring. Platinum and opal. Said she didn't want

222

that either, because her daughter had told her that opals are unlucky unless you're born in October. Not that you need to worry about that, of course."

"Oh?"

"As you're one of the favoured few."

"Oh, yes."

"It's rather a lovely ring. The opals are a perfect match for your eyes, if I may say so. Anyway, would you like to have a word with Mr Butter about it? Then perhaps he could telephone me. I'll hold it for a day or two. It's always a particular pleasure to oblige an old customer."

"Yes, thank you. Goodbye."

I put down the phone and walked home. A platinum and opal brooch. Charles knew I didn't like platinum. Then the opals: unlucky unless the wearer had been born in the month of October. My birthday was in March. And how could opals match my eyes? They are brown. Finally, Mr Caterford had spoken to me as if he knew me. But until this afternoon I had never heard of him.

The following morning, I found the rat. The rat-catcher had warned me this might happen. "That's the trouble with rats, look," he had said. "You can never tell where they're going to pop up."

The rat was lying on the path that led from the old stable to the road. It was dark, with a long tail. There had been a frost in the night and its fur was dusted with droplets of ice, like sugar. Actually, it looked rather sweet. Because of the frost, the ground would not be easy to dig, so I decided to bury it after lunch – my lunch with Marina Harper.

Marina lived in Raglan Court, a block of modern flats overlooking Jubilee Park. The place looked very nice, I'm sure – if you like hard, modern furniture and American gadgets. There was a lounge-cum-dining room with a huge picture window overlooking the park and a serving hatch to the kitchen. The place stank of garlic.

"I've just made dry martinis," Marina said. "You don't mind if I put the finishing touches to lunch, do you? We can talk through the hatch."

As she poured the drinks, light glinted on a silver brooch she was wearing. Rather a pretty brooch with opals set in it.

Not silver – platinum?

"That's a lovely brooch," I said.

"Yes, it is pretty, isn't it?"

"Aren't opals unlucky?"

Marina laughed, a gurgle of sound like water running out of a bath. "Not if you're born in October. Then they're lucky. Now, why don't you sit here while I finish off in the kitchen?"

I watched her through the frame of the hatch – the flash of a knife, the glint of platinum – and all the time she talked.

"I thought we'd have *filet de porc en sanglier*. It's one of my Elizabeth David recipes. Pork that tastes like wild boar. The secret is the marinade. It has to be for eight days. And you can't skimp on the ingredients either – things like coriander seeds, juniper berries, basil. There's a little shop in Brewer Street where you can get them. I think it must be the only place in England."

Black market ingredients, I thought. *Pork and all. The bitch. The cow.*

While Marina talked, the rich, unhealthy odours of the meal wafted through the hatch into the living room. My hands were sweaty on the cold glass. In my nervousness, I finished the drink more quickly than I should have done.

"Can I get you a refill?" Marina called.

I stood up. "I wonder if I might— Is it along here?"

"Second on the left."

In the hall, I opened my handbag and took out Charles's

224

Yale key. Holding my breath, I opened the front door. I slipped the key into the lock and twisted. The key turned.

I drew it out of the lock, closed the door quietly and darted into the sanctuary of the bathroom. Marina was wearing the brooch. The jeweller in Cardiff had thought that Marina was me, had thought that she was Charles's wife. So they must have been in Cardiff together, and acting as if they were a married couple. The key in Charles's pocket fitted Marina's door. There could be only one explanation for all that.

It is strange how in a crisis one finds reserves of strength one did not suspect existed. Somehow I went back into the living room and accepted another strong dry martini. Somehow I made myself eat the ghastly, overflavoured pork which Marina served up with such a triumphant flourish that I wanted to throw the plate at her. I even complimented her on her cooking. She said that she would give me the recipe.

The meal dragged on. It was far too heavy and elaborate for lunch. Marina served it in the French way, with salad after the main course, and then cheese before the pudding. So pretentious. What was wrong with our way of doing things?

When at last it was time to go, Marina came into the hall and helped me on with my coat. Then she bent forward and kissed my cheek.

"I have enjoyed this," she said. "Let's do it again soon. I'm running up to town for a night or two but I'll be in touch as soon as I get back."

I walked home through the park and down Victoria Road. The rat was still lying on the path between the house and the stable. After I had taken off my hat and changed, I went outside and manoeuvred its stiff body into a bucket with the help of a spade. The ice had melted now, so the fur gleamed with moisture. I carried the bucket into the stable. I looked at the various places where the rat-catcher had left the poison. All of it had gone. I wondered if there were more rats. It was then that the idea came into my mind. I remembered the Kipling story.

Nigel and Charles thought Kipling was the greatest writer of the century. They were particularly fond of the Stalky stories, which are about schoolboys at a boarding school near the sea. I had read them in our early days, when I'd been friends with Charles and Nigel, just before Charles and I became engaged. A wife should try to like the things the husband likes. But I hadn't liked these stories.

In one of them, the boys kill a cat with an air gun. They push its dead body under the floorboards of a rival dormitory. The cat decomposes, and gradually its smell fills the dormitory, growing stronger and stronger, and more and more loathsome. If a cat could do it, so could a rat.

It was just a silly idea – childish, undignified and in any case impossible to carry out. I left the rat in the stable and went inside for a cup of tea. During the rest of the day, however, I could not help thinking about the rat. And about Marina.

Marina was going to London. I had a key to her flat, which she did not know I possessed. If I went there tomorrow evening, after darkness, there would be very little risk of my being seen as I went to or from the flat. There was a little gate from the park to the communal garden of the flats – I could go that way. People kept to themselves at Raglan Court so with luck I would not be noticed. In any case, I could take the precaution of wearing a rather bright headscarf, a pre-war present which I had never used, and an old mackintosh which had belonged to Charles.

As the evening slipped past, the idea seemed more and more attractive. Well, why not? It wouldn't harm Marina to have another smell in that evil-smelling flat. And it was a way of making a point about her beastly behaviour. There was no excuse for adultery. There was no excuse for stealing my husband. The following evening, I decided to act.

I put the rat, wrapped in brown paper, in my shopping bag, slipped a torch into my pocket, walked up to Raglan Court and let myself into the flat. I was not afraid. Indeed, I had the oddest sensation that it could not be me, Anne Butter, doing this. I felt as if I were watching rather than doing.

I went straight into the kitchen. This was where the nasty smells came from – so this was the place for the rat. I did not turn on the light, but used the torch sparingly. I unwrapped the rat and let it fall to the linoleum.

The gas cooker was raised on legs a few inches above the floor. I found a floor mop and used it to push the body under the cooker to the wall. The torch proved to be a blessing. With its help I was able to see that there was a gap between the wall and the back of the cupboard beside the cooker. With a little manoeuvring of the broom, I managed to push the rat into the gap. Even if Marina looked under the cooker she would not be able to see anything. I did not think it would be long before the rat began to smell: the flat was centrally heated, and the kitchen would be the warmest room.

I went home. Then it was simply a matter of waiting. Waiting for Nigel and waiting for the rat.

A few days after I had left the rat at her flat, Marina arrived on my doorstep with a small parcel in her hand.

"For you," she said, smiling. "Just a little something."

I asked her in for coffee. The parcel contained a copy of Elizabeth David's *A Book of Mediterranean Food*.

"The lovely thing about cooking is that when the pleasure's shared it's somehow doubled," Marina said. "You won't be able to get a lot of the ingredients in Lydmouth. Perhaps I can find what you need in London."

During the next two weeks, I saw Marina regularly. I even asked her to lunch. Many of Elizabeth David's recipes were really very simple. I found one – *tarte à l'oignon et aux oeufs* – which turned out to be very like the flans I used to cook Charles. Marina said my *tarte* was quite marvellous.

Why did she do all this? Why was she such a hypocrite? There were two possible explanations: either she felt guilty about stealing my husband, or she was doing it because she derived a malicious pleasure from pretending to be my friend. On the whole I thought the latter explanation was more likely.

On the second occasion I had lunch with her, I was sure I could smell something in the living room. It was a faint *blueness* in the air, an uneasy hint that lingered in the nostrils. After the meal, I helped Marina carry the plates into the kitchen. I sniffed.

"Can you *smell* something?" Marina asked.

"Well . . ."

"I keep thinking I can. Something rather unpleasant. I really must turn out the cupboards soon. And the larder."

No more was said about it until a day or two later, when Marina drove me up to Cheltenham for a matinée at the Everyman. In the interval she brought up the subject again.

"Do you remember that smell in the kitchen? I think it might be the drains."

"Have there been complaints from the other flats?"

"Not as far as I know. I've got someone coming to have a look."

Two days later, she came to tea and gave me the next instalment. Unfortunately the plumber had turned out to be rather good at his job. He soon realised that the smell was not from the drains. He pulled out the cooker and found the decaying body of the rat squeezed between the cupboard and the wall.

"It was quite disgusting," Marina said. "It looked as it smelled, if you know what I mean. Anyway, the plumber was marvellous. He got the wretched thing out of the flat and now things are beginning to return to normal."

"Isn't it odd having a rat in a modern block of flats?"

"Unusual, I suppose. But apparently they are very agile creatures, and you never know where they are going to turn up. The plumber suggested that I get the rat-catcher." Marina shivered, rather theatrically. "Just in case there are any more."

"We had rats in the stable," I said. "The rat-catcher soon sorted them out. I've got his address if you'd like it."

Marina took out a little leather-bound diary and made a note of the details. As she jotted them down, the brooch gleamed on her cardigan. Platinum and unlucky opals.

The rat man came and left poison under the cooker and in the larder. Marina told me all about his reluctance to leave the poison in the kitchen, about the strictness of his instructions to her. This was just before she went up to London for the weekend. She was going to a party, she said, where she hoped Elizabeth David might be present.

"I know I've only met her once, but I feel I know her really well – as well as I know you – just through her writing." Marina patted my arm – she was always touching me, which was one of the things I disliked most. "I'll tell Mrs David I've been making converts in Lydmouth. I'm sure she'll be delighted. I'll be back on Monday, so I'll come and tell you all about it on Tuesday."

I was in a quandary. Should I or shouldn't I? It was such a good opportunity, presented to me, as it were, on a plate. It would make up for the rather tame performance of the rat. I didn't want to hurt Marina, of course, not seriously. But there would be very little risk of that. The amount of poison that would kill a rat would surely give a human being nothing more than a mild bilious attack.

All weekend I toyed with the idea. *What if? What if?* On

Sunday evening, when it was dark, I put on the headscarf and the raincoat and left the house. I had the torch and the key to Marina's flat in my pocket.

Everything went as smoothly as last time. In the refrigerator was a saucepan containing what I now knew was ratatouille. It looked and smelt quite disgusting. The rat poison was on saucers, one under the cooker and the other in the larder. I took a little of the poison from each and rearranged what was left on the saucers so that they both looked untouched. I stirred it into the ratatouille. To my relief, it seemed to dissolve very quickly. I wondered if the poison would taste. Even if it did, I thought that the ratatouille was so strongly flavoured that it would mask any additions.

What if? What if?

I went home. That night I dreamed of Nigel. Funnily enough I had always dreamed more about Nigel than about Charles. On Monday morning, I woke with a light heart. Now I could put the past behind me and look to the future. In a sense, there was nothing personal in what I'd done at Raglan Court the previous evening. There was no reason to gloat. It had not been a question of being vindictive – merely of doing my duty. Someone had to teach the woman a lesson, and the someone had happened to be me.

I was washing up after breakfast when a man walked past the kitchen window and knocked on the back door. A plate slipped from my hand and broke when it hit the sink. I dried my hands and went to answer the door.

It was the rat-catcher, a grubby little man with a baggy tweed jacket and a collarless shirt.

"Morning, ma'am. Just come to see how the little fellows are getting on."

"I really don't know."

"No dead 'uns?"

"Who knows?"

230

The Woman who Loved Elizabeth David

"Shall I take a look? See if they need a second helping?"

"Yes, please."

The rat-catcher went down to the stable. I cleared up the broken plate and tidied the kitchen. A few minutes later, the man came back.

"They've eaten it all. I put down a bit more."

"Good." I opened my handbag and took out my purse. "Were there – were there any bodies?"

He chuckled. "Gone back to their nests. Give 'em a choice, they like to die in their own beds, just like us, eh?"

I paid the man. He wanted to stay and gossip – in my experience, men are far worse gossips than women – but luckily we were interrupted by the ring of the front doorbell.

It was a telegram. My heart lurched because telegrams usually mean bad news, apart from those connected with births and weddings; and I had nothing to do with either. I tore it open.

BOAT DOCKED LATE LAST NIGHT. COMING DOWN TODAY. IN CIRCUMSTANCES HAVE BOOKED ROOM AT BULL. SEE YOU ABOUT FIVE. NIGEL.

That was typical of my brother-in-law. Nigel could be very thoughtful. When Charles was alive, Nigel always stayed at the house. But now Charles was dead, the situation was different. Lydmouth wasn't London. If we were alone under the same roof, tongues might wag. People might even remember that before I became engaged to Charles, I had seen a good deal of Nigel.

By half-past four I was as ready as I could be – the lounge fire burning brightly, the brasses in the hall gleaming, the water near boiling point in the kettle, the tea tray laid. As I sat waiting, all sorts of foolish thoughts chased through my mind. *What if? What if?*

231

Nigel rang the doorbell at twenty past five.

"Anne – wonderful to see you." He swept me into his arms. "I'm so sorry about Charles." He hugged me, then stood back. "Sorry I'm a bit late. Train was delayed. Nothing works properly in this country."

Nigel was taller than Charles had been, and age had been kinder to him. As a young man, he had been gawky and had had difficulty in talking to a girl without blushing. The war had changed all that. I brought the tea in and we chatted for a while, mainly about Charles.

"You must be wondering about the money side," Nigel said. "No need. As far as I am concerned, you can stay in the house for as long as you like. You own fifty per cent of it now, anyway. And Charles's share in the shop comes to you, so that should give you a decent income, even if we have to pay out a bit more in wages."

I asked him how long he was staying in Lydmouth.

"Only a couple of nights, I'm afraid. I'm popping over to Paris on Thursday." He grinned at me. "I'll see if I can find you some perfume."

"It's a shame you can't stay longer."

His eyes met mine. "I'll be back."

"I wonder – could I ask you to help me with Charles's things? There're all his clothes, for example. And I've not really been through the business papers in the bureau."

"Of course I will. When would suit you?"

"Come to lunch tomorrow – we can sort everything out afterwards."

He hesitated.

"I'll see if I can do something interesting," I said brightly. "I've been experimenting lately. I love Elizabeth David. Her recipes are mouth-watering."

"Yes." He glanced at his watch. "Elizabeth David, eh? You've been acquiring cosmopolitan tastes in my absence."

"I try." I smiled at him. "Even with all the shortages, there's no excuse not to be adventurous in the kitchen."

Nigel stood up and tossed his cigarette end in the fire. He ran the tip of his index finger along the spines of the Kipling editions in the bookcase. I shivered. He turned to face me.

"Oh, by the way, I owe you some money."

"Really?"

"I asked Charles to pay a debt for me. He mentioned he'd done it in his last letter. A hundred and ninety-odd pounds."

A hundred and eighty-nine pounds, nineteen shillings and eleven pence?

"Oh – oh yes." I felt as if a horde of insects were crawling across my skin. "I'd noticed the cheque. To a jeweller's, wasn't it?" With immense effort I forced a smile. "Who was the lucky lady? If it *was* a lady."

Nigel's cheeks darkened. The young man I had known before the war was suddenly not so very far away. "I – I suppose I'd better tell you. The thing is, when I've come down to Lydmouth in the last year or so, I've had a sort of friendship with a woman. A special friendship."

"And Charles knew?"

He nodded, took out his cigarette case and fiddled with the catch. "And then I went to Paris on a business trip in the spring, and I met Ghislaine. One thing led to another – well, in fact we're going to get married."

He paused, looking at me, as if waiting for congratulations. I couldn't speak.

"But there was still this – this other lady. That had to end. But I wanted to give her something as a keepsake. Then I had to go to Tanganyika . . ." He managed to open the case at last. He took out a cigarette and rolled it around in his fingers. Crumbs of tobacco dribbled down to the hearthrug.

"I asked Charles if he'd buy her a present. It was while

233

Andrew Taylor

you were in hospital. A piece of jewellery – something quite decent. So I gave him a rough idea of how much I wanted to spend and left him to get on with it. We were going to settle up when I got home. I do hope you don't think too badly of me."

He looked at me. In the end, I shook my head, which seemed to satisfy him. Men are easily satisfied.

"It wasn't serious," he said, as if that excused it. "Men tend to sow a few wild oats before they settle down. Women are different."

Were they? If all women were different, how could the men sow their wild oats?

He looked at his watch again. "Oh lord, I must go. I'll see you tomorrow. What time would suit you?"

"About twelve-thirty?"

"Splendid."

We went into the hall. He bent towards me and his lips brushed my cheek.

"You've always been a good pal. You're not shocked? Charles thought you would be."

"Don't be silly." I smiled up at him. "Boys will be boys."

We said goodnight and I closed the door behind him. I went back into the lounge. The room was empty and desolate. There was nothing left of Nigel except crumbs on a plate, a puddle of tea at the bottom of a cup and golden flecks of tobacco on the hearthrug. I went over to the bookcase and ran my finger along the spines of the Kiplings. What would it feel like if Nigel's finger ran down my spine? I tried to think about Ghislaine but she was too abstract, too foreign for me to grasp. She wasn't flesh and blood like Marina. Marina, I thought idly, would be home by now.

One of the books was a little out of line. It was *Stalky and Co*, the schoolboy stories which had been Nigel and Charles's favourite. *Boys will be boys*. There was a slip of

234

paper protruding from the pages, presumably a bookmark. I took it out, suddenly curious to re-read the story about the dead cat and the smell. The bookmark was buff-coloured. I pulled it out and discovered it was a telegram. For a moment, I thought that Nigel's telegram to me had somehow found its way into *Stalky and Co.* But that was still propped up on the mantelpiece behind the clock. This one was addressed to Charles and dated in September, while I was in hospital.

YOU'RE WELCOME OLD BOY. WHILE THE CAT'S AWAY. HAVE FUN. NIGEL.

I sat down beside the bookcase in the chair that was still warm from Nigel's body. I read and re-read the telegram. It had come all the way from Suez. Nigel must have sent it on his way down to East Africa. Suddenly many things were clear. Nigel, Charles and Marina – they had all betrayed me in their different ways, even Nigel.

Nigel worst of all.

It was growing very cold. I stood up and put more coal on the fire. *A Book of Mediterranean Food* was on the sideboard. I riffled through the pages, looking for a suitable recipe for tomorrow. I knew I would find something. And I also knew that, whatever I cooked, Nigel would eat with apparent relish because he felt guilty.

A little later, I went outside. It was a cold night, with stars like diamonds. The moon gave a hard, clear light. Frost gleamed on the path to the stable. I opened the door. Moonlight streamed across the floor and showed me a saucer in the corner. I picked it up and left the stable.

As I was walking back to the house I heard the sound of an ambulance. The bell drew closer and closer. It was coming down Victoria Road from the direction of the park and Raglan Court. In the freezing night air, I stood still and listened to the sound of the ambulance as it slowed for the junction with the Chepstow Road, turned left and sped towards the hospital.

What if? What if?

BIOGRAPHICAL NOTES

Catherine Aird is the author of seventeen crime novels and a collection of short stories, *Injury Time*. She has also been awarded an honorary MA from the University of Kent and was made an MBE for her services to the Girl Guide Association. She is a former Chairman of the CWA and in 1992 she was the first recipient of the CWA/Hertfordshire Libraries Golden Handcuffs Award for her outstanding contribution to detective fiction.

Mat Coward is a freelance journalist and crime fiction reviewer who has published a number of short stories. He contributes columns to the crime fanzines *A Shot in the Dark* and *Deadly Pleasures*. Formerly London-based, he now lives in Somerset and has recently been appointed as editor of a new mystery magazine, *Crimewave*.

Eileen Dewhurst was born in Liverpool, read English at Oxford, and has earned her living in a variety of ways, including journalism. When she is not writing, she enjoys solving cryptic crossword puzzles and drawing and painting cats. Her nineteenth and latest novel is *Roundabout*. Her other works include *A Private Prosecution*, *The House that Jack*

Built and *Death in Candie Gardens*. She wrote five novels featuring the policeman Neil Carter; currently, her principal series detectives are actress Phyllida Moon and the Guernsey policeman Tim Le Page.

Marjorie Eccles was born in Yorkshire and spent her childhood there and on the Northumbrian coast. Later, she lived for many years in the Midlands, where her crime novels are set. Her series featuring Detective Chief Inspector Gil Mayo has achieved an enthusiastic following; the most recent title is *Killing Me Softly*.

Martin Edwards has written six novels about the lawyer and amateur detective Harry Devlin; the first, *All the Lonely People*, was short-listed for the CWA John Creasey Memorial Award for the best first crime novel of 1991. The series has been optioned for television. He has published about twenty short mysteries, including several with a historical setting, and is also the author of six non-fiction books on legal topics. His latest novel is *The Devil in Disguise*.

Susanna Gregory is a pseudonym. Before she earned her PhD at the University of Cambridge and became a research fellow at one of the colleges, she was a police officer in Yorkshire. She has written a number of non-fiction books on subjects including castles, cathedrals and historic houses. She and her husband live in a village near Cambridge.

Biographical Notes

Edward D Hoch has dominated the market for short crime fiction of quality for over the past forty years. Although he has written occasional novels, it is his gift for (and ability to make a living from) the short form that has earned him a unique reputation. In the course of writing many hundreds of stories, Hoch has employed a wide range of pen-names and created series characters such as Captain Leopold, Dr Sam Hawthorne, the cipher expert Rand, Ben Snow and Simon Ark, who claims to be 2,000 years old. The first dozen of Hawthorne's cases have recently been collected in *Diagnosis: Impossible*.

HRF Keating has written many novels and works of non-fiction, but is perhaps most famous for the Inspector Ghote series set in India, the first of which, *The Perfect Murder*, won the CWA Gold Dagger and was subsequently made into a film by Merchant Ivory. He has been President of the Detection Club since 1987 and in 1996 received the CWA Diamond Dagger. His most recent book is *The Soft Detective*.

Gillian Linscott set the first of her mystery novels in a French nudist colony and in her twelve subsequent books she has continued to specialise in the quirky and the unexpected. In recent years, she has concentrated on writing about the suffragette sleuth Nell Bray, whose latest adventure is chronicled in *Dance in Blood*. Nell also appears in a novella, *In at the Death*.

Edward Marston is the author of ten novels in the Nicholas

Biographical Notes

Bracewell series set in an Elizabethan theatre company; and of eight Domesday Books set in the eleventh century. Under his own name of Keith Miles, he has written several other crime novels as well as plays, short stories, literary criticism, biography, sports books and children's fiction. His latest book is an architectural mystery set in Chicago in the 1930s and featuring Frank Lloyd Wright. He is a former Chairman of the Crime Writers' Association.

Amy Myers was born in Kent. After taking a degree in English literature, she was director of a London publishing house before becoming an author. She is married to an American and lives in Kent. She also writes under the name Harriet Hudson.

Anne Perry was born in London and spent many years abroad before settling in her present house in the Scottish highlands. Her Victorian mysteries divide into two distinct series, featuring Thomas Pitt and William Monk respectively. They have achieved enormous popularity in the United States in particular, where she regularly features in the bestseller list.

Ruth Rendell, under her own name and as Barbara Vine, has achieved both critical and popular acclaim for her achievement in showing the rich potential of the crime novel. Her first book about the Kingsmarkham policeman, Reg Wexford, *From Doon with Death*, appeared in 1964, and the most recent, *Road Rage*, in 1997. Her non-series novels under her own name include *A Demon in my View*, which won the CWA Gold Dagger in 1976, and the even more remarkable *A Judgement in Stone*. *Lake of Darkness* won the Arts Council National

Biographical Notes

Book Award for Genre Fiction in 1981. The much-praised
Vine novels include *A Fatal Inversion* (another CWA Gold
Dagger winner) and *The Brimstone Wedding*; the most recent
is *The Chimney Sweeper's Boy*.

Andrew Taylor grew up in East Anglia and went to the
universities of Cambridge and London. He now lives in
Gloucestershire with his wife and two children and writes
full time. His first novel about William Dougal, *Caroline
Minuscule*, won the CWA John Creasey Memorial Award
and the third, *Our Father's Lies*, was short-listed for the
Gold Dagger. He has also written an espionage trilogy,
books for younger readers, non-series novels such as *The
Barred Window* and three mysteries set in the post-war era
and located in the border town of Lydmouth. Most recently,
he has embarked on the Roth Trilogy, which opened with
The Four Lost Things.

Alison White was born and bred in Liverpool, but returned to
the north-west after some time living and working in London
and is now based in Southport. She has published many stories
in magazines and her work has also been broadcast on BBC
Network Northwest, Radio 4 and the World Service. In
recent years, she has concentrated increasingly on crime
fiction, writing for magazines such as *Ellery Queen's Mystery
Magazine*. She is now at work on her first mystery novel.

Tony Wilmot has been a newspaper reporter, book publisher's
editor and feature writer on *Weekend* magazine (interviewing
everyone from public hangman Pierrepoint to Salvador Dali).
He has published a novel about Modigliani and won a CWA

prize for a murder story set in a flea circus. Several of his short stories were televised in *Tales of the Unexpected* and broadcast on Radio 4. He has been a full-time writer since the late 1980s.